Hunting Grounds
A Julian Mercer Thriller

G.K. Parks

Copyright © 2020 G.K. Parks

A Modus Operandi imprint

ISBN: 1942710240
ISBN-13: 978-1-942710-24-0

For my mom and dad

ONE

"Are you sure the kidnapper is still operating in the area?" Bastian Clarke asked.

Julian Mercer wrapped his hands around the glass mug, warming his palms. He raised an eyebrow at his second-in-command. "Correct me if I'm wrong, but shouldn't you know the answer to that question? You've been analyzing the intel for the last few weeks."

Bastian grumbled to himself and snagged a chip from the side of Julian's plate. "Jules, I'm asking your opinion. Do you think he's still here?"

"Yes." Mercer sipped his tea and studied the promenade, as the locals called it, filled with shops, tourist attractions, restaurants, and lodgings. This was the quintessential sleepy town. The tourists outnumbered the residents three to one. "These are ideal conditions. The perfect hunting grounds. He can slip in and out, operate as he chooses, and no one notices. The locals probably have no idea what's going on, or they turn a blind eye. They wouldn't want the bad publicity. Their economy depends on tourism.

They'd have a difficult time surviving without it, and he's careful. He's never taken any of them, just the outsiders. He does his homework. He watches, waits, and then strikes. That's why he hasn't moved on."

"You think they're covering up his crimes?"

"It's possible." Mercer sighed. "Surely, one of his victims would have gone to the police, but the bobbies I've spoken to deny having any knowledge. I don't necessarily believe them."

"You never do."

Mercer reached for the dossier on the table. "The victims never reported anyone stalking them or receiving any threats while on holiday. And since the actual crimes took place elsewhere, none were reported until much later on, if they were reported at all."

"It's poor form to publicize a ransom or kidnapping. That just invites other riffraff to try the same," Bastian said, "just like blackmail. The rich don't want to attract that kind of attention and with good reason."

"Still, we need to know what's what. This is rubbish." Mercer gestured at their incomplete files. "The only reports we have were filed by family members when their loved ones weren't returned. And by then, it was too late. It doesn't give us much to work with."

Bastian reached for another chip, toying with the edge of the file. "At least the insurance firm gave us their internal memos regarding the ransom insurance payouts. We know some of the victims survived the ordeal. That's something."

"Not bloody much. We don't know a thing about the kidnapper, or even if he works alone. But this is where he operates, even if the authorities haven't realized the connection yet. Everything links back to this place. This is where he chooses them, despite what local law enforcement and the tourism brochures would have us believe."

"You can't blame them, Jules." Bastian chomped down on another chip. "The bodies of his victims were discovered elsewhere. Nothing directly links them to this town."

"Except they were here. This is the only place they have in common. This is where the kidnapper selected his victims, even if he didn't abduct them until days or weeks later. He followed them back to their homes, to their everyday lives, and then he struck when they least expected it. They never saw it coming."

Bastian eyed Mercer cautiously, wondering if the commander was projecting his own personal tragedy onto these victims. "Maybe they did. Didn't you speak to the few who survived?"

"Yes, but they had nothing helpful to add. They never saw him. He waited for a chance to grab them from their homes, schools, the market, wherever, and then he took them to some other location until he was paid."

"He's not particularly consistent."

Mercer glanced up, scowling at Bastian over the rim of his cup. "Didn't I just say this place is the only consistency among the kidnappings?" Putting down the mug, Mercer sat back and took in their surroundings. "He's here, somewhere, waiting for his next target."

"Do you think he's local or just another tourist?"

Mercer cocked his head to the side. "He's too familiar with the people in the area to be a tourist. Even a frequent flyer wouldn't know every person in town. He'd make a mistake at some point and pick the wrong target, but that's never happened. He lives here. He must."

"Or maybe he likes to ski and picks tourists at random. Maybe he and his targets share the same hotel or chalet." Bastian reached for the placard on the table and flipped it over. The back had an advertisement for a ski shop. "Apparently, in a few weeks, we'll be in the throng of tourist season. It'd be easier for him to prey on another unsuspecting chap when the place is crawling with travelers."

"No shit." Mercer rubbed his temples. That's why he felt added pressure to find and stop this guy. But in the last few weeks, the team had accomplished next to nothing. Though they'd explored the town and retraced the dozen victims' travel itineraries prior to their abductions, they found few commonalities and no one in town willing to speak to them about strange oddities or disappearances. "We need to focus on building a profile. We need to identify this bastard."

"Based on what? No one's seen this guy's face. The victims who survived never saw him without a ski mask, and he always wore winter weather gear." Bastian placed the placard back on the table. "If he's local, he could work in one of the ski shops or clothing stores. That could be where he first happened upon his victims and discovered they were tourists."

"Perhaps."

"Jules, we're doing what we can."

"It's not enough. We still have nothing to go on."

"Well, we know this is a wonderful place to holiday, minus all that bloody business with being abducted and murdered. That tends to put a damper on things."

"Yeah, minus that." Mercer reread the intel on the latest victim. "We have to stop him before he takes another one."

"The last abduction was nearly five weeks ago. He might have moved on. It'd be the smart thing to do. He made bank on the last ransom. He has no reason to continue. If it's skiing he enjoys, he could move to the Alps or some other resort town. He doesn't have to stay here."

Mercer quirked an eyebrow. "He's a greedy bastard. This place has been lucrative for him. He's been lucky here. Why would he stop? He doesn't know anyone is on to him. He thinks he's safe. He's clever, which is why it took us this long to notice. He'll only stop if we put an end to this. To him. This is what he does. And this is where he likes to do it." Mercer tapped the radio clipped to his ear. "Hans, anything on your end?"

"All's quiet on the western front," came the reconnaissance expert's cheeky response. "Are you sure I can't invite Maggie to stay the weekend? She'd love it here, and it'd shut her up about wanting me to prove I'm committed."

Thoughts of Michelle, Mercer's late wife, sprang to mind. His expression soured. "It isn't safe. Do you want something to happen to her? We know a kidnapper is working in the area. He has no problem killing. Do you want to give him a beautiful doctor to target?"

"No, Jules. Of course not. I just thought two days wouldn't hurt, and it might be nice. We've been here for nearly a month. If something were to pop off, don't you think it would have by now?"

Mercer stared across the table at Bastian. "Is that the consensus? Am I the only one who thinks another abduction is imminent? Donovan, do you want to weigh in on this?"

"I'm with you, commander," the tactician said. "Apex predators do not abandon fertile hunting grounds. And this place is perfect. According to our research, ten abductions have happened here in the last year. He's not going anywhere. He's biding his time, carefully choosing his prey. I can feel him."

Mercer gave Bastian a pointed look. "So can I."

Deep down, the analyst felt it too. "The insurance firm that hired us to investigate did so because they are tired of paying out ransoms, but they're growing impatient. They want to pull the plug. Our mission is too costly an endeavor for them to bankroll."

"Our fees aren't nearly as exorbitant as what another abduction and ransom payout will cost them. I don't care what they say. The value of a human life can't be quantified in dollars and cents." Mercer finished his tea and put down the mug. "We didn't get into this line of work for a paycheck. Right?"

"Aye," Bastian said.

"So we stay and wait," Mercer said. "Does anyone object?"

"Bugger," Hans muttered. "It's one thing to work. It's another to do it without support or even the slightest hint of appreciation. A simple 'thanks, mate' every now and again would be nice. It's been too long since I've heard that."

"Thanks, mate," Donovan said through the radio. "Feel better now?"

"Piss off," Hans replied, laughing.

Bastian chuckled, nearly choking on a mouthful of chips. "Jules, I wasn't suggesting we abandon our assignment. Quite the opposite, actually. I was thinking we should expand our search parameters and increase our grid. Since we'll be operating solo, we don't have to worry about accounting to any institution or worry about following orders. We can branch out and find this bastard faster, before he narrows in on his next target."

"How?"

"I'm still working on that."

Mercer thought for a moment. "Any idea where he

goes when he isn't here?"

"Not yet, but he follows his victims home or to their next destination before he strikes. Either way, he must leave a trail. Once I find that, I'll find him."

"But they've used different methods of transport," Hans argued. "By air, by sea."

"Well, private jet, helicopter, commercial airlines, some even fancied a lengthy road trip," Donovan chimed in. "That won't make tracking him any easier."

"Still, there must be a trail. I need to find the first breadcrumb." Bastian picked up another chip.

"You might want to work faster." Mercer watched a large family shuffle down the sidewalk a few meters from their table. "We're weeks away from the peak of tourist season."

"I'd wager he'll strike then," Donovan said. "We have to find him before that."

Mercer watched a mother and daughter enter one of the shops. The girl held her mother's hand as they browsed. The child pointed to the glistening crystal figurines inside the cases, leaning so close her breath fogged the glass. "Have you noticed any patterns with the victims?"

"Aside from the fact they all came here on holiday?" Bastian asked.

Mercer swallowed a growl. "Did they stay at the same resort? Shop at the same stores? Frequent the same pubs?"

"Half of them were underage, so the pubs are out," Hans said.

"This isn't London or New York, Jules. This is a tiny ski town. With only a handful of restaurants and resorts, everything is a bloody commonality," Bastian said. "The ski lift, the shops, the restaurants, it's all the same for each of them. His victims went to the same places. Did the same things. Crossed the same paths."

"Crossed paths with our kidnapper," Donovan mumbled.

"So he could be watching from anywhere." Mercer glared at one of the shop owners. "He could be right under our noses, and we'd never know it."

The girl and her mum left the shop and strolled down the walkway. The girl couldn't have been older than eight. She wore a light grey knit cap embroidered to look like a kitten, complete with ears and pink pom-poms which bounced up and down with every step she took. She waved at Bastian and Julian as she went past the table.

"He's only taken the affluent," Mercer said. "How does he figure out their net worth?"

"Only the rich can afford the lodgings here. Have you seen the price list for a room at the resort? It's why he targets tourists," Hans said. "It's also why we're in that freeze-your-balls-off cabin in the middle of bloody nowhere." The reconnaissance expert let the thought percolate for a moment. "Jules, you're right. He must be a local. It's how he can tell the difference."

"That doesn't narrow the possibilities for determining his future victims," Bastian said, "though it explains why he leaves the locals alone. He probably knows everyone in this town by name."

"I hate small towns," Donovan mumbled.

"Surely, not everyone who holidays here has enough money to pay his ransom demands. Some must scrimp and save to have a posh holiday." Mercer reached for his mug, only to find it empty. He waved down the server for a refill. "He must have a way of determining the crème de la crème. Have you evaluated the hotel and resort registries for potential breaches?"

"I didn't find anything on their servers. I even

checked the inns and the cabin rentals," Bastian said. "Even the online sites. But it's a no-go."

Mercer flipped through the dossier, skimming the intel they had on the kidnapper's previous victims. Most stayed at the resort, but a smattering had rented private cabins, chosen an area hotel, or visited the B&Bs.

"What about room and apartment rentals? Timeshares? Things like that?" Hans asked through the radio.

"Nothing," Bastian said.

"Those wouldn't be his primary targets," Mercer said. "People traveling on a budget wouldn't have the kind of money he demands in his ransoms. And he knows it. He only targets the rich." He closed the dossier. "The resort would be his best bet, but he hasn't stuck with it. He selects them another way." Mercer glanced at one of the souvenir shops. The cheap trinkets could be purchased by anyone, but the same didn't hold true for the jewelry store on the other side of the promenade. "He could work in a high-end shop or restaurant."

"Which one?" Bastian asked. "There are several. It'd be impossible to track. We don't know which of his victims might have paid cash and what shop or restaurant the survivors failed to mention when we questioned them about their itineraries. With the overlap, I'm not even sure it matters."

"Then we check them all."

"For what?"

But without a profile or description, such a search was pointless.

"Not to be contrary," Hans said, "but couldn't he be choosing his victims when they catch a return flight home? He'd have an easy enough time targeting first-class ticket holders."

"Except they all didn't fly here," Donovan pointed out.

"Most did, and some of the ones who didn't still had to check in at the airport. The nearest one has a helipad and private runway. That would cover the private jets and helicopter crowd."

Mercer looked at Bastian, waiting for the analyst's response.

"Airport security is rather strict. They'd notice some bloke hanging around the private lounges or checking tickets at the gate."

"He could work at the airport or for one of the airlines," Donovan suggested. "He'd have access. He might load luggage or work at the ticket claim. Then it'd be his job to check tickets. That'd give him names, addresses, a look at their passports. He could even work in one of the shops or pubs in the airport, possibly in one of those first-class lounges."

Mercer stared at the tall, snow-topped mountains. It was cold, but it hadn't snowed yet. It would soon, which would bring couples escaping for romantic weekends, families desperate to enjoy some skiing, and groups of young men and women searching for fun and casual hookups. "That's a gamble. I'd wager he's a local who works somewhere in town."

"I'd say so," Bastian agreed. "None of the bodies were found anywhere even remotely close to here. Most kidnappers operate where they are comfortable. They want to exploit every advantage possible."

"That's precisely what he does," Hans said.

"Yeah, but his victims came from all over. It'll make it that much harder for us to stop him if he takes another one. We'll be here, and he'll be wherever," Donovan said.

"That's why we have to intercept him before he makes his next move." Mercer thumbed the corner of the file. "He's most active during tourist season. Ninety percent of the abductions happened then."

"Actually," Hans interrupted, "if he works locally, his absence would be missed during peak times when all of the locals are back to work. Wouldn't that sound some alarms? Maybe you can flag him that way, Bas."

Bastian reached for another chip. "That's brilliant. If we ask around, sneak a peek at the employee records for the resort and other high-end shops, attractions, and restaurants, and check for patterns, we might be able to identify him that way. It'll just take time. Of course, that's assuming we're right in our assumption that he's a local."

"Then you should get started." Mercer pushed his plate across the table and leaned back in his seat. "We've been here long enough. It's about time we make some progress."

TWO

Bastian pulled the laptop out of the bag by his feet and placed it on the table. He took another handful of chips off Mercer's plate and chewed while scanning for nearby networks. Since they were situated in the center of the promenade, which was a lengthy cluster of shops nestled between two large resorts, he could access the individual networks without moving from the table.

"I'll see what I can pull too," Hans offered, having recently honed his hacking skills while recovering from a near-amputation.

Mercer watched the tourists move from shop to shop while his dining companion worked. The server brought another plate of chips, refilled Mercer's mug with hot water, and placed an assortment of teas on the table beside him. She topped off Bastian's coffee and asked if they needed anything else.

"No, love," Bastian said, his eyes fixed on the screen. "But thanks."

She smiled and walked away, her ponytail swinging

as she went.

Mercer selected a packet of earl grey, ripped it open, and submerged the tea bag in his cup. The surrounding outdoor tables had emptied, and only a few people dined inside. He checked the time. It was just after two. That explained the sudden lull at the café.

"Shit." Hans' curse sounded loud in Mercer's ear.

"What is it?"

"The bloody network detected an intruder and kicked me out." Hans cursed again.

"Where are you?" Bastian asked.

"Checking the back-end of the Wonderland Resort's mainframe."

"No wonder. They have added encryption. I was saving them for last. Just back out and leave them alone. Hopefully, you didn't trigger any additional protections and their security won't pay too much attention to your failed intrusion." Bastian gnawed on the end of a chip. The soggy, greasy potato wedge hung limply from the corner of his mouth, like those bloody cigarettes he'd been so fond of. "Hand me that."

Mercer slid the dossier closer, and Bastian turned to the timeline. He narrowed his eyes at the dates and double-checked the screen.

"Did you find something?" Mercer asked.

"I don't know. Maybe."

Mercer went around the table and peered over Bastian's shoulder at the screen. "What's his name?"

"I don't know. I just have an employee number."

"Where does he work?" Mercer asked.

Bastian nodded at the ski lift. "He might sell tickets, day passes, or he operates the lift. I'm not sure. Nothing's broken down. It's all very mechanical."

"But you found him?" Mercer asked.

"It's too soon to say." Bastian wrote down the pertinent information on the inside cover of the folder. "I'll need more time to analyze it and better access to the rest of my equipment and the databases. But Jules, I've only hacked into the town's main database. I haven't had time to check each and every shop, restaurant, and hotel. I'm sure we'll have dozens more possibilities."

"Keep at it."

"Let me download the network information." Bastian tore his eyes from the screen. "I need to note the networks around here. It'll make getting into each individual system easier, but I'll need better computing power and decryption software."

"Is it at the cabin?"

"Aye."

Mercer tapped the radio clipped to his ear. "All right. We're heading back."

"Copy that," Donovan said.

"On my way," Hans replied.

Bastian packed up his computer and stuffed a fistful of the remaining chips into his mouth, washing them down with the rest of his now cold coffee. He tucked the folder into the bag beside the laptop. "I have to start eating better."

Mercer snorted. "I concur."

Bastian glared at him. "This would be easier if you didn't order a sandwich with unlimited chips when you rarely eat the chips."

"You like the chips."

Bas chuckled. "Sure, clog my arteries with grease while forcing me to give up cigarettes."

"They'll kill you." Mercer looked at the empty plate. "But so will that, I suppose."

"And so will a bullet to the head." Bastian pushed

away from the table. "Seems to me everything I do is likely to result in my demise. Shouldn't I enjoy my final days?"

"These better not be your final days." Even though Bastian was joking, Mercer didn't want to contemplate the possibility of losing his best friend or any of his teammates. He'd already lost enough, and it broke him once. Another tragedy would destroy him. "That's an order, Clarke."

Bastian grinned. "I always knew you cared."

An engine revved in the distance, somewhere on the other side of the row of shops. Mercer turned to look, but the storefronts blocked his view of the parking lot and roadways. He listened as the vehicle barreled away, the tires screeching. A chill went through him. Perhaps the wind had picked up, but Mercer didn't believe that was the case. He turned, examining the few people milling about on the promenade. No one else seemed to care.

"Hans, Donovan, anything to report?" Mercer asked.

"There's a bird with a see-through sweater at your nine o'clock," Hans said.

"Donovan, do you see anything?"

"No," Donovan said uncertainly. "Should I be seeing something?"

Bastian cocked his head to the side. He was used to Mercer's paranoia, but this was different. "What is it, Jules?"

"I'm not certain." He removed several bills from his pocket and placed them beneath his mug, ensuring they wouldn't blow away. "Come on."

The two men headed down the path, the thick wood planks giving slightly beneath their feet. They passed several shops selling everything from ski equipment to souvenirs. Near the end, where the boardwalk gave way to resort property, Mercer noticed a grey knit cap beneath the railing.

Bending down, he picked it up. Two pink pom-poms hung from the garment. He scanned the area, searching for the girl and her mum.

Bastian stared at the smiling face and ears stitched to the cap in Julian's hand. "We would have seen the child or her mum. Neither of them went past us." The resort towered in front of them, the grounds expanding in all directions. "I'll check the resort. Maybe she dropped it on her way inside." Without waiting, Bastian sprinted toward the sprawling property, regretting every greasy chip he ate.

Mercer turned, cursing his own incompetence. How could a child and her mum vanish only meters from him? The kidnapper had never struck like this before. Why would he now? What changed? Had he caught on to the kidnapping and ransom specialists' investigation? They'd been operating in the area for nearly a month. If their target was a local, he must have noticed them. But why would he act out when he knew he was under scrutiny? It didn't make sense. *Surely, I'm mistaken*, Mercer thought. *Paranoid, like Bastian always accuses me.* But his instincts told him otherwise.

"Bloody hell." He sprinted down the few steps, across the path, and into the parking lot, barking orders to Donovan and Hans to get eyes on nearby traffic. "Find the vehicle with the screeching tires. He must be driving erratically, which should draw someone's attention."

"Commander?" Donovan questioned.

"I don't know," Mercer said, "but it's possible a little girl was taken." Someone must have noticed the kidnapper's escape. After all, Julian heard it. He described the girl and her mum to the best of his recollection to his teammates. Normally, he didn't concern himself with the people around him, but he was always aware. He was too well-trained not to be. But the little girl had caught his eye. Perhaps, it was because she waved, or it was the ridiculous knit grey cap she wore. Whatever it was, Mercer had seen her, and now she was gone.

He searched for signs of foul play, but he didn't find any dropped packages or blood. He checked each of the empty parking spaces in the resort's lot, but nothing indicated a car had been idling or had just pulled away. Spotting a few resort valets, he jogged over to them.

"Have you seen a little girl? She's this tall," he gestured with his palm, "and has flaxen hair just past her shoulders. Her eyes are bright green." He squinted, recalling the unimportant details. "She has freckles on her nose."

The two men shook their heads.

"Bugger." Mercer tried again, this time describing the woman who'd accompanied the child. "She's around forty. Thin, dark blonde hair swept into a bun." Mercer squinted. "She wore sunglasses and knee-high, high-heeled boots with fur lining."

"Sorry, sir, we didn't see either of them. We'll keep an eye out."

"What about vehicles? Did anyone leave?"

The two valets exchanged a shrug. "No one's picked up a car. In case you haven't noticed, the place is dead."

Mercer cringed at the word. "Some tosser revved his engine. Surely, you heard it."

Before either man could answer, a woman screamed something from the promenade. Mercer raced back the way he came, leaping up the two steps to the boardwalk. The woman screamed again. This time, he understood what she said. "Annalise."

"Madam, is everything all right?"

Her eyes were the same sharp green as her daughter's. But her hair was darker, and her freckles less pronounced. "Have you seen a little girl?" Her gaze fell to the light grey mass crumpled in his hand. "Where did you find that?" She yanked it from his grip, smoothing the wrinkles out of it. "Where's my daughter? Where did she go?"

"Does that belong to her?"

"Yes. Where did you find it?"

Mercer swallowed. "Tell me what happened."

The woman took a step back, sensing something was wrong. "Annalise," she yelled again.

"Madam, please."

"Where's my daughter? What did you do to her?"

"Nothing." Mercer held up his palms. "Please, let me help you. We're wasting valuable time. What happened? Where was she? Where were you?"

The woman came to a decision. "I wanted to get a new sweater. I went to try it on. Annalise was looking at the mittens." She pointed to the display near the front window. "I told her I'd be right back. She knew not to go anywhere."

Mercer didn't wait to hear the rest. He burst into the clothing shop, the chiming bell announcing his presence. He stormed to the counter. "Who took her?"

The clerk looked back at the frazzled mother a few steps behind Mercer. "I don't know, man. I told the lady that. I didn't see anything."

"Bugger." Mercer turned back to the woman. "Did you hear the bell?"

"Yes."

"How many times?"

She shook herself, growing more frantic by the second. "Just the once."

He turned back to the clerk. "Did you see anyone outside the shop? Anything abnormal? Anything at all?"

"I wasn't paying attention."

"Where are your security cameras?"

The clerk pointed vaguely toward the ceiling.

"I need to see the footage." When the clerk didn't move fast enough, Mercer said, "Now." He tapped his ear. "Bas, I need you to get back here. Pull everything you can from outside the clothing shop. Donovan, Hans, follow the paths away from the resort, see what you can find. You have her description." Mercer looked back at the harried mother. "The child's name is Annalise." He waited for the woman to fill in the blank.

"Van der Berg," she said.

He repeated it for his teammates as he followed the clerk down the hallway, past the dressing rooms, and into a tiny office. An ancient black and white monitor sat on top of a filing cabinet. Mercer rewound the footage.

"There she is." Mrs. Van der Berg pointed to the screen.

Annalise knelt down, sorting the mittens on the rack. She had found some with a similar design to the kitten on her cap and tried them on, animatedly moving her hands back and forth as if they were puppets. Abruptly, in the midst of her playing, she stopped and peered out the front window. Returning the mittens to the rack, she ventured closer to the glass and pressed her nose against it.

"What's she looking at?" Mrs. Van der Berg asked, but the unhelpful clerk had left them alone in the room.

Briefly, Mercer considered he could be involved and split his focus, concentrating on the telltale chime of the bell. If the clerk tried to escape, Mercer would break his legs. "I don't know."

Approximately thirty seconds later, Annalise went to the front door, pushed it open, and disappeared. The camera didn't cover outside. Bastian would have to find a camera that did. It was the only way.

"She knows better than to wander off on her own, especially in a strange place." Mrs. Van der Berg hurried out of the room and out of the shop. "Annalise," she screamed, desperate to find her daughter. "Answer me."

Mercer moved through the store, giving the clerk a warning look before stepping outside.

"Annalise," she yelled again, each time, her voice becoming shriller and more panicked. "Annalise." She shrieked until her words were nothing but a strained whisper, barely even a squeak. Then she turned on Mercer with the same ferocity as a ravenous wild animal. "Who are you? You had her hat in your hand. What did you do to my daughter? Where is she?"

Bastian charged onto the wooden walkway. He must have been searching the far side of the resort. He approached, but Mercer shook his head, waving off the analyst. "I'm sorry," Mercer said, "but I promise, we'll get her back."

The blood drained from the woman's face. She stared at him as if she must have misunderstood what he'd said. "What have you done to her?"

"Nothing." Mercer held up his palms, his unzipped jacket shifting in the process.

She stared at the Sig Sauer holstered at his hip. But she didn't look afraid. She looked angry. "Who the hell are you?" She shoved him. "Answer me."

"I'm Julian Mercer. I'm a kidnapping and ransom specialist. My team and I were asked to determine if a kidnapper was working in the area."

The woman teetered. Mercer reached for her, afraid she might pass out, but she batted his hand away. "This can't be happening. This is a dream." A sick understanding contorted her features. "Did my husband put you up to this? Did he do this?"

"Who's your husband?" Bastian asked.

Before the woman could reply, her phone rang. She reached into her pocket, a brief look of triumph on her face, as if she expected the call to be from Annalise. But quickly, the expression evaporated, replaced by confusion. "Hello?"

Mercer met Bastian's eyes. They were too late. The pair wordlessly communicated, and Bastian ducked over to the side to update Hans and Donovan on the situation. They had to start the clock. They'd never arrived to an abduction this quickly before. They weren't prepared. Though, they should have been.

"This is Zoe Van der Berg," the woman said. Mercer glanced at Bastian, making sure the analyst heard it. They'd need that information to build the profile. "I don't understand." She paused. "Let me speak to her."

Mercer's throat tightened. He moved half a step closer, desperate to grab the phone and take control.

"Annalise, are you okay?" Zoe asked. The woman sniffed, her tense expression relaxing ever so slightly.

The child hadn't been harmed, at least not yet.

"Annalise?" Zoe asked, panic quickly returning. "Why are you doing this? What do you want?"

Mercer debated if he should intercede. He'd handled many negotiations, but he didn't know enough about the kidnapper or the Van der Bergs to know how the family wanted to proceed. So he waited, hating every moment. On his best day, he despised himself and the pain his existence had caused the woman he loved. Right now, he loathed himself for being unable to stop the abduction. He and his team had come here with this exact purpose, and already, they failed. In fact, he wasn't positive their presence hadn't exacerbated the situation.

"I'll give you whatever you want," Zoe said, "just let Annalise go. You don't understand. She's sick. She needs me. She needs her medicine."

Mercer reached for the phone and tugged it free from Zoe's grip. "Sir, please listen to what I have to say. I'm a professional negotiator." But by the time he said those words, the kidnapper had hung up. "Shite." He passed Zoe's phone to Bastian.

The woman's eyes went wide, and her knees buckled. Mercer pulled her into his chest before she collapsed to the ground. She held the soft grey cap in a vise grip and sobbed.

"Easy," Mercer soothed. "We'll get her back. You have my word."

Bastian eyed him. Normally, they didn't make promises unless they knew they could keep them. And from the limited knowledge they possessed on this particular kidnapper, a positive recovery wasn't guaranteed. Annalise had a fifty-fifty shot of surviving, depending on her mother's willingness and ability to pay.

"Madam, let us help you," Mercer said softly.

She bit her lip, swallowing down her sobs. "Why should I trust you? I don't know a damn thing about you. For all I know, you could have taken my baby. You could be behind this."

"We're not," Bastian said. "We didn't take her. But we're your best chance of getting her back alive."

THREE

"Here, love." Bastian tried to hand the steaming mug to the distraught woman. Mercer had led her to a nearby bench where they could keep an eye on the area in case they missed a clue or someone wandered by who had witnessed the abduction. Bastian had gone to the nearest coffee cart and gotten the woman a hot cocoa to sooth her frazzled nerves.

She didn't reach for it, so Bastian placed it on the bench beside her. She stared at him with cold, dead eyes. "I don't know about any of this. Maybe I should let the police handle it."

"That's your prerogative," Bastian said. "You have to do what's in Annalise's best interest, whatever that may be." Mercer gave the analyst a look, but Bastian ignored it.

The woman blinked rapidly. "I don't know what to do. He said if I notified the authorities, he'd kill her." She sniffed. "Why did I leave her alone in the store? Why didn't I make her come into the dressing room with me?"

"You can't change that now," Mercer said. "You

didn't know."

"I should have. No one leaves a seven-year-old alone in a strange place."

"You're not local?" Bastian asked, though they already surmised as much.

"We needed to get away for a few days. I remembered coming here with my parents as a kid. I always thought of this place as a winter wonderland. That's probably how the resort chose the name." Zoe shook her head. "I don't ski, but it's nearly ski season. I figured most of the attractions and shops would be open. It snows a lot up here, so I thought we might get to sled or build a snowman or something. Annalise loves wintertime with fluffy sweaters and cute mittens." She looked down at the smiling kitten on her daughter's knit hat. "This is all my fault."

"No, it isn't," Bastian said.

It's mine, Mercer thought. The kidnapper must have been keeping tabs on their progress. Perhaps he overheard them talking or detected the network intrusion. He must have wanted to make one last score before fleeing, or he had some other plan in mind. "What is he thinking? Why would he take her?" Mercer rubbed a hand over his mouth to conceal his words from the girl's mum. "This doesn't make sense."

"What?" Zoe asked.

"Let me check on something. Bastian, stay with her. If the bastard calls again, take care of it."

"Sure, Jules."

Mercer moved along the promenade, searching in all directions, but he didn't see anything out of the ordinary. Wouldn't he have felt someone watching? He backtracked to the café and spoke to the server. Perhaps another party had lingered, but she didn't recall anyone. It had been a slow day, which is why Bastian and Mercer had camped out at the table since lunchtime.

"It was just you and the man you were with," the server said. "No one else stuck around, except for an elderly couple who came in early this morning. But they were gone before you got here." She twirled her ponytail absently. "They were cute. They did a crossword puzzle together."

"Bollocks." Mercer took a breath. "What about people walking by?"

"Um..."

"Dammit." Not waiting, Mercer ran the entire length of the strip. "Hans? Donovan?"

"Nothing to report. Still looking," Donovan said.

"Same," Hans added.

"You checked everywhere?" Mercer's lungs burned from the cold air.

"No sign of the girl."

But Mercer didn't give up. He ran faster, as if he could catch the bastard on foot, slowing only to ask anyone he passed if they'd seen a suspicious looking man or a vehicle racing away. He described Annalise, but all he got were headshakes and confused looks.

When he reached the other end of the strip, he moved away from the enclosed boardwalk and checked the joint parking lots. Without plates or any details on the make and model of the getaway vehicle, or what he assumed to be the getaway vehicle, he had nothing to go on.

With a final deep breath, he took the streets back, sticking to the sidewalks as much as he could. But he didn't find any indication of the sinister crime that happened only moments ago. Hans and Donovan had spread out to search the rest of the town for any hint as to who took Annalise or where they might have gone. Unfortunately, they had few workable details. Bastian was pulling area footage from outside the shop, but he hadn't made any progress before Mercer began his search. Hopefully, that would change by the time he got back.

Twenty minutes later, Mercer returned, winded. He let out a few huffs, his breath crystallizing in the air.

"What?" Zoe asked. "Did you find her? Did you find the man who took her?"

Mercer shook his head. He rubbed his side, sore from the cold and possibly previous injuries and surgeries. Then he explained his failed attempt to find answers and the man responsible.

Zoe listened to Mercer's ramblings, the distrust in her eyes easing. She reached for her phone, which Bastian had placed beside the hot beverage. "I have to call my husband. He needs to know what's happened."

Mercer moved to intercede, but a sharp look from Bastian held him off. They'd have time to ask more questions later. They listened while Zoe told Charles about their daughter's disappearance and the threatening phone call she received. Two minutes later, she put the phone down.

"He's on his way. He'll be here in a few hours." She shivered. The promenade was nearly empty. In an hour, the sun would set and the temperatures would plummet. "I can't wait that long. Annalise can't wait that long." She reached for the mug, her hands shaking from the cold and nerves. She turned her focus to Mercer. "I don't think I should trust you, but I'm not sure I have a choice. Annalise is diabetic. Without her insulin, she could die."

"Bloody hell," Bastian murmured.

Mercer remained stone-faced. He knew it was best to avoid getting emotional in front of the client, if at all possible. "What did the kidnapper say when you spoke to him? What does he want?"

"He didn't say much. He asked for my name, said

Annalise was safe for now, and if I wanted her to stay that way, I'd follow his instructions." She held the mug against her chest, letting the steam rise and warm her face. "Then he put her on the phone."

"How did your daughter sound?" Mercer asked.

"She was scared."

"But unharmed, right?" Bastian asked.

Zoe nodded.

"Did he ask for money? What were his instructions?" Mercer asked.

"He didn't ask for anything. He said he'd call back, so I should sit tight."

"And that's when he warned you not to contact the police?" Bastian asked.

The woman nodded again.

"He already hung up by the time I took the phone." Mercer checked his watch. Depending on how long it took to receive a second call, they might be able to determine the kidnapper's location. "The sooner he calls back, the closer he is."

Mercer stared down the lengthy boardwalk. Shops and restaurants filled in the gaps left between the various ski resorts and hotels. On the other side of the boardwalk, the tiny town sprawled out. Inns, B&Bs, cabin rentals, and other necessities, like grocery stores, pharmacies, and local attractions littered the zig-zagging streets. This was a tiny place, but the kidnapper could be anywhere. With all those rental places and constant tourist turnover, it'd be nearly impossible to narrow down the search, not to mention the mountains themselves with their wooded paths and hidden trails.

Zoe wiped her eyes on her sleeve. "I can't lose her. Annalise is my everything."

"You won't," Mercer said. "But time is of the essence. We need to prepare for his next call. Do you trust me to handle this? I will get her back alive."

"Jules," Bastian warned, but Mercer maintained eye contact with Zoe.

"You better," she said.

"Where are you staying?" Bastian asked gently.

"At one of the resort's private chalets."

"Sounds perfect," Bastian said. "When did you check in?"

"Sunday."

That meant the kidnapper could have been observing the mother and daughter for the last four days. "When did you make the reservations?" Mercer asked.

"Last month. This was all rather spur of the moment." Zoe's lip quivered, her face contorting in anger. "I wish we'd never come here."

"Bas, how's it coming on security footage?" Mercer asked.

"Nothing yet."

"We need a place to set up. More than likely, he's been watching you. We need to check the chalet for surveillance devices," Mercer said. They'd also need to check their own cabin, but that wasn't important now.

Zoe almost laughed, the situation too surreal for her to comprehend. "This can't be happening."

"I'm sorry, love, but it is." Bastian shrugged out of his jacket, pulling his sweater down over his exposed gun, and putting the insulated slicker around her trembling shoulders. "Let's get you out of the cold. Once you warm up, you'll be able to think better. I'll make sure your lodgings are safe and secure, and then we'll get down to business. The sooner we get started, the sooner we can negotiate your daughter's safe return."

"Okay."

FOUR

The trio abandoned the outdoor café and headed toward the resort. As they passed the scene of the abduction, Mercer slowed. The clerk inside the clothing shop appeared just as oblivious now as he had earlier. The man didn't care a child had gone missing, and that apathetic attitude made Mercer both angry and suspicious. Were missing children so common an occurrence the clerk couldn't even pretend to care? Or was he a bloody accomplice? He couldn't be the predator, but he could work with him. For all Mercer knew, a team could be conducting the kidnappings. That would explain a lot of the discrepancies.

According to their research, the town didn't know a kidnapper was operating in their midst, but maybe that was a lie. The paranoid part of his brain feared the entire town could be in on the conspiracy, profiting from others' miseries.

"Jules, are you coming?" Bastian peered into the store. "Do you think now's the best time to ask more questions?"

"It can wait." Mercer would find out everything he needed to know later, but for now, he had to get moving. The clock was ticking. They had to prepare for the kidnapper's next call. He glanced at his watch. Annalise Van der Berg had been taken thirty-five minutes ago. It was fresh. Too fresh. Hans and Donovan hadn't returned or radioed in any updates. They were still searching.

As they passed the parking lot, the valet called out, "Did you find her?"

"No," Mercer said. "We're still looking."

"I'll keep an eye out."

Shock registered on Zoe's face. "You knew this would happen. You knew she was gone before I did. Why didn't you stop it? Why didn't you warn us?"

"Shh," Bastian soothed, leading her further down the path and away from the concerned parking attendants. "We knew he was here. We just didn't know what he had planned or when he would strike again."

"Again?" Her volume increased.

"We've been over this," Mercer said, though he wasn't sure it was true. "But you're right. We failed to protect Annalise. However, I won't let that happen again."

Zoe considered his words as the three went past the main building and headed for a tiny outcropping of smaller dwellings. The chalet Zoe rented was the fourth in the long row. She removed the key and stuck it in the lock.

Bastian put a hand on her forearm and met her eyes. "Let us go in first and make sure it's safe. We'll only be a moment."

He and Mercer entered with guns at the ready. After a quick sweep, they found the chalet empty.

Mercer tucked his gun away, examining the view from each of the windows before closing the drapes while Bastian used an RF reader to scan for hidden surveillance devices. Once they were positive the place was secure, they allowed Zoe to enter.

"Do you mind if we set up shop in here, love?" Bastian pulled a laptop from the bag he'd been carrying. "We'll need to stay in close proximity to make sure we don't miss his next call."

"It's fine, I guess. Actually, nothing's fine, but you know best. I hope. You said you do this for a living, right? You've done this before, so you know what to expect. Right?"

"That's right. Now isn't the best time to hand you our CV, but I've given you numbers. You can contact MI5, Interpol, the Met, or several firms which specialize in ransom insurance and security. They'll all tell you the same things I have." Bas nudged his phone closer to her. "Make some calls if you have other questions about who we are or what we do. We want you to be comfortable. If you're not, we'll go. It's imperative you trust whoever you hire to handle this situation."

Mercer turned away from the window, a million questions running through his mind. Annalise didn't have time for her mother to second-guess these things, but pushing Zoe to make a decision wouldn't help matters. As it was, she had every reason to believe he and his team could be in cahoots with the kidnapper or responsible for her daughter's disappearance.

Zoe studied Mercer carefully. Then she picked up the phone and dialed the Met. After speaking to several DCIs in London who vouched for Mercer, she hung up. "No, it's okay. I trust you."

"Good." Mercer had to prioritize and focus on the

most important details first in order to anticipate the kidnapper's next move. The rest of his questions would have to wait until they had some time to flesh out every minute detail. "Tell me about Annalise's condition. You said she's diabetic. How severe is her illness? Does she have medication with her? What kinds of warning signs indicate she's experiencing distress?"

"Since her diagnosis, she's been lucky. It hasn't been too bad, but she has to monitor her blood sugar. She gets daily injections. Most of the time, she can go hours without a problem."

"How many?" Mercer didn't want to push it, but he needed a reasonable timetable by which to work.

"Twelve, but that's only if she's very careful about what she eats, how much she eats, and when she eats."

"Tell me about your daughter's diet, what it entails, what it doesn't. I'll have to pass that information on to the kidnapper."

"I better write it down." Zoe reached for the resort stationery and pen. "Annalise can't consume large amounts of sugars or carbohydrates. She has to eat balanced meals and keep her stress down. That's what this trip was for, but obviously, that's not the case now."

"I'm sure not," Bastian said. "But it sounds like she's rather resilient."

"She's had to be," Zoe said. "She wears a medical alert bracelet, just in case. But she doesn't carry any insulin pens with her. I carry those. When she's at school, the nurse has them, along with strict instructions on what to do. We've never had a problem. Until now."

"When's the last time she had an injection?" Mercer asked.

"Right after lunch. Maybe two hours ago. We ate

late, but her sugar was fine the last time we checked. She has to make sure she eats when necessary and gets her insulin when necessary. She's a good kid. She understands the better she takes care of herself, the fewer injections she needs, so she does good. Better than most adults I know."

"It's a balancing act." Bastian glanced up from the screen. "How do you spell your last name, love? E or U?"

"E."

"Could she make it until the morning without her medication," Mercer asked, "if push came to shove?"

"Probably. It really just depends."

Mercer thought for a moment. "She's only seven. Does she know how to give herself injections?"

Again, Zoe nodded.

"Okay." Mercer ran a hand down his face. This complicated matters, and something told him the kidnapper didn't care for complicated. That's probably why he killed half of his victims. The easier Mercer could make this situation, the better Annalise's chances were of surviving. "We need to find them. Bas, I need that footage ASAP." He tapped the radio in his ear and stepped into another room. "Hans, how's the traffic?"

"I have no bloody idea who he is or where he went. Does Bas have the details on the car yet?"

"Negative," Mercer said, not wanting the analyst to have to answer in front of Mrs. Van der Berg.

"That would make it easier," Hans said. "I've asked around. A few people remember hearing it, but no one's seen it."

"What about you, Donovan?" Mercer asked.

"A few people thought they saw a girl matching Annalise's description in the back of a silver sedan. They didn't notice the plates or get a look at the driver. But half the seven-year-old girls around here fit her description. I backtracked to the promenade. He lured her out of the clothing store somehow. Perhaps someone saw him do it."

"I don't think so. Bas and I couldn't have been more than a few minutes behind him. No one was around. I spoke to the parking attendants and the store clerk. They didn't see anything, or so they say. I scouted the entire strip. No one saw anything."

"I'll check again, and then I'll speak to the servers at the outdoor cafés and see if anyone noticed anything. They're always outside. If Annalise screamed, they might have heard her. I'm sure they heard her mother."

"I did that too," Mercer mumbled. But since they didn't have any better ideas, it couldn't hurt. "The entire town must have heard Mrs. Van der Berg screaming." But Mercer knew that wouldn't lead to anything either. "Finish it up. Unless you find something solid, we don't have the luxury of time. The kidnapper said he'd call again soon. I'm guessing he'll do it once his hostage is secured."

"Another call should help narrow the possible locations," Donovan said. "We can use the time between calls to determine how far away he could have traveled. Then we can establish a search grid and hunt this bastard down."

"That's what I'm counting on. Rendezvous with us, and bring the rest of our gear. We're setting up inside the Van der Bergs' chalet." Mercer gave Hans and Donovan the chalet number and disconnected. Taking a deep breath, he pushed his shoulders back. He had to think clearly. Right now, Annalise's life depended on it. And he wouldn't let her down again.

Reentering the room, he went to the phone and checked for a dial tone. Then he grabbed the equipment from the bag Bastian carried and set up a trap and trace on the resort's phone in case the kidnapper called the landline instead.

"How did he get your cell phone number?" Bastian asked, glancing up at Zoe.

"I don't know." Zoe pulled her legs to her chest, only to drop them to the floor and rest her elbows on her knees.

"Does Annalise have a cell phone?" Mercer asked.

Zoe shook her head. "No. Her father and I thought she was too young."

"No trackers either?" Bastian raised an eyebrow.

"Like you'd put in a dog or cat?" Zoe made a face. "Do people really do that to their children?"

"Not exactly. Usually, it's in a piece of jewelry or an app on a tablet or cell phone." Bastian glanced at Mercer. "I did chip him, but that's because he tends to wander."

However, Zoe didn't find that amusing. She just frowned.

"Tell me about your husband," Mercer said. "Earlier, you accused me of working for him. You thought he orchestrated this. Why would you think that, especially when he was the only person you called for help?"

"He was angry we took this vacation. He doesn't like it when I take Annalise out of school. He doesn't like a lot of things."

"Is he violent?" Mercer doubted he misread the situation, but if this wasn't the work of a professional kidnapper and instead a domestic dispute over child rearing, it'd be best to determine that now. Coincidences were unlikely, but they did happen.

"No. Charles loves her very much. He'd never hurt her. We don't always agree. He might do something to scare me or hurt me, but he wouldn't abduct her.

She's his everything. Our everything. That's why I called him. He has a right to know. He'll fix this. He always fixes everything. Well, almost always."

Mercer watched her carefully. In the heat of the moment, the mother had exhibited quite the opposite opinion. But he didn't point it out.

"When the phone rang, I thought Charles was calling to tell me he picked Annalise up. That he was taking her back home. He might mess with me, but he wouldn't go to these lengths. If he had her, he would have told me," Zoe said. "He wouldn't be on his way here now. Someone else took her." Her words came out strangled, and she gasped, on the verge of hyperventilating.

Bastian reached over and rubbed her back while he worked the computer with his free hand. "He doesn't sound particularly stable, love."

Zoe snorted. "No kidding, but none of that matters. What matters is finding my baby. Charles is coming. He said he'll help in any way he can. I can't do this without him. I won't."

Her phone rang, and all three of them looked down at the display. *Blocked.*

Mercer reached for it, but Zoe grabbed it off the table. He held up a hand, gesturing for her to wait. "Before you answer, I need you to listen to my instructions. Remain calm. Listen to what he has to say. Then tell him you want to avoid any mistakes or miscommunications, so you think it's best if he speaks to me. Tell him who I am. That I'm a K&R specialist. And we'll take it from there. Okay?"

Zoe nodded and pressed the green button. "Hello?"

FIVE

"What's your name?" the kidnapper asked.

"Julian Mercer."

"K&R, huh? That must mean you were either military or law enforcement. Which is it?"

"Military."

"Private?"

"No." Mercer watched Bastian gesture to keep the conversation going. The trace would take time.

"Royal Navy?"

Mercer almost agreed, but something told him this was a test. The kidnapper wanted to figure out if Mercer could be trusted. "No. Special Air Service."

"Those guys are hardcore. You ever kill anyone? You must have. Probably lots of people."

"I did what was required to resolve the situation."

"That's an obvious yes. Me too, in case you're curious." The kidnapper snickered. "Confession time. Did you enjoy it?"

"No."

"Really? Not even a little bit?"

"Sir," Mercer began, hoping to derail the conversation before it could reach a threatening conclusion, "you know who I am, what I do. It's your turn. This is about give and take. That's how negotiations work. So tell me your name."

"Eh, I'm not sure about any of that. Y'see, I take, you give. That's how this works. I took the girl. Now you're gonna give me what I want. It's simple. I'm sure you've done this a lot. It's old hat to you. Am I right?"

"There is nothing old hat about this. Every case is unique." Mercer inhaled to keep his voice even. "What do you want? What are your demands?"

Again, the kidnapper hedged. "I'm not sure we're there yet. I need to feel you out first. You're a professional. Obviously, you have me at a disadvantage. How did you arrive so quickly? Do you live around here? Or are you on holiday?" He made a pathetic attempt to emulate Mercer's accent.

Bollocks. The kidnapper wasn't an amateur. He just wanted to jerk Mercer around. He wanted to see if the K&R specialist would explain himself or the reason for his presence. Mercer rubbed a hand over his mouth. He had to choose his words carefully. But nothing came to mind. When he didn't answer, Bastian looked up from the computer screen.

How close? Mercer mouthed.

Bas shook his head. *Not yet.*

"Cat got your tongue?" The kidnapper laughed. "Or maybe it's a cat on a hat, or a girl with a cat? Shit, man. I just realized I missed my true calling in life. I could have been a modern day Dr. Seuss. I could have made millions."

"It's never too late," Mercer said.

"Oh, it might be."

"I'll do my best to ensure my client meets all your

demands, but that is dependent on Annalise remaining unharmed. That's my only condition. As long as she's okay, I'll do everything in my power to get you what you want. Do you understand?"

"Sure, but now I'm thinking I missed out on making millions with this innate talent of mine. I mean, c'mon, you have to admit, this is some talent. My rhymes could be children's books or rapper's lyrics. I'm gonna have to make up for it somehow."

Mercer glanced at Zoe. He didn't know what the Van der Bergs were worth, but it had to be a lot. "I'll see that you're appropriately compensated."

"Let's not talk about money yet. First, I want you to answer my question. How'd you get here so fast?"

"Jules," Bastian shook his head, "careful."

"I was already here."

"Now we're getting somewhere. But I won't push you, Julian. I'd hate to confuse your client and give her the wrong idea. After all, she might start to think we're conspiring together. I'm sure that wouldn't work out very well for you. I mean, you get paid a fee for your service, and according to you, I'm gonna get paid whatever my heart desires."

"I didn't say that."

"You might not have said it, but you meant it. We both know it. Is your fee charged by the hour? By the day? Based on the recovery?" The kidnapper took a breath, his nonstop rambling bordered on manic. "Never mind. That's not my business. That's yours. It must suck for the Van der Bergs though. They pay me. They pay you. We're both screwing 'em, right? If we worked in tandem, we'd have the perfect racket going. I make problems, and you make solutions. We could rule the world."

"Sir," tension ran down Mercer's shoulders and into his arms, "to simplify the negotiation, how should

I address you?"

"Address me? Are you mailing me a Christmas card now?"

"When I speak to you," Mercer clarified.

"No shit. I'm just yanking your chain. Do you think I'm a moron?"

Mercer gripped the phone tighter, the plastic case creaking under the pressure. "Quite the opposite."

"Good."

"So what do I call you?"

"Sir works. Actually, I kinda like it. Sir. It sounds respectable. Royal, even. Especially with your accent. What is that? North London? You're one of the upstairs people, aren't you? Like the show. None of that 'aye, guv'na' bullshit."

Bastian shook his head, hoping Mercer wouldn't get dragged into a debate on the class system. Mercer eyed him, raising an eyebrow as if to say, *Well?*

Bastian's focus returned to the data on the computer screen, but he couldn't get a fix on the kidnapper's location. The signal bounced around the globe. This would take a lot more time and patience.

"Is Mrs. V listening in on this conversation?" the kidnapper asked. "Does she have any questions for either of us?"

"We need to discuss terms. We need to talk about Annalise," Mercer insisted, seeing Zoe's ears perk up at the mention of her daughter's name. He intentionally looked away, afraid to see the hope in her eyes. He made a promise. He just wasn't sure he could deliver.

"Sure, sure, but time's almost up. I can't spend too long on these calls. That's how they get you." The kidnapper laughed again. "Since you're a professional and all, you must have a VoIP number to conduct business. Give it to me, and I'll call you back. I am dealing solely with you now. Right, mate? Mummy is out of the picture for now?" He embellished on the mocked accent. "Oh, wait, that's Australian, isn't it? Shit. You'd think by now I'd know my countries."

Bastian scribbled down a number and slid it across the table. Just as Julian read off the last digit, the call dropped. He stared at the end call message for a moment before placing Zoe's cell phone on the table.

"That's it?" Zoe asked. "What did that accomplish? He didn't tell us anything. You didn't tell him about Annalise or her condition."

"He'll call back. He didn't want details. He wanted to establish his presence, but he couldn't waste too much time. He was afraid we'd trace the call." Mercer went around the table and stared at Bastian's screen. From the looks of it, they hadn't even gotten close to pinpointing the kidnapper's location.

"He's using an internet phone number," Bastian said, "probably shielded behind a—"

Before Bastian could complete the thought, the notification popped up in the center of the screen. They had an incoming video call. "Jules," Bastian warned, but Mercer was ready.

The two men switched places. Mercer checked behind him to make sure nothing damning was visible. Then he clicked accept.

The screen filled with the image of a man in casual winter dress, wearing a navy blue ski mask over his face. The mask only showed his hazel eyes and chapped lips. That didn't give Mercer much from which to work.

"Is that you, Julian?" the kidnapper asked.

"Yes." Everything about this man's demeanor grated on Mercer's nerves, but he filed it away for later consideration. Even the tiniest detail could lead to the man's identity and location. And that was all that mattered.

He cocked his head from side to side. "I pictured you in a tuxedo or desert camo. I'm not sure why. We're in the middle of a snowy forest. Did you pack the arctic camo or the forest camo?"

Mercer didn't answer, his patience waning. "Is the girl unharmed?"

"See for yourself." The kidnapper flipped the screen around. Mercer watched a white, interior door open into a bedroom. It looked basic, possibly even commercial. He clicked a key, taking a screen grab for later analysis. Annalise sat on the bed, her back against the headboard and her legs pulled up in front of her.

"Smile at the camera, honey," the kidnapper instructed. The child looked up for a split second before tucking her face down behind her knees.

"Annalise?" Zoe asked. Bastian put his hand on her shoulder, keeping her from getting off the couch.

"It's okay, love," Bastian whispered. "Jules will handle this."

"I want to see her. She needs to know I'm here."

"She does," Bastian insisted.

"Satisfied?" the kidnapper asked, pulling the door closed and blocking Mercer's view before he could communicate with Annalise.

"We want to know your demands. We'd like to sort this matter out as swiftly as possible. Annalise is sick," Mercer said. Normally, he wouldn't divulge weaknesses, but time was of the essence.

"She looks fine to me." The kidnapper winked.

Mercer's blood boiled. "I want to make sure you get what you want as quickly as possible. Playing games only wastes valuable time. As long as Annalise remains unharmed, I will do my best to meet your demands, whatever they are."

"Whatever they are." The kidnapper stroked his chin in an exaggerated fashion. "I like the sound of that. Let me think about it. I'll call you back. Stay by the phone. Or computer. Whatever. Just stay put." He disconnected before Mercer could get a word in edgewise.

"What just happened?" Panic crept into Zoe's tone. "Why didn't he tell you what he wants? Why aren't you making arrangements to pick up Annalise? Why didn't you do anything?"

"That's not how negotiations work," Mercer said.

Bastian spun the computer around. After a few seconds, he looked up. "He pinged in India. He's hiding behind a VPN or some other network protocol to bounce the signal around. He knows what he's doing."

"Bugger." Mercer tapped the comm in his ear. "ETA?"

"Knocking now," Donovan said, followed by a gentle rapping at the door. With gun in hand, Mercer went to the front entrance and unlocked the door.

Donovan stood on the other side with several large bags thrown over his shoulder. He nodded to the commander and entered the chalet. "Where do you want to set up?"

"Kitchen." Mercer pointed to the dining area, and Donovan strode across the room and dropped the bags on the table. "Do you have the files?"

"Of course." Donovan pushed one of the bags closer while he opened the other and removed another laptop and more of their gear. "Bas, a little help, if you're not too busy."

"Coming." Bastian offered Zoe a reassuring nod and joined his two colleagues at the table.

"Did you find anything?" Mercer asked as they separated their gear, hooked up the computer equipment, wired the phones, and assembled the other necessary tools of their trade.

"A waitress remembered seeing a man with a box of kittens earlier in the day. She doesn't recall much about him, but she thought it was odd he kept changing locations," Donovan said.

"I'll start pulling footage," Bastian said. "I didn't get much from outside the store, but if someone was around all day, I might spot him farther down the strip."

"What about the car? Anything on that?" Mercer asked.

Donovan shook his head. "I described the girl to every shop owner and tourist I came across. Half of them said they saw her, but those are probably false positives. A lot of the girls around here fit that broad description." Donovan glanced into the living room where Zoe remained poised on the couch, prepared to grab the phone should it ring again. "I hate to ask, but do you think he had a specific target in mind? Or would any little girl do?"

"His other victims varied in age and gender," Mercer said. "He doesn't have a type, except rich."

"That sums up every tourist on this bloody mountain," Bastian mumbled.

"We still don't know how he's choosing them." Donovan reached for the dossier on the kidnapper and his previous victims. "Shall I pin these up?"

"Not yet. We'll play it close to the vest for now. We don't want to frighten the poor woman any more than she already is." Mercer wasn't sure how much Zoe trusted him after the things the bastard said on the phone. Until he was sure they wouldn't get kicked out or arrested, he didn't want to commit to the chalet becoming their new base of operations.

"She doesn't trust us," Bastian said, "and with good

reason."

"I'll see if I can change her mind," Donovan offered.

"Have her call a few of our friends at Interpol and MI5. Maybe they can persuade her that we're here to help," Bastian suggested. "She's already spoken to our friends at the Met. But we need her on board. There's a lot she isn't saying. I just don't know what it is. But it could be important."

"Right-o." Donovan crossed the room and introduced himself.

SIX

"Nothing on the car." Hans ran a hand down his face. "I drove around this entire bloody tourist trap of a town and examined every silver sedan I found. No sign of the girl. We don't even know if that's the proper vehicle."

"It's all we have to go on," Donovan said.

Mercer narrowed his eyes. "Kittens."

"It looks like that's the reason Annalise left her mum inside the shop." Bastian pointed to the video feed he'd pulled from the resort's security system. The angle was utter shite, but a man in shabby ski gear, minus the skis, had stopped within view of the front window. He put a tattered cardboard box on the ground and waited. A small grey furball climbed out of the box and dropped onto the boardwalk. It froze in place, timid at first. The man scooped it up before it could run away and put it back in the box.

A few seconds later, it climbed out again, but this time, Annalise intercepted the cat before it could escape. She picked it up and stroked its soft fur. The kitten batted at the pink poofs hanging from her cap.

Annalise put the cat down on the ground and took off her hat, dangling it just out of the kitten's reach. The kitten pawed at the pom-poms. The man moved closer, blocking the camera's view, and then the trio disappeared, box and all, leaving only the grey knit hat behind.

"Show her mum," Mercer said. "Mrs. Van der Berg will want to see that. Let's make sure that's Annalise."

Lifting the laptop off the table, Bastian returned to the living room where Zoe was pacing to show her the footage he found. Unfortunately, the angles didn't show Annalise exiting the shop or where the girl and man disappeared. They simply vanished off the side of the screen.

Hans lifted the knit cap off the table, holding it up for Mercer and Donovan to see. "Obviously, the bastard knew his audience."

"Doesn't take much," Donovan said. "What child doesn't like animals?"

Mercer stared at the smiling face embroidered on the garment. If Hans was right, Annalise had been specifically targeted. They needed to go back to the profile. Somehow, the Van der Bergs had gotten onto the kidnapper's radar. Mercer had to find out how.

"That's Annalise," Zoe said, appearing a few steps behind Bastian. "She loves cats. I promised her we'd get one after we got back from vacation."

"Who knew you were going on holiday?" Donovan asked.

"No one, really. The school. My parents. The neighbor next door, who said he'd collect our mail and keep an eye on the house." Zoe took the cap from Hans' hand and held it against her chest. "That's about it."

"What about Annalise's father?" Mercer asked.

"Charles?" Zoe glanced at the digital display on the microwave. "He should be here soon."

"That's not what I meant. Did he know you were taking his daughter on holiday?"

"Of course. He just didn't like it. He has an aversion to fun or at least having fun with us." She chewed on the inside of her cheek. "He always imagines worst case scenarios. *What if there's a plane crash? What if there's an avalanche? What if you get stuck on the chairlift?* Until now, his constant worrying sounded like the ramblings of a madman. Now, it doesn't seem so stupid."

"Is that why you thought he might have been behind your daughter's abduction?" Mercer asked.

She nodded. "It'd either be his misguided attempt to protect her from the world or a way to prove he was right and I was wrong."

"That doesn't sound like a healthy marriage," Hans said.

"It isn't." Zoe put the cap down on the table and wandered toward the fridge. She opened the door and stared inside at the takeout cartons and plastic containers of premixed salads and other grocery items. Eventually, she settled on a bottle of sparkling water, took one sip, put it back, and shut the door.

"From the looks of it, you went to the market. We'll need a list of every place you've been since you arrived. If you can include the dates and approximate times, that will help speed this up," Bastian said.

"I don't know. I can't even think of all the places we've been or the things we've done."

"I know we're asking a lot, love, but you have to make a list. It'll give us some idea if the kidnapper's been following you and for how long." Bastian retrieved the notepad and held it out to her. "It's only been four days. Try to think back."

"Following us?" She stared at him as if that was the most ludicrous thing she'd ever heard. "Why would anyone follow us?"

"That's what I'd like to know." Mercer leaned against the counter. "What does anyone have to gain by taking your daughter? How much are you worth?"

Zoe let out a bitter laugh. "I'm not worth much of anything."

"You're a beautiful woman. I have trouble believing that." Hans appraised her. She wore fashionable jeans tucked into designer boots. Her sweater was cashmere, and the logo on her coat indicated it set her back quite a few quid. "Renting a private chalet for any length of time means you have disposable income. How much is nestled away as part of the Van der Berg fortune?"

"The Van der Berg fortune?" She snorted. "Last I heard, ten million."

"I'd consider that quite a lot." Hans gave her a funny look. As a rule, he tried not to flirt with married women, more so now that he had an ongoing fling with a doctor he met while rehabbing his shoulder. But he couldn't always help himself, even after surviving several vicious bar fights and getting banned from some of the best pubs in Europe. "But that has nothing to do with your actual worth. You're a knockout. Obviously. Smart, loving, and a good mum. Anyone can see that."

Mercer cast a look at the younger man, wondering where this was leading. Frankly, the dining room table didn't look sturdy enough for where most of Hans' conversations with women led.

"You're wrong," Zoe said. "If I were any of those things, Annalise would be safe and sound."

"No, I'm right. And I'd wager the kidnapper can see it too. That's why he knows you'll do anything to get your daughter back. He knows you'll pay. That's a good thing. It means he'll think twice before hurting her." Hans hoped the sentiment would encourage her, but Zoe looked away, fighting to control her rage.

Mercer knew that feeling. He understood the internal anger and blame. "Help us find Annalise." He shoved the pad of paper at the woman. "Give us that list. We can't do anything until we know where to look. In the meantime, we'll scour our records for details on the kidnapper. He's done this plenty of times before. You're not the first. You might not even be the last. This is his career. As soon as he calls back, we'll know more. But until he does, we're flying blind, unless you fill in the blanks." He stabbed at the notepad with a pen. "Right now, the only thing keeping us from finding him is you."

"Jules," Bastian warned, turning to Zoe. "Love, he didn't mean that."

"I bloody well did," Mercer said.

Zoe gawked at the men for a moment, shocked anyone would speak to her in such a fashion, and then she took the pen from Mercer's hand. "You're lucky you have friends at the Met and Interpol. Their assurances are the only reason I haven't called the local cops and had you and your friends arrested. I heard what the kidnapper said on the phone. It sounded pretty damn reasonable to me, but they said you're my best shot. Maybe Annalise's only chance. So tell me what to do, and I'll do it. But if I find out you're part of this, I'll fucking kill you."

"I'm not." Mercer stared into her eyes. "My team was sent here to hunt him, not help him. We will find him, even if it takes us to the ends of the earth."

"The list," Bastian urged. "Every location you've visited. We need to know when and where."

Zoe thought for a moment. "I have receipts. Will

that help?"

"Immeasurably." Bastian took the computer and followed her into the bedroom.

"Finally." Mercer exhaled. "We can't afford to waste any more time. Annalise doesn't have it. By morning, her health will be at risk, if it isn't already. We need to have a plan before then. This wanker is a cocky shit. He's flippant. Obsessed with unimportant details. He treats this like a game. Like it's all one big joke. He doesn't even seem to care if he gets paid or not. Frankly, he doesn't care about anything."

"Maybe he wants to be aloof. Cold. Distant," Hans suggested. "You know, professional."

Mercer shook his head. "He's anything but professional."

"His actions beg to differ," Donovan pointed out.

Mercer thought for a moment. "Find out where he got the kitten or kittens. Pet shops, animal shelters, breeders, those should be your priority. He might have used the animals to lure out all of his victims. We need to explore the possibility. I'll contact his previous victims, the ones who survived the ordeal, and ask what they remember."

"You already spoke to them when we first took the case," Hans pointed out.

"Yes, but we didn't have specifics. We asked about him. About where he took them. How long they were held. How they were treated. Where they were taken. We didn't ask what led to the abduction. All we know is it involved a sack being tossed over their heads and being thrown into the back of a vehicle. That's how most who survived the ordeal described it, but maybe he used kittens to lure them out. That's why we need to know where he got them."

"Children like animals," Donovan repeated. "While you work on that, I'll reach out to area locations and see if I can find out who's recently adopted a kitten."

"What should I do?" Hans glanced toward the bedroom.

"Grab that duct tape and secure your fly," Donovan teased. "We need you to keep it in your pants."

"No worries. I have Maggie."

"Doesn't seem to matter much." Donovan tapped on the tablet and scribbled down a list of addresses for area pet shops.

"Enough," Mercer snapped. "Focus. We have to figure this out. I promised Zoe we'd save her daughter. I don't want to go back on my word. Hans, work on building a list of local employees who missed work when the abductions occurred. We have to identify this bastard. It's the only way."

Over the course of the next hour, the men worked. Mercer made call after call. Only a handful of the victims would even speak to him. No one wanted to rehash the traumatic event. Of the few who tried to help, only one recalled seeing a cat. Not a kitten, but a large, orange tabby that mewled at the door for food. When the woman opened the door, she was attacked by a masked stranger and dragged from her apartment.

Another of the kidnapper's victims, this one a twelve-year-old boy, recalled a man asking for help to find his lost dog, but that had been days before the abduction. Still, it could be something. Mercer wrote the details on a notecard and clipped it to the outside of the folder.

In the meantime, Donovan made a list of every pet store, shelter, and breeder within a hundred kilometers of their location. He made as many calls as possible, compiling a list of new cat owners. Only a couple of them had adopted a kitten that fit the description from the video, so Donovan flagged those.

He'd conduct a follow-up as soon as he could.

"Do you have that list yet?" Donovan asked Hans. "I'd like to cross-reference names."

Hans cursed, slamming his palm on the keyboard. The computer let out an angry beep. "I don't bloody understand how Bas gets this to work."

"Do what you can," Mercer said.

Hans assessed the resort's security footage again and clicked each of the opened tabs Bas had left on the screen, scanning the nearby footage for any sign of where the kidnapper came from or where he went. But the security cameras covering the promenade left much to be desired. They only glimpsed the shabby coat and tattered box for brief moments before the man disappeared from view.

"The bastard knows where the cameras are positioned," Hans declared. "We won't be able to track him that way."

"This is his playground," Donovan said. "He knows everything about it. Every camera, every street, every weakness."

"Every bloody place a person can go to get a hissing, scratching, biting, crazy ball of fur," Hans added.

"Pretty much." Donovan quirked an eyebrow. "You got a problem with cats, mate? I would have thought with your affection for pussy, this wouldn't be a problem."

"Sod off," Hans mumbled. "I had a traumatic experience once with a wild cat in the jungles. Ever since, I haven't trusted any of them and with good reason. Look what this little fellow did to help a maniac grab an unsuspecting child."

"I'm not sure the kitten realized it was an accomplice." Donovan turned to find Mercer scowling at the aerial map of the town. "Jules, we won't find him unless he makes a mistake."

"Bollocks." Mercer knew the information was here—in the files, in the previous abductions, in whatever secrets and enemies the Van der Bergs were hiding. The answers had to be here. "He chose the wrong victim. None of the others had any type of physical malady. This one does. That will require effort on his part, possibly sacrifice. He doesn't want me to believe he cares one way or the other. He wants to make it clear he doesn't like problems, that he won't do the extra work. If that were true, he wouldn't have taken Annalise Van der Berg, unless he had a reason. And a bloody good one."

"What if it was a mistake?" Hans asked. "What if he meant to grab a different child and got this one instead?"

"Then he'll kill her and be done with it."

"Let's hope he didn't make a mistake," Donovan said. "Or he doesn't care who he takes as long as the family pays."

SEVEN

Mercer glanced at the steaming cup of tea. "I don't want it. I don't need any distractions."

"Pish." Bastian slid into the chair beside him. "What do we have so far?"

"Shite." Hans rubbed his eyes. "Utter shite."

"Where's Zoe?" Mercer asked.

Bastian glanced toward the closed bedroom door. "I told her to rest, but I doubt she'll listen."

"You can't expect her to sleep with her child missing." Hans reached for the tea since the commander didn't want it and took a sip. He made a face and went into the kitchen to get some milk. When he couldn't find any, he settled for sugar and returned to the dining room table. "I couldn't find anything on nearby camera feeds. No one spotted the car, and without any traffic cams in the area, we have no way of tracking this bastard."

"What about the employee records? Have you made any progress on that?" Bastian leaned over so he could see the screen. "I got you past the firewalls and security protocols."

Hans blew on the surface of the scalding liquid. "Nothing."

Mercer climbed out of the chair and reorganized the files on the table. The dossier they had was incomplete. No matter how many times he spoke to the surviving victims, he couldn't figure out who took them or where they were kept. From each of their descriptions, no two kidnapping victims had been taken to the same location. And they weren't taken from the same places or under the same circumstances either. "Do you think our hacking triggered this?"

"Jules, come on," Bastian said.

"I'm serious. Did we cause this?" Mercer's gaze flicked to the bedroom door. "Is this our fault? You heard him during our internet call. He knows damn well we came here to find him."

"That'd be an ass-backward reason to take the girl from right beneath our noses." Hans leaned back. "He's lucky we missed him."

"Not if he made us at the café." Mercer laid out photos of the kidnapper's last few victims, hoping to find some similarity he missed.

"That would mean he had to be close or, at least, close enough to watch us." Bastian slid the computer around, minimized the open windows, and scanned the camera footage.

"He had a shabby coat and a box with at least one kitten," Hans offered.

Bastian nodded, but he could only come up with the same bits of limited footage they'd already reviewed. "Honestly, I don't remember seeing him."

"Neither do I." Mercer closed his eyes, forcing his mind to focus. He thought about the crisp breeze, the scent of coffee and chips mixing with the heady, outdoor winter air, and the swish of the server's ponytail. He recalled Annalise and Zoe going from shop to shop, a few other tourists, and that large group with matching outfits, which must have been a family. He didn't see anyone who didn't belong. In this opulent wonderland, a shabbily dressed man toting around a cardboard box would have caught his attention. "He wasn't out there."

"The footage begs to differ." Hans put down the mug and held up his palms when two sets of laser-focused death stares settled on him. "I'm just telling it like it is. You can't argue with cold, hard facts."

"According to Donovan, the server remembered seeing him," Mercer said.

"See?" Hans asked too exuberantly, earning another withering stare.

"I'll check the timestamps." Bastian played the footage again. "This bastard's an expert at avoiding surveillance."

"He's had years to figure out where the cameras are," Mercer said. "I told you he's from here."

"Yeah, I guess." Bastian checked the angles and footage. "He never came near us while we were at the café. According to this, he should have been on the far eastern end of the promenade. He would have had to go past us to get to the sweater shop."

"But he didn't," Mercer insisted.

"Which means he went around. On the other side are more parking lots, a few 'off the strip' attractions, and some other roads," Hans said.

"Brilliant," Bastian said.

"No need to be snotty about it," Hans said.

"No," Bastian shook his head, "I'm serious. That is brilliant. Though, it's not good news." Bastian entered more commands. "Again, no bloody cameras to cover the area. What is wrong with this town? The rest of the world has a security camera every few meters. Here, nothing."

"And they probably leave their doors unlocked at night too," Donovan said. "It's no wonder they have a psycho in their midst. They're all daft."

"He intentionally went around us." Mercer drummed his fingers on the table, lost in thought. "He must have spotted us and sensed the danger, just like we sensed him. How long do you think he's been watching us?"

"You're the one with the keen sixth sense about these things." Bastian waited for an answer. "Earlier today, you said you felt him. Care to elaborate?"

"It was just a bloody feeling. I haven't noticed anyone suspicious around us." Mercer thought back. "No one's been to our cabin. We have traps set. You have surveillance. We would have known if someone paid us a visit."

"I checked when I grabbed our gear," Donovan said. "Nothing had been touched. No one's been there but us."

"Didn't you feel it too?" Hans asked Donovan. "You sided with Jules about his presence."

"Yes, but I never saw him. I would have said something if I did."

Mercer got up from the kitchen table, desperate to be in motion. He stuffed his hands into his trouser pockets to hide his clenched fists. But no matter how quickly he paced, he couldn't escape the one thought in his mind. "Did this wanker abduct Annalise Van der Berg because of us?"

"Jules, come on," Bastian said. "Don't go there."

"I don't have a choice. He might have taken her to test out a theory. To test us. To see if we'd come to the rescue, show our true nature, or our reason for this excursion." He licked his lips, which had gone dry. "She waved to us this afternoon. That might have been enough to set him off. That could be why he targeted her. And if that's the case, this isn't about the family or her illness or anything else. It's about us. Which means she's meaningless to him."

"You're jumping to conclusions," Bastian warned.

"I have to." Mercer fought to keep his voice down. He didn't want to alarm Zoe. "Until we have a profile and know precisely what this bastard wants or where he is, we can't do anything but wait for his next call. In the meantime, the little girl is on a clock. We don't have time for this. We have to consider every possibility. Any one of them might bring us one step closer to finding him."

"If that's the case and Annalise was taken because of us, wouldn't we have what the kidnapper wants?" Hans asked. "His demands would be centered around us, around our facts and intel, around our mission. He'd want that stopped. It'd be easy enough to give him what he wants. Shouldn't this help us reach a resolution faster? This could work in our favor."

"It depends." Mercer rested his palms against the tabletop, forcing his fingers to unclench.

"Until we know more, might I suggest we tackle this from every angle?" Bastian asked. "Donovan can check the pet shops. Hans can continue to search employee records and backgrounds on locals who left town during the previous abductions."

"If anyone called in sick today or doesn't show tomorrow, that ought to be telling," Mercer said. "Most of the townsfolk work at the resort, and we know which restaurants and shops Zoe and Annalise visited today, so you should start there."

"I'll stick with pinning down this bastard's location," Bastian got up from the table. "He's concealing his IP address. Once I crack that, I should be one step closer." Bastian checked the progress bar on the screen. "Jules, build a profile on the Van der Bergs and see who might want to hurt them." He looked down at the stack of previous victims. "We'll cross-reference everything again. Maybe there's some sort of overlap that we missed. Maybe Zoe can make a connection for us." Bastian collected a few photos and the sheet with names. "All right, Jules?"

Mercer nodded, his mind a million miles away. They'd find this bastard and get Annalise back. They had to. Mercer couldn't be responsible for another innocent losing her life. Not on his watch. Not this time.

EIGHT

"How's that list coming along?" Mercer asked.

"About the same as the last time you asked." Hans picked up the mug and took another sip. "Since you have nothing better to do, why don't you grab me a refill?"

Mercer ignored him, leaning over his shoulder. "Can you sort them by eye color?"

"How the bloody hell do you expect me to do that?"

"Bas does it."

"Then get Bas to do it."

"Bas doesn't have time." The analyst gave them both a look. "I'm not a bloody octopus. Pick a priority."

"Locating this bastard," Mercer said. They could always identify the corpse after they found him and saved the girl. The real trick was to find him.

Mercer circled the dining room table, taking in every bit of intel they had collected. He'd spoken to Zoe again and built a basic profile of the Van der Bergs. But she didn't think this had anything to do with her family. The family didn't have any enemies and hadn't received any threats. Her husband ran some kind of charity. Mercer hadn't been too concerned about the details. In his gut, he knew this had nothing to do with the kidnapping. Annalise was just in the wrong place at the wrong time.

Static burst in his ear, and he removed the communication device. They'd been getting a lot of interference lately. Between the mountains and weather, the service was shoddy. Mercer checked his cell phone. He had two bars. No, one. No, two. "Bugger."

"What's wrong?" Hans asked.

"How's your internet speed?"

"Better once we hardwired it." Hans glanced at Bastian.

"Signal strength is weak, both for phones and internet. This town doesn't have much going for it. The tourist bureau claims it's a great place to disconnect." Bastian snorted. "It's a great place to die of exposure or from a bear attack after getting lost in the woods."

Mercer closed his eyes, the intel swirling around his head. "How did the kidnapper make the internet call? Is he hardwired too?"

"If he was, this shouldn't be so bloody difficult." Bastian stroked the side of his screen. "C'mon, baby. Papa needs answers."

"Maybe we should leave the two of them alone," Hans muttered, his own fingers flying over the keyboard. "All right, I've got the list of city employees or whatever you want to call them who were absent during the previous abductions. I'm pulling up their photos now."

Mercer took a breath and studied the photo array on the screen. "He has hazel eyes."

"Average height," Bastian added. "I can't get much

on his weight. With the added layers, it's a tough call."

"Hazel." Hans pushed away from the computer while Mercer clicked through the images. "They could look brown or nearly green, depending. That doesn't help us much."

Hoping his instincts would pick out the bastard from the line-up, Mercer was disappointed when he got to the end of the potential unsubs and didn't feel confident about any of them. "We'll have to dig deeper. Check their travel history, financial transactions, and see if any of them have previous criminal records."

"Background checks came back clear on criminal history. No felonies anyway," Hans said. "That is one of the few requirements the local government has for hiring."

"That doesn't mean anything." Mercer blinked. "What about that bloke you found, Bas? The one who operates the ski lift. Which one is he?"

"I don't think he had hazel eyes." Hans minimized the window and opened another one where Bastian had made a note of the employee number. He typed it into the local government's employee database, but nothing popped up. "Huh, that's odd. It could be a glitch."

Bastian pushed away from his computer and slid in front of the laptop Hans was using. "You're looking in the wrong place. You want to look under the tourism bureau." He entered the employee number again. "Shit."

"What?" Mercer asked.

"It's a contracted position. It might not even be the same bloke." Bastian pulled up the history. "He must work for one of the ski shops. They hired the operator to work the lift. It'd make sense since without the lift they wouldn't make any money."

"Which shop is under contract?" Mercer asked.

Bastian read the scrolling data on the screen. "I'm not sure. They don't keep that information in the same database."

"Can you find it?"

"It's bureaucracy, mate. They might have it filed away under janitorial supplies for all I know. I don't even know where to begin. Searching the front end won't get us there, and working through the back end like we are, nothing connects in a logical manner. The network's piecemeal." He blinked a few times. "I'm seeing at least seven different programmers' signatures. So much for bloody transparency."

"It's government." Mercer checked the time, but it was too late to call the tourism bureau or forestry department to ask if they had any idea who had been hired to operate the ski lift. "Someone in town might know."

Reaching for the radio, Mercer tried to contact Donovan, but he couldn't get a clear message out through the static. Instead, he picked up the cell phone and dialed.

"Did he make contact again?" Donovan asked.

"Not yet. Any progress?"

"Not much to report. I started at the shelters and pound. They believed my story and gave me a list of names and numbers of people who recently adopted a kitten matching the description on the video. But it's been harder to get pet shops and breeders to answer my questions. I can't exactly tell them I lost the beloved family pet and was hoping they found it."

"Bollocks."

"I'll come up with something," Donovan said. "I'll just have to get creative."

"Where are you?"

Donovan rattled off an address. "Considering

there's not much in this blasted town, I'm surprised they have so many pet places. They even have a doggie day care center and a cat café."

"What's a cat café?"

"I don't bloody know. But it's next on my list."

Mercer glanced back at Hans and Bastian who were bickering over something while rapidly working the computers. It was a strange sight to see his recon expert behind a screen, but until they locked down this bastard's location or determined his identity, Hans would fill in where he was needed most. But when the shooting started, Mercer knew Hans would want in on the action. Even though his arm may never be a hundred percent, Hans would find ways to compensate. He wouldn't let a little thing like a near-amputation let him stop working the long guns. Mercer just hoped letting him back in the field wasn't a mistake. "I'll meet you there."

"Copy," Donovan said.

"Going out?" Bastian asked.

"I'll help Donovan work the cat angle since we hit a dead end on the employee list, at least for tonight."

"Just on local government positions. I got Hans into the Wonderland Resort system. We should have more possibilities soon." But Bastian knew Mercer was wound too tightly after speaking to the kidnapper. He was liable to break something or put his fist through the wall during their next communication if he didn't do something to actively search for the girl. "Be careful, Jules. It's bound to be a long night. And we're just getting started."

Nodding, Mercer grabbed his parka and headed for the door.

NINE

"This can't be sanitary." Donovan leaned closer to Mercer. The two had been in a lot of questionable establishments over the years but never anything even remotely close to this. "Shouldn't the board of health shut this place down?"

Mercer eyed the fat calico draped across the edge of the counter warily. It snored loudly, the tip of its tail flicking up and down. He turned, finding several other cats positioned around the café. Green eyes peered out at him from all around the room. He felt them watching. His instincts said they were the enemy, which was ridiculous. They were nothing more than domestic cats. Scratching posts, cat towers, and tree condos stood in rows throughout the room with tables and chairs dispersed in the middle.

A Siamese sat on a woman's lap while she drank her hot cocoa and chatted with a friend who petted a fluffy white kitten while animatedly gesturing with her free hand while she spoke. In the back corner, a teenage boy sat in an easy chair with a book while a cat slept curled up on the seat beside him.

Donovan chuckled. "When this mission's over, we should bring Hans here."

Mercer glanced at the long-range tactician from the corner of his eye. "Agreed, just disarm him first."

"You think that's necessary?"

Mercer shrugged. "I don't want to find out."

"I'll be with you in a moment," a woman called as she bustled out of the kitchen. The door swung wide, and Mercer caught sight of three other people baking in the back. She went to the sink and washed her hands, dried them, and turned around with a friendly smile plastered on her face. "What can I get you?"

Mercer studied her, sensing the friendliness was faked. Something about the frazzled look on her face gave him the sense she was annoyed. He just wasn't sure if it was because of their interruption.

Donovan studied the chalkboard. "It all looks rather wonderful." He looked away from the menu and returned the woman's smile. "My mate and I have never seen a place like this before." He leaned in close, as if this was a well-guarded secret. "You have cats."

Apparently, this wasn't the first time she'd heard that line. "They're part of the service. You pay for the interaction." She pointed to the sign beneath the counter with hourly rates. "It's like an internet café but without the internet."

"You don't have internet?" Mercer asked.

"Actually, we do, but that's on the house." The woman cocked her head at them. "You're not from around here. I take it they don't have cat cafés where you're from."

"No, we don't have any novelties like this." Donovan looked around. "Do you have any kittens, grey ones, with little white paws? I always like those the best. They look like they're wearing wee socks."

If the woman thought it odd a full-grown man was asking about a kitten with socks, she didn't let on. "You mean Franklin." She searched the room. "He usually likes to hang out in that middle tower. But I don't see him. He might be asleep in one of the boxes or hiding. He likes to play in the supply boxes. I can look for him. In the meantime, why don't you order a beverage and have a seat? Maybe another furry companion will wander by that'll strike your fancy."

Before Donovan had to commit to drinking something he suspected would be laced with cat hair, a loud bang sounded from the kitchen.

"Excuse me for one second." The woman dashed back through the door.

"Wee socks?" Mercer whispered, but his gaze remained on the commotion in the kitchen.

"It worked, didn't it?" Donovan slipped behind the counter, feigning fascination with the handmade cat treats which could also be purchased. He picked up one of the wrapped packages and gave it a careful sniff, convinced the patrons must be on drugs. "Let me know when she's coming back."

"Aye." Mercer kept one eye on the kitchen door while he paid attention to the customers in his periphery, but the few people inside the café had no interest in the pair. One man inside the kitchen kept glancing in their direction. Mercer busied himself with examining the cat coasters, pens, and keychains hanging from a tree rack on the counter. But the man in the kitchen remained suspicious. The cat café probably didn't see many men, at least not men who carried themselves the way Mercer and Donovan did. "We're not doing a great job of blending in."

"Try on the cat ears," Donovan teased, jerking his chin toward the display of headbands while he searched the photographs of cats the restaurant had to offer for one matching the description from the video. He found the grey kitten near the bottom row and slipped the photograph into his jacket pocket. "This might be where the bastard picked up his bait."

"How can you tell?"

"I'm not sure, but the markings may match. We'll have to compare it to the video."

Mercer turned around. "I'll see if I can spot him." He wandered through the café, checking each of the towers and hiding spots for the grey kitten, but he didn't see any with white socks. The closest he came was to a brownish grey kitten, who batted at his sleeve when he picked it up to check for similar markings. He stepped away, and the cat pounced on his boot and attempted to climb his trouser leg. He picked it up, put it on one of the platforms, and made his way back to the counter.

The change in angle showed that something had happened with one of the ovens. Smoke billowed up from a pan on the counter. The woman who had tried to sell them on the whole coffee and a kitten experience was on the ground, checking something at the side of the oven while a man held a flashlight, and a second woman fanned the smoke with a pair of oven mitts with a similar design to Annalise's hat.

"It looks like we're in no rush," Mercer said. The third worker remained at his post, icing cookies or cat treats. Considering how similar the cutesy desserts looked, Mercer couldn't be sure if they were meant for humans or felines. Perhaps they were interchangeable. "Do you think Annalise and her mum came here?"

"Zoe didn't mention it." Donovan continued to search behind the counter while Mercer noted the other cat-themed items for sale. He expected to find Annalise's hat here, but he didn't see any like it. "But she said her daughter loved cats. You'd think this would be one of their favorite spots."

Mercer leaned against the counter, lowering his voice, even though they'd been speaking quietly the entire time. "Any luck on finding those receipts yet? The bloke in the back is getting suspicious."

The calico sneezed, letting out an odd noise before stretching. It looked up at Mercer and meowed loudly. He reached to pet it, figuring that might make the man in the kitchen less suspicious, but the cat would have none of that.

It sniffed Mercer's gloved hand as he rubbed its side, and then it latched its mouth around his fingers. Mercer pulled his hand away, and the cat meowed again.

"You're doing it wrong." Donovan didn't bother looking up. He had found the stack of receipts, along with a list of previous orders. "Gentle. You're not petting Cynthia."

Mercer had limited experience with animals, but the team had taken in a dog for a few weeks while its owner had been on the mend. He'd gotten used to having the spaniel around, and the two had come to a peaceable arrangement. His home in London now had a fence in the backyard which they'd built just for her.

Unwrapping a bag labeled cat treats, Mercer shook a few out and put them on the counter beside the calico. The cat sniffed each one, gave Mercer a suspicious look, as if to say 'about damn time', and gently picked up one of the treats.

While it crunched away, leaving crumbs on the counter, Donovan ducked behind the register. "Found it."

"Good." Mercer turned back to the kitchen, but the third worker who'd been watching him had moved to another part of the kitchen that Mercer couldn't see from his position. He moved down the counter and peered through the tiny window cut in the swinging kitchen door. The third worker was now unboxing more supplies while the woman who'd assisted them wiped her hands on an apron. "We're out of time."

Donovan shoved the entire book beneath his jacket, zipping it as he stood. He maneuvered around the counter, coming to stand at the far side just as the woman returned.

"Sorry about that. The pilot light went out." She shook her head. "It's been one of those days." She smiled at both of them. "I see you fed Thomas." She nodded down at the calico.

"He was hungry." Mercer pulled out his wallet and took out some cash. "Did you happen to notice if a little girl and her mum have stopped by in the last few days?"

"Sure, lots of girls and their moms stop by." She scooped Thomas off the counter and cradled him against her chest, absently rubbing behind his ears.

Mercer described them, but the woman didn't react to his description. "The Van der Bergs?" Mercer asked. "Annalise and Zoe?"

She shook her head. "The names don't ring a bell."

"Do you sell hats?" Donovan asked. "Y'know the little knit ones with ears and cat faces?"

"No, but I know which ones you're talking about. Are you buying a gift for your daughter?" She looked from Donovan to Mercer, deciding the two men must be a couple.

"Something like that," Donovan said.

"Try Sullivan's. They have a whole section of snow outfits and accessories for kids. I bet they have some."

"Thanks," Donovan said.

Mercer turned to leave.

"I thought you wanted to order." The woman

sounded confused.

"Oh, we'll be back," Donovan winked at her and hooked his arm through Mercer's, "but this one forgot we agreed to meet some friends for dinner. Maybe tomorrow afternoon." He made a show of looking around the room. "Hopefully, you'll have found Franklin with his wee socks by then."

She smiled. "I'll see you tomorrow. Have a wonderful evening, gentlemen."

"You too." Donovan tugged on Mercer's arm. "Come along, darling. We mustn't keep the others waiting."

"You lost your bloody mind," Mercer whispered once they set foot outside. "But you have the receipts and the photo, so I can't complain." Donovan let go of Mercer's arm as they headed back to the resort. "There's something seriously off about that place."

"Aye. We'll know more once we find out if the kidnapper's accomplice had been taken from there."

"I didn't see any grey kittens inside, but it might have crawled into the oven to get away from the insanity."

"Also a strong possibility," Donovan agreed. "I have a few more shops to check in the morning, but something tells me the café is our best bet."

Mercer couldn't tell with all the strange occurrences and oddities that existed in this place. "The entire town is bloody batty. But we'll have Bastian or Hans run background checks on the employees. I spotted three more in the kitchen. They were cooking something."

"Edible hallucinogens?"

"I wouldn't doubt it." Mercer slowed his pace. The hairs at the back of his neck prickled. He put a hand out, and Donovan stopped. But the footsteps continued to crunch behind them. By now, it was dark.

Mercer and Donovan split up. The tactician entered the nearest shop while Mercer continued toward the resort. The footsteps continued to follow him. He tried to make out a figure reflected in the windows he passed, but their pursuer was too far away.

The kidnapper had no reason to think they'd search for the kitten, but maybe he retraced his steps. Or maybe he had gone to the café to return the animal and noticed Mercer and Donovan. After all, the kidnapper knew precisely what Julian looked like, not that Mercer could say the same about him.

But something about that seemed off. The kidnapper should be with Annalise, unless his base of operations wasn't that far away. The timing of the phone calls had given them a search area consisting of the entire town and a large portion of the surrounding area. Mercer estimated the kidnapper could have driven a hundred kilometers from town in the time it took between the first two calls, assuming the first was made while on the road, but Bastian had cut that number down based on driving conditions. Either way, the bastard could have come back. Maybe he wanted to eliminate Mercer or grab the girl's mum.

He tried the radio, but all he heard was static. By now, Donovan should be tailing their tail. But without open communication, Mercer didn't know how far behind they were. Deciding it'd be best to lead the bastard into a trap, Mercer set out for the chalet. He wanted to warn Hans and Bastian to prepare for an uninvited guest.

TEN

"Bastian, take Zoe into the bedroom. We have incoming." Mercer stood by the front door, holding his gun in both hands.

"Bloody hell. Now what did you do?" Bastian didn't wait for an answer. He gave Zoe a sympathetic look. "Come on, love. It's best to do what he says." He took her by the arm and led her down the hallway and into one of the back bedrooms. The chalet had four. Two upstairs and two downstairs. Leaving the door open a crack, Bastian took up a position against the jamb. He held his gun down by his thigh and nodded to Mercer. They were set.

Hans had gone out the back door. He'd find a position outside in case they needed to set up a crossfire or to assist Donovan. Mercer took a breath. Time slowed. It was the calm before the storm. In this moment, everything was sharp and clear.

Hearing a noise, he pushed the curtain out of the way, just as someone knocked on the door. From his position, Mercer could see a dark figure in front of the door. Donovan remained behind him, far enough back he didn't think the man on the porch had even noticed the tail. His focus remained on the entrance to the chalet. Mercer caught movement near the trees. It had to be Hans. A green laser sight cut through the darkness and stopped directly on the back of the man's head.

Realizing it was safe, or as safe as it could be, Mercer opened the door.

"Zoe," the man shouted, oblivious to Mercer's presence. "Zoe?"

Mercer shoved him back before he could enter, aiming his gun directly in the man's face. "Who are you?"

The man nearly wet himself. He raised his hands. "I'm Charles Van der Berg."

Hans broke from the tree line, heading for them. Mercer lowered his weapon and reached into the man's breast pocket for his wallet. While Mercer checked his ID, Hans frisked him for weapons, confiscated his cell phone, and handed it to the commander.

Mercer tapped on the screen, noticing it required facial recognition. He turned it around and held it in front of Charles Van der Berg's face. The device unlocked, and Mercer stepped back, scrolling through the calls and texts. When he didn't find anything suspicious or damning, he checked the saved numbers and moved on to voice messages.

"Zoe?" Charles called again, but he didn't move a muscle. "What's going on? Where's my wife?"

"He's clean." Hans holstered his weapon.

"Why were you following us?" Mercer asked.

Charles looked even more bewildered. "Following you? Who the hell are you?"

"You were behind us, mate. On the promenade," Donovan said. He closed the distance, but he hadn't put away his gun. Donovan was one of the best shooters in the world, at least as far as Mercer was concerned. If this man made a move, Donovan would put him down in a fraction of a second.

"Behind you? I parked at the main town center. That's where the GPS in my car led me. Well, that's where it died." He looked at the three men suspiciously. "Are you the police?"

"Not exactly," Mercer said.

"Charles?" Zoe appeared in the bedroom doorway. Bastian stood beside her, his gun still at his thigh. She sighed in relief and pushed past Bastian, shoving her way around Mercer, and throwing her arms around her husband. "Thank god, you're here."

"Of course." He squeezed her hard, pressing his nose against her neck. His glasses tangled in her hair, pulling strands of it when she released him, but neither seemed to notice. "Where's Annalise? What do we know so far? How is she? I'm sorry it took so long to get here. I got turned around twice, I think. I don't know. The satellite signal is so buggy. Stupid mountains. Why did you come to the stupid mountains, Zoe?"

"I needed to get away. It's supposed to be good to disconnect."

"Not in an emergency." Charles turned to Mercer. "Who are these people?"

Mercer held up a finger to silence him. After playing each of Charles' saved voicemails, Mercer handed the man back his phone. "We're waiting for the kidnapper's next communication. He should be compiling a list of demands. Has he contacted you? Have you received any threats?"

"No." Charles narrowed his eyes. "And you are?"

"Julian Mercer." He pointed to the rest of his teammates. "That's Bastian Clarke, Donovan Mayes, and Hans Bauer."

"Sorry about the guns," Donovan said. "We can't be too careful."

"You're cops?" Charles asked again.

"They're kidnapping and ransom specialists," Zoe said. "It's a long story, but I checked them out. They're legit. They'll get our baby back."

Charles nodded slowly. "Yeah. Okay." He ran a hand through his unkempt hair. "How did this happen? Weren't you with her?"

"I didn't... I just." Tears sprang to Zoe's eyes. "I went to try on a sweater. I told her not to go anywhere."

"So someone took her when you weren't looking? You shouldn't have left her alone."

"I know." Zoe sniffed.

Charles took her hand. "At least you had the foresight to contact the experts. Specialists. Whatever these gentlemen are." He looked uncertainly at the group assembled. "Shouldn't we call the police?"

"He said no police," Zoe said.

"Who cares? We do whatever it takes to get our baby back."

"The authorities aren't prepared to handle these types of situations," Mercer said. "They have training, but their recovery rates are abysmal. Their primary goal is making an arrest." Mercer stared into the dark. The bright lights from the resort and neon signs from nearby restaurants kept things from being pitch, but it was still too dark to see if anyone was watching them. "Let's continue this inside." He waited for the group to enter the chalet and locked the door.

"What's wrong with arresting the asshole who kidnapped my daughter? That sounds reasonable to me," Charles said. "This man deserves to be arrested or worse. Don't we want that?"

"No, mate. We want to get your daughter back alive. The rest is icing on the cake," Bastian said.

"How many of these recoveries have you performed?"

"Dozens," Mercer said. "Possibly hundreds. We've lost count."

"How many were successful?"

"More than those that weren't." Mercer wasn't sure what he thought of Charles, but based on the man's appearance, he figured Charles worked behind a desk most of the time. "What do you do, sir?"

"I manage a nonprofit. Why does that matter?"

Mercer had only started researching the family, believing it to be a dead end, but he could be wrong. "What you do might not matter. But until we know more about the kidnapper and the reason your daughter was taken, everything matters. Considering your organization is a nonprofit, how did you come by your wealth?"

"It's family money. My father started a pharmaceutical company and sold it off years ago. Me and my siblings each got a portion of the proceeds. Pharmaceuticals were how the Van der Bergs amassed their fortune. But now we have to find interesting ways to keep it, I suppose. I took my trust fund and invested it. While that's being maintained by competent accountants, it's allowed me to pursue more charitable endeavors and not worry too much about providing for my family."

"Providing was never the problem," Zoe muttered.

Charles' gaze traveled over the lush furnishings. "I'm assuming it also paid for this vacation rental." His tone didn't sound nearly as friendly when he said that, but Zoe didn't respond. He squeezed her hand, forcing her to look at him. "How long has it been since you checked Annalise's blood sugar?"

"About six hours."

"Shit." Charles exhaled. "She needs to eat, and she might need another shot." He turned his attention back to Mercer. "I'd really appreciate it if you could expedite things. I'll pay whatever. Just get her back."

"We're waiting for the kidnapper to call again. Then we'll get things underway. Until then, we're working on building a profile and collecting intel," Bastian said. "The more we know about him and this situation, the greater our chances of getting your daughter home sooner, rather than later. We'll need a list of anyone who might want to hurt you or your family."

"I can't think of anyone. Who would want to hurt us?" He looked at Zoe. "Can you think of anyone?"

She bit her lip and shook her head.

Mercer watched the exchange. Something wasn't quite right between the couple. Bastian picked up on it too. The analyst painted a sympathetic smile on his face. "Why don't we try this another way? How many people do you employ, Mr. Van der Berg?"

"At the hospital?"

"Hospital?" Mercer raised an eyebrow.

"That's my nonprofit. It's a hospital. We rely on donations. Our staff and doctors are kind-hearted souls. We have hundreds of employees. Plenty of full-timers, dozens of part-timers, and a bunch of interns and volunteers. I want to help those who can't afford care."

"That's a lot of possibilities," Hans said.

"Make a list of anyone who knows you and knows what you're worth." Mercer sized up the man. "Are you a doctor?"

"I never made it that far. The MCATs kicked my ass. My dad wanted me to go to pharmacy school. Y'know, part of the family legacy, but biochem wasn't my thing." He sobered. "I regret that now. Had I known my little girl would need constant care, I might have sucked it up and tried harder."

"Constant care?" Hans asked. "I thought her disease was well-managed."

"She doesn't need constant care," Zoe said. "That's just Charles being overprotective."

"Overprotective?" He stepped away from his wife. "Have you ever considered you might be underprotective? That's how some lunatic managed to nab our daughter, isn't it? You weren't watching her. If you had been, none of this would have happened."

"Charles," she warned.

"Enough." Mercer stepped between the two of them. "Hans, take Mr. Van der Berg into the kitchen and get him settled. I'm sure he could use a drink."

"I don't drink," Charles said.

Maybe you should start, Mercer thought. "Tea then." Mercer nodded to the recon expert, who gently took Charles by the arm. "Start on that list. I want a complete timeline of everywhere you went and anyone you encountered in the last month. This arsehole's probably been watching Annalise for a while. I want to know when it started."

"We should go over the same, love," Bastian said to Zoe, more to appease Charles and force his acquiescence than anything else. He led her into the living room while Hans took Charles into the kitchen.

Donovan gave Mercer a look. "I'll update Bas so he can run our latest intel, and I'll see what Zoe knows about the cat café."

Mercer nodded, his eyes on the man seated at the counter. He doubted Charles Van der Berg had anything helpful to add since the kidnapper chose his victims once they arrived on holiday, but he needed to do something to keep the man occupied. Charles was a lit match tossed into an armory. His presence would make something explode. Mercer could feel it.

Once Hans got him settled with a cup of tea and a fresh sheet of paper, he crossed the room and took up a position beside Mercer. "Something's going on between Mr. and Mrs. V."

"I noticed."

"How'd it go on your end? Did you find anything?" Hans asked. "Bas and I hit a wall with the employee records. The non-government jobs don't require photo IDs, except for resort security, so Bas started checking DMV records, but at this point, it's a shot in the dark. We decided it'd be best to focus on the IP address and the kidnapper's location instead."

"Aye."

"Any luck finding the furball from hell?"

Mercer chuckled despite the situation. "There are a lot of places one can go to get a kitten. Most of the adoption agencies run background checks and require forms. Donovan has a list, but we stumbled upon a cat café. We believe the furball from hell came from there."

"What about the kidnapper? Did he come from there too? Did you get a description?" Hans watched Donovan and Bastian exchange whispers at the far end of the living room while Zoe tapped the end of her pen against the pad of paper, clearly annoyed to be asked to repeat the same pointless task.

"We didn't get that far. The woman working there didn't seem to notice the kitten was missing, and if she did, she didn't want to share that information with us."

"She could be involved."

"Possibly." Mercer suspected half the town was involved. Hearing Hans voice a similar belief made him feel a little less paranoid for thinking such things.

"Have you or Bas made any more progress?"

"It's the Wild West around here. The old time, pre-computer age Wild West. I think we're going to have to check every location. But until we know what this wanker looks like, I'm not sure how much good it'll do."

Mercer hated having his hands tied. "The girl's running out of time. Why hasn't this bastard phoned with his demands? Running out the clock is foolish."

"He wants us desperate. It'll guarantee we agree to his terms without quibbling."

"The bastard needs to give us his demands while the girl still has a fighting chance. If he waits too long, the only thing he'll get is a bullet to his brain."

ELEVEN

An hour later, the phone rang. The bastard had taken his time to call back, and now he wanted to end the call. The kidnapper knew what he was doing. After all, he had plenty of practice.

"You don't understand." Mercer stood in front of the webcam. "It will take time to meet your demands. Time we don't have. Time *you* don't have. We need to meet before the ransom exchange."

"I have all the time in the world." The masked man on the other side of the screen rocked back in his chair, folding his arms over his chest and resting one of his legs on the edge of the table. His left sleeve inched upward, revealing the lower portion of a tattoo. Mercer hit a key, saving the image. "You're the one with the problem, pal. You better find a way to fix it."

Mercer inhaled through his nose, resisting the urge to utter the words running through his mind. "The only way you get paid is if the package is unharmed. She could die without food and medicine. And then you get nothing. Do you want to risk that?"

"Package? Shit." The masked man snorted. "And people think I'm a bad guy. You're talking about a little girl. Shouldn't you refer to her by name? Isn't that your job? You have to humanize the victim, right? That way I'm less likely to, y'know," the guy made a gun with his right hand and snapped his thumb down, "do something crazy."

"You don't care about her. Nothing I say is going to change that. What you care about is getting paid. I'm here to make sure that happens and that you understand the terms."

"I make the terms."

Again, Mercer found his patience thinning. "Yes, but make no mistake, if the girl is harmed, you won't see a dime. That's why we need to meet ahead of schedule. We have to meet tonight. Before the exchange."

"There's an easier solution. Get me my money faster."

"It's not possible."

The kidnapper let out an audible sigh. "That seems more like a you problem than a me problem."

"It's going to be your problem if something happens to her." Mercer would make sure of it.

"Take it easy, dude. She's fine. Nothing's gonna happen," the kidnapper continued to rock in the chair, scratching at the edges of the ski mask where it brushed against his upper lip, "assuming you do what I say, when I say it."

"That's not the issue."

"It sure sounds like it is. I want you to bring me money, but instead, you want to bring me dinner. You gonna serenade me by candlelight too?"

Mercer glanced away from the screen, his gaze stopping on his teammates who were doing everything they could to console the bereft parents. He'd worked dozens of these cases but never with such an arrogant and mouthy unsub. "It's not for you. It's for her. She's sick. We've been over this. She needs to get the proper nutrition. Check her wrist. She's wearing a medical alert bracelet. I'm not lying. Without food and her medication, she could die. And a dead child is worthless to you. Be smart about this. She stays healthy. You get paid. Everyone wins."

"You sound like a broken record. Let me think about it."

The screen went blank, and Mercer tugged the earpiece out and tossed it onto the desk, cursing. Emotional manipulation wouldn't work on this unsub. Within the first minute, it had become clear the kidnapper was a sociopath. He had no empathy for the girl or her family. Emotions didn't play a part in his decisions, and if they did, he concealed them well behind his glibness. As far as Mercer could tell, the guy didn't feel a thing. This was just business as usual. The kidnapper didn't care about his victim, but he cared about getting paid. At least, that's what the research suggested.

"Since this is just a job to him, another payday, why is he making this so difficult?" Mercer flipped through the materials on the desk. It didn't make sense. He was missing something.

Bastian stepped into the room, partially closing the door. "He knows the playbook. That's why he won't give in that easily. He wants to make sure you know he's in control and unpredictable. It's possible he's dealt with other negotiators in the past. There are other agencies. There could be other victims and recoveries we don't know about. That might be how he knows so much about this."

"You were listening?"

"Of course." Bastian cocked his head to the side. "I know we haven't worked one of these in a while, mate, but it hasn't been that long. You should remember how it goes."

"It normally doesn't go like this. He's too chatty."

"That is odd." Bastian stepped behind the computer. "May I?"

Mercer gestured to the device, taking a step back. "Do you think he'll agree to the drop? I offered to leave her medicine and a balanced meal at a location of his choosing, but he wouldn't give me a straight answer. He's afraid it's a ploy. That we're making it up."

"Or he doesn't want to stay on the line that long." Bastian clicked a few keys and squinted at the screen. "He'll come around."

"You don't know that." Mercer flexed his fingers, surprised to find his hands balled into fists again. This wasn't supposed to be personal. Not for him. But seeing the Van der Bergs in pain pulled at that fractured piece of his soul, especially since he was now convinced it was his fault.

"It's just business," Bastian said, distracted by the numbers scrolling across the screen. "Letting us drop off her medication is a smart business decision. He should say yes."

"What he should do isn't necessarily what he will do. Does he seem apathetic to you?"

"Towards Annalise?"

"No, towards his payday. Towards everything."

"It's part of his game. Part of how he's exuding control over the situation. The less he cares, the more you will." Bastian met Mercer's eyes. "And might I add, I think it's working."

"He's behaving like an errant teenager on purpose?"

"Perhaps."

But Mercer wasn't convinced. "Any luck tracing his location?"

"Not yet. His network protocols are topnotch. According to this, he's now in New Zealand."

"The first time you said it was India."

"It's neither, mate. We know he's in town or somewhere close by. He can't be more than sixty kilometers from here."

"Bollocks." Mercer reached for one of the files. "We have to find him."

"I'm doing my best, but it'll take time." Bastian closed the window on the computer. "Jules, we have to proceed blind. Annalise can't wait for us to get this sorted. The intel her parents gave us is worthless. Even if he stalked the family from their California home all the way here, they didn't notice. Whatever I can pull off area surveillance and local networks is still our best bet."

"I know." Mercer watched Hans and Donovan check the rest of the house while Mr. and Mrs. Van der Berg remained on the couch, whispering to one another. At least the couple made up. "The kidnapper's close."

Bastian raised an eyebrow. "We've already established that, but his network protocols make it appear he's halfway around the world."

"I know, but he's never taken anyone from town while they were still in town. This is new. Different. He doesn't play in his own backyard. That was the only consistent thing we knew about him. Now we don't know anything."

"That's not true," Bastian argued. "And maybe we should consider this a fortunate turn of events. If he'd waited to abduct her after they left, we might not have been around to intercede."

But there wasn't a single fortunate thing about this situation. "Do we know why he targeted them?"

"Not yet."

"Did you ask Zoe about the cat café? Had she and Annalise been there?"

"No. They passed by it for the first time today. Annalise wanted to go in, but Zoe didn't like the looks of things. She told her daughter they had to schedule an appointment to play with the kittens. She wanted to do more research."

"Was Annalise disappointed?"

"She's a seven-year-old with a love for kittens. What do you think?"

Mercer thought about the setup. "The café is on the corner. It's nothing but picture windows on two sides. He could have been inside with the kitten when Zoe and Annalise went by. Maybe that's when he decided to target them."

Bastian shrugged. "We don't know enough yet about him or the situation."

"Care to speculate, Bas? I thought you said we knew something. So what do we know?"

"That you can be bloody insufferable." Bastian's tone held a hint of sarcasm. He knew Julian's moods better than anyone, and when frustrated, Mercer had a tendency to lash out at everyone and everything. Most of the time, Bastian simply ignored it. "What do you think he wants, Jules? He didn't ask anything else about us, our presence here, or our mission, and he didn't ask to speak to the Van der Bergs. That basically rules out our current theories."

"It doesn't rule anything out. He's only mentioned money. Nothing else. Aside from the original message he gave to Zoe Van der Berg, warning her not to go to the authorities, he hasn't bothered with additional threats toward the family. Not really. But he doesn't have to. I told him Annalise has a health condition. He doesn't have to make threats. Time is already of the essence. He hasn't asked me to relay any messages either. It goes back to my reasoning." Mercer glanced out the door again to ensure they had their privacy. "He did this to find out more about us, specifically how we function and why we're here. Normally, these bastards want to threaten and taunt the family. But he seems content doing nothing more than irritating me."

"Mission accomplished." Bas closed the various tabs and dropped into the chair. Picking up a pen, he gnawed on the end. "So it's just about the money, then. That should be easy enough. We get it. We pay him and get Annalise back." But Bastian's face reflected a certain level of unease.

"What's wrong, Bas?"

"This should be easy, unless it isn't."

"Meaning?" Mercer asked.

"They're divorced." He nodded out the door. "Zoe and Charles separated a year and a half ago. It's been rocky ever since. Three weeks ago, everything became official."

"She never mentioned it."

"Aye." Bastian drummed his fingers on the desk. "You'd never know it by looking at them now, but the court transcripts were rather vulgar. Money's one of the big things they fought about. When Zoe said she wasn't worth much, she meant it. Charles didn't give her a dime more than necessary to provide for their daughter's care. But from his reaction, I'm guessing she found a way to force him to pay for this elaborate trip."

"How?"

Bastian shrugged. "It's a necessary excursion for her child's mental health? I don't know."

"Do you think she's behind this?" Mercer watched the woman wipe away the silent tears that hadn't stopped falling since the phone rang. He had trouble believing she'd jeopardize her daughter's health. "He could just as easily be behind it. If he proves she's unfit, he could get sole custody and have to shell out even less."

"Possibly, but he's willing to pay the ransom. He started making calls before he even knew the amount. That's not the kind of behavior I'd expect from a cheapskate."

"It could be an act."

"I don't know. He's worried about the strings attached to getting such a large sum in such a short amount of time. The funds have to be approved by his accountant and withdrawn from his investments. That will complicate matters and delay things."

"We don't have time for that."

"I know."

Mercer replayed every interaction he had with Zoe and her ex-husband. "All that aside, this explains why Zoe took her daughter on holiday in the middle of the school year. Do you think Zoe needed to escape the stressors, or do you think this trip was designed for Annalise's benefit?"

"Have you been reading self-help books in your spare time?" Bastian teased.

Mercer narrowed his eyes, staring pointedly at the pen hanging from his best friend's mouth. "You might benefit from a few on how to control that addictive personality of yours."

"Have you ever considered you may be the reason I started smoking in the first place?"

"Was I?"

Bastian shrugged, an amused glint in his eye. "No, mate, but you're the reason I quit. Someone's gotta stick around to keep you out of trouble. So whenever I'm particularly insufferable, that's your fault. As for the reason behind this mother-daughter trip, I don't know. But if they despise each other so much, isn't it odd Charles was the first person Zoe called after the abduction?"

"He's Annalise's father. That trumps everything else." Mercer thought back. "But at first, Zoe thought he was behind it." This case had them all on edge, and they'd only been working on it for four hours. Mercer watched the Van der Bergs through the open doorway. They huddled together on the couch, far too comfortable with one another for unmarried people. "What do we know about their custody agreement?"

Bastian lowered his voice to make sure they weren't overheard. "They have joint custody, but based on the court transcripts, they fought quite the battle over Annalise. It was brutal. Each accused the other of being unfit."

"Most kidnappings have to do with custody. Any indication that might be the case now?"

"Not that I've found. But you've already pointed out a possible motive. Most kidnappings are personal. Ransoms aren't. And this pisser is in it for the money. He doesn't care about the girl. Plus, that wouldn't explain all the previous abductions."

"Assuming we're dealing with the same kidnapper. This one could be a copycat or a professional the Van der Bergs hired."

"Then why the emphasis on the payday?"

"To convince me he's a legitimate kidnapper," Mercer suggested.

"Do you really think it's an act, Jules? Or that we're dealing with some other bloke? Or do you just hope that's the case so you don't have to feel responsible?"

"It's too soon to say, but it's another possibility we

ought to consider."

"Ransom demands are typically delivered by professionals or bloody idiots. From what we know of Mr. Ski Mask, he could fall into either category. But it's doubtful we're dealing with an unknown third party. More than likely, this is the bastard we've been pursuing."

"That's what I was afraid of." Mercer rubbed his hands down his face. "Regardless, make sure you check their financials. Either one could have hired someone to abduct Annalise to keep the former spouse from having joint custody. I'm sure the courts would reconsider the terms of their agreement in light of a kidnapping. And with their divorce still fresh, emotions are running high."

"Tell me about it. Being too close to either of them will cause whiplash. But Jules, if one of them did this, the kidnapper would have known to take Annalise's medication with him. She's diabetic. He wouldn't have taken her without grabbing her insulin too."

"Maybe he thought she carried it with her, or maybe he already has her prescription stockpiled. It could be why he's taking so long to get back to us." Mercer glared at the phone. "Her father runs a bloody hospital for fuck's sake. The Van der Bergs must have plenty of friends capable of writing prescriptions. That could explain why the kidnapper isn't in a rush to pick up food and medicine for his captive." But even as he said it, Mercer knew it was rubbish. "Just make sure this isn't something her mum or dad orchestrated."

"Hans is already on it," Bastian said. "He's picked up some wicked computer skills while he was rehabbing. I think he's vying to replace me."

"I wouldn't worry. He likes operating the long guns and serving as overwatch a bit too much for that. He was ready to shoot Charles the moment he stepped foot on the porch."

Bastian chuckled. "We should get him drones then. A whole fleet. That way, he can coordinate tactical strikes without compromising his shoulder again."

"The kidnapper is mouthy enough. I don't want to deal with you too."

Bastian smiled. "Just wanted to cheer you up. We're only four hours in. This will be a long negotiation. You need to keep your wits about you. If you lose your cool with this guy, we'll have problems. I can tell you that now. His laissez-faire attitude is meant to push your buttons. He wants you desperate and on edge, reactive instead of proactive. Don't give in."

"I know how to conduct a negotiation."

Bastian held up his palms. "Fine, so how should we proceed in the meantime?"

"Keep the Van der Bergs in the dark, just in case Zoe or Charles is to blame. I will update them personally on our progress, but until we are absolutely sure they aren't responsible for this, we don't tell them how close we are to making a recovery."

"Do you think we're close?"

"No." Mercer rubbed his temples. "This pisser's relaxed. Calm. He doesn't care one way or the other. That worries me. If he doesn't care about the payday, he'll kill her and walk away. And we can't do anything about it."

"He does this for a living. It has to be about the payday, unless he has an ulterior motive." Bastian's fingers flew over the keyboard. "Annalise isn't his first. For him, this is just another Thursday."

"Then why didn't he do his homework? He didn't know about the child's condition. His demands are basic, even a little on the low side. He's not asking for an exorbitant amount. He wants two million. This feels different from his other victims. Something went wrong."

"We're here. He didn't expect that, or he took her just to test us. Either way, he probably wants to get paid and bugger off. Or he wants us to bugger off. He knows the larger the sum, the longer it'll take. Two million is enough to make it worth the risk, but small enough that it can be collected in a matter of days and delivered easily."

If that was true, Mercer should be able to convince the kidnapper to accept even less. This wasn't about saving a few bucks. It was about determining the kidnapper's motive. And if Annalise's health wasn't at risk, the K&R specialists would have more time to hammer out these details and build a profile. But with the added stress, the girl could have an episode and possibly even go into a coma. "You're right, Bas. This is how he earns a living, so he'll move on to his next victim if this one proves to be too much trouble or if her health takes a sudden nosedive. He might not call back. He could just eliminate her and start over with his next target. He's done it plenty of times before."

"Give it time." Despite Bastian's optimistic words, he gnawed more furiously on the end of the pen. He'd reached the same conclusion Mercer had. They had to make this as easy as possible, or Annalise wouldn't survive.

"All right. Let's go back over the few things we know. There might be something to it." Mercer looked around the vacation rental. The chalet was a commercial property, like so many others he'd seen in the past. "Mr. Ski Mask didn't take her from her home. He targeted her after she arrived here, so how did he know she'd be here? How did he know this opportunity would present itself?"

Bastian climbed out of the chair. "I'll speak to Zoe

again and find out exactly when she planned to go on holiday."

"While you're at it, find out if anyone has a reason to hold a grudge or get revenge on either of the Van der Bergs. Run their coworkers, business partners, associates, neighbors, friends, relatives, whatever. They made lists. Let's use them."

"Right-o."

Mercer glared at the blank screen. Going over the same facts wouldn't help. But he didn't know what else to do. They needed the kidnapper's location, and Bas had yet to figure out a way to get it.

The kidnapper said they'd only communicate via internet calls. "He's using a satellite uplink," Mercer mumbled. He and his team had used them before on missions. It made it nearly impossible for the enemy to intercept the signal or determine their locations.

"That'd be my guess," Bastian agreed on his way out the door. A thought struck him. "We need to get a cell phone number or some other electronic signature. I could probably find a way to triangulate his location by using multiple sources."

"Easier said than done." Mercer looked around the spare bedroom which they'd turned into their office. "Tell Donovan I want to speak to him. And Bas, we should make this our primary base of operations. I want to stay here and maintain eyes on the family, so you'll have to fetch the rest of our gear from the cabin. Something tells me we're going to need it."

"For the record, I don't like the sound of that."

"Neither do I." But a part of Mercer itched for the action. He'd never met a kidnapper who didn't rub him the wrong way, but this one was worse than the others. Ski Mask's attitude and chattiness gave him the air of invincibility. He'd gotten away with abducting and ransoming children before, which meant he might get away with it again. Until Mercer knew more about him, he had no way of knowing why some survived the ordeal while others perished.

Bastian saw the look in Mercer's eyes. "You think he's going to kill her."

"I made a promise to her mum. We have to stop him." Unfortunately, Mercer didn't know how. "We need to figure out who he is and what he wants. For all we know, it may already be too late. She was taken this afternoon. If she doesn't get her insulin by morning, he might not even have to waste a bullet."

"You might be on to something."

"What are you going on about?"

"I'm not sure yet." A spark ignited in Bastian's eyes. He had a plan. "I'll let you know what I find."

Mercer nodded, afraid to allow the tiny glimmer of hope to comfort him. Perhaps he was no longer desensitized to these crimes. It'd been several months since he and his team had worked one of these cases. The last had nearly cost them their lives and Hans' right arm. But they were finally back after a brief hiatus and an assignment in the service of Her Majesty.

However, a few lingering fears remained in the back of Mercer's mind. The team was his family. All he had left. His thumb traced the wedding band around his finger. He almost forgot to take it off. Almost. He didn't want to lose anyone else. And he sure as hell didn't want to break his promise and cause anyone else to feel the excruciating grief to which he had grown accustomed.

"Jules, are you all right?" Donovan asked, stepping into the room.

"Brilliant." Mercer slipped off his ring, pressed it against his lips, and tucked it inside his wallet. "We need to find Annalise. And we need to do it now."

TWELVE

Ten minutes later, the kidnapper rang again.

"I need a number where I can reach you," Mercer said.

"What are you? My girlfriend?" the kidnapper asked. "Take off your shirt and spin for me, sweetheart. I'll let you know if I want to swipe right."

"Piss off."

The kidnapper snickered. "Why do you need my number? You gonna send me dick pics?" He glanced down at his trousers. "Give me a few minutes, and I'll send you some of mine."

Mercer's temper flared. "I want to keep an open line of communication. It's in everyone's best interest."

"Not mine, snook-ums."

"Jules," Bastian warned from the doorway.

Mercer blew out a breath. He couldn't let this bastard rattle him. "I'll bring her dinner and medicine to the agreed upon drop. The insulin needs to be kept cold. I'd prefer to make the hand-off in person. Maybe even see the girl. Make sure she's okay."

"That's not happenin'. It's colder than a witch's tit out there. It'll be kept plenty cold. Don't you worry your pretty little head about that. What you need to worry about is following my instructions. If you try anything and I mean anything, the deal's off and the girl's dead."

"I assure you we'll meet your demands. No trackers. No surveillance. Nothing. Just make sure Annalise is fed and has access to her medication. We'll hold up our end, but you have to hold up yours."

"Yeah, yeah." The kidnapper waved his hand in front of the screen. "I'll send you her blood sugar levels before and after she eats. And again after she gets a shot."

"Only if she needs it."

"I know. I heard you the first time. Damn, you're such a nag, just like my girlfriend. Nag, nag-nag, nag, nag." Abruptly, he cut communication, and the end message box popped up on the screen.

Mercer spun and punched the wall. Letting out a huff, he stalked the enclosed space for a moment, forcing his emotions away. He needed to be calm when he spoke to the Van der Bergs.

"I told you he'd agree," Bastian said.

"Don't be smug." Mercer went past him. "Any luck getting his location or the bleeding internet number he's using?"

"No, mate. Nothing on the number. He's taken measures to keep us blocked. I have yet to find a way around them. But I've narrowed his location to somewhere in North America, so we're making progress."

"Not enough."

"A few more calls, and we can probably knock it down to a state, maybe even a city."

"We know what city he's in. He's here. Isn't he?"

"Probably, or just on the outskirts. Based on the background, he's stationary. He's called from the same location every time. He's been in the same room for each of his calls, minus when he showed you Annalise. But it's too vague for me to pinpoint the location. It could be a hotel room, a house, a cabin, anywhere."

"That doesn't help."

"It might. That's probably his base of operations, maybe even his home. It appears he hasn't left since the abduction. That means he's holed up for the duration."

"Good. It'll make it easier for us to perform a recovery."

"Or a breach," Donovan said, catching the tail-end of the conversation.

"Where are her parents?" Mercer asked, realizing the chalet had grown quiet.

Donovan pointed to the enclosed patio. "Hans convinced them to get some air. We thought it'd be best to have them out of the way while you negotiated the drop."

Mercer opened the fridge and took inventory. At least they didn't have to make a run to the market. He opened the cupboards, finding a food storage container with a lid. "Tell Zoe she needs to prepare dinner for her daughter." He checked the time. "I'm to make the drop in an hour and twenty-three minutes."

Before Donovan or Bastian could say anything, the computer chimed.

Mercer ran into the bedroom. But it wasn't a call. It was an e-mail. He clicked open, and a blown-up shot of an erect penis filled the screen.

Mercer's blood boiled. This wasn't a joke. For a moment, he feared what the image might mean. Annalise was a little girl. That sick fuck better not touch her, or Mercer would castrate the kidnapper and shove the offending appendage down the bastard's throat and let him choke to death.

"Shite." Bastian came up beside him, reading the commander's thoughts. "Give me a minute." He sat down, running a reverse lookup on the image. "It's pornography."

"I can see that," Mercer managed through gritted teeth.

"No," Bastian pointed, "that image came from a pornography website."

"So the kidnapper's a porn star?"

"Doubtful. He probably found it and sent it to you." Bastian opened a dialog box and executed several commands. "I might be able to use this. Perhaps he isn't as clever as he thinks he is. The metadata might give me details about his computer. I might be able to track his location."

"He thought he was clever, but he isn't." Mercer examined the photo again, wondering what Bastian hoped to accomplish. "He's suicidal. He's begging me to shoot him by sending threatening images."

"I doubt he sees this as threatening. He wants to push your buttons. It may have never crossed his mind how you'd interpret it."

"Or he knows exactly what he's doing. You said it yourself, Bas. He wants me reactive, but he's going to regret it." Mercer stormed out of the bedroom. He couldn't think. He went to the table and dug through the files. None of the previous victims reported a sexual assault. For all Mercer knew, the bastard couldn't even get it up. He probably saved that image out of penis-envy.

"Are you going to the drop alone?" Hans asked. He kept an eye on Zoe, who was pulling ingredients from the refrigerator in a haphazard fashion. Donovan had gone outside to keep Charles company, and Bastian remained in their office/bedroom to work. "I don't think that's a good idea."

Mercer's eyes remained glued to the files spread out on the table. "It doesn't matter. I have to gain his trust. Prove to him that I'm a man of my word. It's the only way. If he senses a double cross, he'll cut ties and run."

"Even with two million on the line?"

Mercer pointed to one of the botched kidnappings. "This was a six million dollar score. The family said they'd pay. They had the money ready to go, and he left her body at the drop site."

Hans rubbed a hand down his face. "What is this wanker's problem?"

"I have yet to figure that out."

"Then it doesn't matter what you do. He plays by his own rules. I'll scout the area. I can blend in. Stay out of sight. Remain at a distance. Whatever you need. He'll never know I'm there. Maybe we could follow him back to Annalise."

"Maybe, if it's not too risky. But without much in terms of traffic, I don't see how you'll avoid getting spotted."

"We could use trackers," Hans said.

"No. Those are too easy to find. A quick scan, and he'll know I lied."

"In that case, I'll just have to keep my eyes open."

Mercer nodded, afraid if they botched this drop, they wouldn't get a second chance. "Don't take any risks. If there's even the slightest chance he'll see you, pull the plug. I mean it, Hans. We'll have more opportunities. He wants to see how this will play out. He wouldn't have agreed to let me drop off her medication otherwise. But he's afraid we'll try something. So he'll have his guard up. He only agreed to one meal. He's keeping us on a clock. He doesn't have to tell us when time runs out. Annalise's body will do that. But if I'm to convince him to accept another drop, we can't screw this one up."

"Understood." Hans palmed a set of keys and knelt down to pack his gear. He tapped the comm in his ear. "Channel three."

Mercer nodded. "Annalise's well-being is our only objective. Remember that."

Zoe turned when Mercer mentioned her daughter's name, though his voice didn't carry into the kitchen. Maybe it was mother's intuition, but Mercer wondered where that had been when her daughter was lured out of the clothing shop.

"Is this a good sign?" Zoe asked. "I mean, he's going to feed her and give her her shot. That must mean he doesn't want to harm her, right?"

"She's valuable. He knows that. We'll take it one step at a time." Mercer regretted the promise he made. "Has the money been transferred yet?"

"Charles is trying to put a rush on it. The bank has a mandatory hold for some reason. It's ridiculous. How can they keep us from accessing our own money? This is bullshit."

"Is your name still on the account?" Hans asked.

Zoe shook her head and turned back to the stove, stirring the vegetables around the pan to keep them from burning. "Charles locked me out of his accounts when we separated. We have a separate joint account, which he adequately funds to pay for household things and Annalise."

"Did it pay for this trip?" Mercer asked.

She didn't turn around, but she nodded.

"Why didn't you mention the divorce?" Mercer asked.

"It wasn't important." Zoe finished sautéing the

vegetables and placed them in a container with the leftover protein from last night's dinner. She searched in the cupboards for some juice boxes. "In case Annalise's blood sugar drops too low," she explained, putting a few in the insulated bag beside the food storage container.

Mercer watched her bustle around the kitchen, packing silverware and whatever else she thought her daughter might need. He didn't want to rush her, but he kept an eye on the time. As soon as she finished, he'd head to the drop site.

Hans hefted the bag over his shoulder and let himself out of the chalet. He'd scout ahead. With any luck, no one would spot him or connect him to Mercer.

Zoe rubbed her sweaty palms on her jeans. "Okay, I guess that's it." She opened the fridge again and took out one of the insulin pens. From the freezer, she removed an ice pack and put it in the box. "He said only one, right?"

"Yes."

"What if she needs more in the morning?"

"For now, it's best if we follow his instructions. Where's her monitor?" Mercer asked.

"Oh, right." Zoe went to the counter and pulled out the device, making sure it had ample battery strength and test strips. "She'll be okay, right?"

"She's in good hands," Bastian said, looking up from the tablet. "Jules has done this plenty of times."

"Can you go over the terms again?" Zoe asked.

"Sure, but would you be so kind as to get Charles, so I can go over the details with you both?" Mercer forced his own morbid thoughts away. As soon as everyone was assembled, he explained what was going to happen. He'd take the supplies to the drop site and leave them there. The kidnapper would pick them up and give them to Annalise. He would then send photographic proof that she tested her blood sugar and ate her dinner. He'd also supply a second photo afterward. This would serve as proof of life. In the morning, he'd contact them again with the rest of his demands, and they'd negotiate future exchanges. It wasn't perfect, but it'd do in the interim.

"How long is he going to drag this out?" Charles asked. "We just want our little girl back."

"Do you have the money ready to go?" Mercer asked.

"Not yet."

"Then we have nothing to bargain with. He controls everything. Until we have what he wants, we do what he says. Is that understood?" Mercer caught the look on his teammates' faces. They rarely played by a kidnapper's rules. But for now, they'd let the tosser believe he had the upper hand.

"Just bring her home," Zoe said. "That's all I want."

Charles put an arm around her shoulders and pulled her into his chest. Mercer studied the couple, confused by the dynamics. Even now, he wasn't convinced at least one of them wasn't faking it. But perhaps, life had made him jaded.

"I'll be back shortly. Bas, you know what to do if he makes contact again." Mercer headed for the door. "If you get a location, radio immediately."

"Aye."

Mercer zipped his down coat, slung the bag over his shoulder, nodded to Donovan, and stepped out into the frigid evening. Even though it was fairly early, the sun had set and most of the shops had closed. The blistering cold chapped his lips as he headed away from the resort and made his way across the parking lot to one of the vehicles the team had rented.

Initially, the engine protested, but eventually it

turned over. Leaving the heater off, Mercer backed out of the space and headed toward the highway. The bastard wasn't making this easy. He wanted Mercer to leave the supplies outside a diner two exits away.

The drive took over thirty minutes, but Mercer arrived twenty minutes before deadline. He circled the building. The diner shared a parking lot with a petrol station, or gas station as the Americans liked to call it. He spotted several silver sedans, but no sign of Annalise. He memorized the plate numbers and found a place to park.

He and Hans maintained radio silence in case the kidnapper intercepted their communications. At this point, Mercer wouldn't put anything past the bastard.

Hans was close. But Mercer didn't spot the car or any sign of his teammate. That was good. If Mercer hadn't noticed him, he doubted anyone else would either.

Getting out, Mercer looked around. It was cold. Too cold for anyone to linger outdoors, but several people were clustered together at tables inside the diner. He went around the side, past the windows, doing his best to memorize faces as he went. At the far end, he located the cooler which housed bags of ice. Tourists and travelers found this useful in summer, but at this time of year, no one had any interest in buying ice to keep their takeout cold or to bring with them on camping trips.

Mercer opened the cooler door, checked the interior of the freezer for surveillance equipment, and placed the insulated bag inside. The cooler was nearly empty, only four bags of ice remained in the bottom, frozen to the frost-covered floor.

Returning to his car, Mercer fought the urge to stick around or set up surveillance. Hans would take care of it. Instead, Mercer surveyed the diner patrons a final time, but since he had no idea what the kidnapper looked like, he couldn't be certain the man wasn't eating dinner inside the brightly lit establishment. A minute later, Mercer started the engine and drove away. Now he had to wait for proof of life.

THIRTEEN

"We should have heard something by now." Charles rubbed his eyes. "Why hasn't he sent back proof. Did you do what he said? Did you go to the right location?"

Mercer stared at the man. "Yes."

"Well, why hasn't he called?"

"I don't know."

"You must have done something wrong." Charles glared at Mercer, his glasses slowly sliding down his nose. He pushed them back up, sabotaging his best attempt to appear intimidating. "What did you do?"

Mercer massaged his temples and slid out of the chair. Hans had maintained eyes on the cooler for over an hour, but no one had made the pick-up. Finally, Mercer told him to leave. Perhaps, Hans had been spotted, or the kidnapper had a sixth sense about things. Either way, Mercer feared their attempt to locate the kidnapper had sabotaged the mission. But he had no intention of admitting that to the upset father.

Mercer rotated his shoulders a few times and came to his full height. The hard planes of his body evident beneath his fitted shirt. Charles swallowed and took a step back. "Would you prefer to have someone else handle this, Mr. Van der Berg?"

"I might."

Mercer moved closer. "So call him."

"Who?" Charles squeaked.

"Whoever you like. My team has worked for several agencies. Would you like a few recommendations?"

"Yes. Yes, I would." He fished out his phone. "I'll need names and numbers."

"So be it." Mercer turned to retrieve the files. He'd give Mr. Van der Berg the insurance firm's number. They dealt with plenty of negotiators. They could recommend someone, and if another negotiator arrived in time, he could hash out the terms and make the exchange. But Mercer wouldn't give up on his mission or the promise he made. He'd get Annalise back or die trying.

"Do you even care what happens to my baby?" Charles asked.

"That doesn't matter. What I think and feel is irrelevant." The question caught Mercer off guard. "You have to do what's best for your daughter. And you think a new negotiator would be best, so when he arrives, I'll hand the recovery over to him."

"You will do no such thing." Zoe pushed her way between the two men. "You made me a promise, Julian. I trusted you to fix this. So fucking fix it."

"Your husband doesn't think I can." Mercer stared into Charles' eyes. "He should hire someone he trusts. I told you the same thing when we first met."

"Do not turn this into another fight, Charles," Zoe warned. "I'm doing what's best for Annalise. You don't get to second-guess me. We're sticking with Julian

Mercer and his people."

But it was too late. Charles had grown tired of his ex-wife dictating terms. "You dragged my baby girl to this snowy hellhole without so much as telling me where you were going. You left her in the store unattended. You caused this to happen. You, Zoe. This is your fault. So I have every right to second-guess everything you've ever done. You're an unfit mother. You always were, even if the courts can't see it."

Mercer stepped away from the arguing couple. He hadn't intended to trigger a fight, but the tension between them had been boiling beneath the surface since the moment Charles walked through the door. Maybe even before that. There odd exchanges and intimate moments only confused the K&R specialist. But this was real.

"You want to lock Annalise away for the rest of her life. All you've ever done is punish her for being sick. At least I try to make sure she has a normal life. That she has fun. That she isn't afraid of things," Zoe spat.

"I'm not punishing her. I'm protecting her. And she should be afraid. This world is a scary place. I see it every day." He gestured at the files on the table. "Don't you think she's terrified now? Do you think getting kidnapped is normal? Is that the experience you wanted her to have?"

"You know it isn't. You know that's not what I meant. I would never let anything happen to our daughter."

"Too late."

"Fuck you, Charles." Zoe wiped at her eyes. Though she came up with some rather creative things to call her former spouse, she didn't attempt to physically strike him. However, Mercer was considering it as a viable option to end the argument.

When Zoe could no longer speak because her

sobbing was out of control, Charles reached for her. "I'm sorry, honey. I didn't mean any of it. I'm just worried about our baby. You're not unfit. I shouldn't have said that."

Fire ignited in Zoe's swollen eyes, and she batted his hand away. "There's a lot you shouldn't have said and even more you shouldn't have done."

Charles reached for her arm, but she stepped away.

Before she could say or do anything else, Mercer intervened, placing a hand on the man's chest and pushing him backward. "That's enough. Leave her be. You both made mistakes. Now we fix them. Forgive your wife or don't. It doesn't matter. But this isn't helping Annalise."

Charles tucked his hands into his back pockets and paced small circles in the dining room. "How do we fix this? Annalise is gone. It's already too late."

Zoe gulped down some air. "He's right. Oh god." She clamped a hand over her mouth when a wail escaped. Hans came up behind her and pulled her into his chest. She clutched his shirt in her fists, her entire body shaking.

"Shh." Hans stroked her back and led her toward the sofa. "Annalise will be fine. Jules and I will make sure of it. No need for tears. Okay, darling? No more tears. You didn't do anything wrong. The bastard who took Annalise, he's the one responsible. He's the one who deserves your anger. Focus your rage on him. There's no reason to bicker amongst yourselves."

Zoe didn't reply. Instead, she buried her face deeper into Hans' shirt. He held her tighter, rocking her back and forth. Mercer felt eyes on him and noticed Donovan and Bastian standing in the doorway.

What did you do? Bastian mouthed.

Mercer let out an annoyed huff but kept one eye on

Mr. Van der Berg. His dislike for the man had grown exponentially in the last few minutes, and Mercer wasn't positive Charles wouldn't do something to exacerbate the situation further.

Taking a breath, Mercer counted to ten. That trick never worked, but he performed the ritual anyway. Maybe he could understand the man's outrage, but now wasn't the time or place for blame. He already blamed himself enough.

"I will handle this situation to the best of my ability," Mercer vowed.

Charles stopped circling, took off his glasses, and wiped them on his shirt. After replacing them on his face, he looked at Mercer. "You better get my daughter back. From what I've been told, you knew this asshole was here and you didn't do a damn thing to stop him. But you're going to, or so help you."

Mercer held his tongue, nodding. He didn't need to add additional fuel to the fire. Even the slightest spark was liable to set off another explosion, and he despised the drama, even if he had inadvertently caused it.

Satisfied, Charles turned to his sobbing ex-wife. "Zoe, honey, you know I didn't mean it. I'm just angry. This situation has me beside myself. But you have to see it from my side. You brought Annalise here."

"Screw you," she whispered, barely loud enough for anyone to hear her.

When she didn't turn to acknowledge Charles or launch herself into his arms, which she had done numerous times since his arrival, the man quietly excused himself and headed to one of the upstairs bedrooms. "Let me know when the kidnapper makes contact," Charles said, leaning against the railing so he could see the group assembled in the living room below.

"Sure thing," Donovan said.

Charles offered a weak smile and closed himself into the upper bedroom.

"You all right, love?" Bastian asked, but Zoe didn't answer. He looked at Hans.

"She'll be fine, just as soon as we get her little girl back." Hans stopped rocking her, and she pulled herself away from him. Using both hands, she wiped her eyes. "Why don't you get cleaned up and try to get some rest, hmm?"

She bit her lip and nodded. Turning around, she blushed when she found the three men watching her. Quietly, she excused herself and ducked into the closest bathroom.

"What did you say to cause all this ruckus?" Bastian asked.

"Nothing." Mercer shook the thought away and returned to his seat at the table. "Charles isn't satisfied with our lack of progress, and neither am I. I should have never let you go ahead, Hans. Maybe he made us. Maybe that's why he never went to the pick-up location."

"Rubbish." Hans ran his hands down the front of his shirt, finding it damp and wrinkled. "This isn't my fault, Jules. And it's not yours either."

"I believe that makes it unanimous." Bastian placed his laptop on the table. "I ran those plate numbers from the diner, but none of the owners match the vague characteristics we have for the kidnapper."

"What characteristics?" Mercer asked.

"Hazel eyes. Male. Roughly average height. I can't be positive about weight or build."

"Too many layers," Donovan said knowingly.

"Still, it's something," Bastian insisted. "And no hazel-eyed blokes are registered to those silver sedans you spotted at the diner and petrol station."

"He has a tattoo," Mercer indicated the spot on his own arm, "right here."

"I saw the screen capture you made. It didn't reveal enough for us to go on," Bastian said.

"No, but if I spot some bastard waltzing around town with a tattoo on the inside of his forearm, I'll have a few questions for him," Hans said.

Mercer didn't speak. He knew there wasn't much more they could do until morning. Since it wasn't tourist season, most of the shops and restaurants closed at six. That might explain the diner's popularity. With the exception of a few fast food joints, nothing else was available for passing motorists or the townsfolk who worked late or found themselves peckish after dinner.

Donovan sat down across from Mercer, and Hans followed suit. The four men crowded around the table, the dossier spread out in front of them. The kidnapper lived in the region. He was probably home right now, gloating.

"He's not staying at this resort," Hans said, breaking the silence. "Bas and I have gone through the guest registry a few times. Again, we have description issues."

"More with the room and background than anything else." Bastian drummed his fingers on the table.

Mercer nodded. "He's not here. He drove away."

"He could have doubled back," Donovan said.

"I don't think it'd be possible to slip in and out without getting caught on at least one security camera," Bastian said. "He couldn't physically bypass them. There aren't enough blind spots. At the very least, someone would have noticed him dragging Annalise around. He's not at this resort. He could possibly be at another place of lodging."

"What about the cat from hell who lured her away?" Hans asked. "Did you get anything on that?"

Donovan stifled a chuckle. "We have receipts with names. We also pulled the café's information. But without a solid description of the kidnapper, we still don't have much."

"Run down the names of those who might have been in or near the café around the same time Annalise and Zoe passed by. It might be a start," Mercer suggested.

"Already done. But it didn't lead anywhere. Though I will say, the cat in the surveillance footage looks a lot like Franklin," Donovan said.

"That's the same fluffy bastard," Hans said.

"Yeah, okay," Donovan agreed.

"Is there any way to track the kitten?" Hans asked.

"I don't think he's been tagged," Bastian said, "but I'm not entirely sure. I think the café gets their supply from one of the shelters, but I can ask in the morning. They've already closed up for the night."

"Okay." Mercer thought, but his mind kept returning to the lack of communication with the kidnapper.

"I checked the resort's data log. The only network intrusions logged by the system were us. So I know he didn't hack in and delete any video files or database entries," Bastian said. "I don't think he decided to target Annalise by hanging out in the lobby."

"What about the other resorts and hotels?" Mercer asked. "You said he might be keeping her there."

"It'll take time. We're talking dozens of establishments."

"This town doesn't feel that big."

"Just wait. In a week's time, it'll look like London the week of the royal wedding."

Mercer swore. "Do you think that's why he's

dragging this out?"

"It would make escape easier," Donovan said.

"He can't hold Annalise for the rest of the week," Hans said. "She won't survive."

"She might," Bastian said. "As long as she has insulin and can regulate her blood sugar, she won't have a problem in terms of her health. She lives with this every day. It's part of life for her. She might be young, but I'd bet she knows how to take care of herself."

"That's not how Zoe and Charles make it sound," Mercer said.

"They're parents. They worry, and with good reason. But I read up on her condition and checked her medical records. She should be fine, as long as she has medication and adequate nutrition."

"But he doesn't have enough supplies to last the week," Donovan protested, "just enough for tonight, assuming he makes the pick-up."

"He wouldn't accept more." Mercer peered into the empty downstairs bedroom he had turned into an office, wondering why the kidnapper hadn't made contact again. "He made it clear what to include and how much. One meal, a light snack, and a large enough dose of medication should she be experiencing distress."

"She might be able to stretch that into two doses. One for tonight, one for the morning, depending on her numbers," Bastian said, ever the optimist.

"Finicky bastard," Hans mumbled. "I'd like to cause him some distress."

"Wouldn't we all?" Mercer toyed with the ends of the pages.

"He wants to make sure we don't drag our feet on getting the money," Bastian said. "He's holding us to the clock. That's his rationale."

"Then why hasn't he called back?" Mercer's temper flared, but he couldn't be bothered to tamp it down. He had every reason to be irate. He made the drop two hours ago. By now, he should have received proof of life. "I need a way to contact him." Mercer stared at Bastian. "What about the e-mail he sent? Can't we use that?"

"I'm close to pulling his MAC, but with the satellite uplink, I don't know how much good it'll do. It may not be linked to a physical address. It's used to identity the computer on a network. But he probably has all of that turned off since he has a direct uplink. So I don't know if I can use that to trace his location."

"English, Bas," Mercer warned. "Speak English."

"The way he contacts us might not be traceable."

"Bugger. What about the e-mail address he used?"

"The photo he sent came from an unmonitored or closed account. I've tried sending a reply, but it gets bounced back. I called our mates in military intelligence to see if they could pull anything, but I haven't heard back yet."

"So we're dealing with a computer genius?" Mercer asked.

"Possibly."

Hans sighed. "I'm going to take a walk and clear my head."

Mercer looked up. "Stay on comms. Do not compromise this op."

"No worries."

"I'll go with you," Donovan said. "Safety in numbers, mate. And there's a good chance a litter of stray kittens is out there running amok. You might need the protection."

"Sod off," Hans said as the two put on their coats, checked their side arms, and opened the front door.

"Don't forget to be mindful of bears," Bastian called

after them.

"Bears?" Hans asked, surprised. But the door closed, cutting off whatever other questions he might have wanted to ask after that warning.

"Unless he calls, we have nothing." Mercer winced. He hated this. Not having any control of the situation caused him physical pain.

"He'll call."

Mercer let out a disgusted grunt. If the kidnapper was half as clever as he appeared to be, he probably killed Annalise the moment they hung up, dumped her body, and left town. How would they even find her? Would the kidnapper call a final time to tell them where he left her, or would the authorities discover her remains and notify the parents?

"Jules, there's nothing else you could have done," Bastian said.

Mercer looked at him. "You don't know that."

And then the phone rang.

FOURTEEN

"Where is it?" the kidnapper asked.

"Where's what?" Mercer stood in front of the screen. Bastian sat just out of view, running every tracking program known to man.

"The food and the girl's medicine." The kidnapper rubbed his lips, pulling his hand away and flicking off the dried bits of chapped skin that had gotten stuck to his gloves.

"I left it in the freezer outside the diner like you instructed." Mercer couldn't believe this was happening. He'd never botched a drop before.

The kidnapper narrowed his eyes. "You're shitting me, right?"

"I assure you, I'm not."

"Huh." He rocked back in the chair. "Are you sure you left it in the freezer? I checked everywhere inside, man. I didn't see anything."

Mercer wrestled with that thought. Hans hadn't seen anyone check the freezer. The only people who even pulled into the parking lot after Mercer left went straight inside. They didn't wander or dawdle. The kidnapper had to be lying. Or they had a serious miscommunication. "I placed the items in a blue insulated bag, like I told you I would, and put the bag inside the outdoor cooler."

"I don't know. I didn't see it." He cocked his head to the side. "You're trying to pull a fast one. I don't know how, but you are."

"What the bloody hell are you going on about? I want to save the girl's life. I wouldn't withhold food or medicine. That'd be daft."

He picked at the pad on the middle finger of his glove, more interested in the debris trapped in the knit material than the conversation. "Does she really mean that much to you? You called her a package. You don't even refer to her by name."

Mercer bit back his comment. He didn't see the bleeding point in humanizing her to this wanker, but saying as much wouldn't further the negotiation. "She needs food and medicine. Did you go to the drop site?"

"Did you?"

Mercer slammed his palm on the desk, infuriated.

The kidnapper laughed. "Take it easy, dude. Your blood pressure must be through the roof. That vein in the side of your neck," he tilted his head, gesturing to a spot beneath his jaw, "it's pounding like a drum solo. I don't want you to keel over. I still need you to deliver my money."

Bastian looked up, hoping to calm Mercer's temper. "Easy," he whispered.

Mercer jerked, wanting nothing more than to hit something and knowing he couldn't. Kidnappers had never been able to see him during a long-distance negotiation, so his outbursts could be contained or kept away from the prying eyes of the enemy. In this case, he had to control himself. Steeling his nerves, he forced his hands down at his sides. His muscles so tight, they cramped into painful knots. But he didn't react. He remained rigid and still to the point statues would be jealous of his concentration.

"I will make a second drop. Is that acceptable?" Mercer asked, his voice monotone.

"Are you going to go to the right place this time?" the kidnapper asked.

"Give me the location. I will make the delivery."

"Same rules?"

"If you wish," Mercer said, "but I need a way to contact you."

"Working on it," Bastian mumbled so his voice wouldn't be picked up by the computer.

The kidnapper chuckled. "Did you do this on purpose just so you could get my number? I'm flattered. It's the whole leave your sweater behind so you have to go back and get it thing. That's adorable."

Mercer remained still, every muscle in his body clenched.

When the kidnapper was no longer amused by his own rhetoric, he cocked his head to the side and tapped on the screen. "Hey, Julian, are you frozen?"

"No. I'm waiting on your response."

"Oh, goody. I thought the screen froze or you had an aneurysm or something. You weren't moving. Though I suppose a medical emergency would probably involve you passing out or writhing in pain. Maybe I should ask Annalise about that."

"Is she okay?" Mercer asked, panic kicking his senses into high alert.

The kidnapper winked. "Glad to see you care about something besides a workout regimen. Seriously, dude, you're ripped. What do you bench? Two-fifty? Three hundred?"

"When and where can I leave a second delivery?" Mercer asked.

"The same place you left the last one. Are you sure you went to the diner at exit 59?"

"Yes."

"Well, I didn't get it. Maybe some starving, homeless street urchin saw you drop it off and took it. Did you see any starving street urchins?"

"It's bitter cold. No one was out."

"No one? C'mon," the kidnapper wheedled, "even I don't believe that. You must have waited a little while to see if I'd show. You're sure no one else was around?"

"No." Mercer kept his expression neutral, but he suspected the plonker had seen Hans or suspected a trap and hadn't bothered to show up. But that didn't explain why he requested a second drop.

"See, I knew you went to the wrong place. That diner always has at least two cars outside. If you didn't see anyone, then you weren't where you were supposed to be."

"That's not what I meant." Mercer exhaled slowly. "No one went near the cooler. The only people I saw were in the diner."

"Huh, okay. Well, maybe someone wanted dessert. Did you pack any dessert in there?"

"No."

"Not even fruit?"

"Fruit juice boxes. That's what her mum said would help boost her blood sugar."

"You should go with fruit. It'd be better. Healthier."

"Who–" Mercer stopped himself from asking the question. He didn't need to argue with the kidnapper. "I need a way to contact you after I make the delivery. Or we can do it in person. Annalise doesn't have time for another mishap or miscommunication."

The kidnapper shook his head. "You'd like that, wouldn't you? You'd grab me up and torture me for her location. But I'll never tell," he sang. "And I'm not stupid. Don't treat me like I am. This is all part of your plan."

"I don't have a plan. And I don't think you're stupid, sir," Mercer said, his cramped shoulders screaming in pain.

"Ah, there's that sir. I do rather enjoy that. Maybe next time you could say it while trussed up in latex and chains."

Mercer stared straight at the camera. "A number that I can call to reach you. This negotiation can only continue if we have an open, two-way line of communication."

"Two-way. I was thinking three-way or four-way. Ménage à quatre? Is that a thing? We should make it a thing."

"Your number, please."

"I'm gonna stick with four. You can watch. Three women and me. That'd work out nicely. Two could go to town down below and one could–"

"Enough," Mercer snapped.

The kidnapper sighed. "All right, you can join in."

"Your. Phone. Number."

The kidnapper sighed dramatically. "Fine, I'll give it to you. After all, you must have guys running traces and shit. They must be a few seconds away from getting it anyway, seeing as how you've dragged this conversation on and on and on." He faked a yawn. "Frankly, I'm getting kinda bored. Bring another batch of food and some fruit this time. Call me once you clear out. Don't dawdle. The kid's not looking so good. Kinda pasty and sweaty. Actually, a bit like you. Maybe you need to eat something too. Try a banana."

"I'm on my way."

"One last thing, Julian." The kidnapper dropped the teasing tone. His eyes went cold and hard. "If I see you or anyone else around that I don't like the looks of, this entire thing is off. You feel me?"

"Yes, sir."

"Good." The kidnapper rattled off a number and disconnected before Mercer could repeat it for verification.

"Well?" Mercer fought to control his breathing and loosen the tension in his back and arms.

"Same number I traced. It's an internet number, but having it will make it exponentially easier to pin down his precise location, assuming he doesn't change locations." Bastian gave the computer an uneasy look. "He knew we'd get the number. He wanted us to have it."

"We shouldn't assume anything." Mercer turned away from the blank screen. "What do you make of him?"

"I don't know, Jules. I just don't know, but one thing's clear. He likes to rattle your cage. And he knows exactly how to do it. We need to change our tactics."

"He knew Hans was there," Mercer declared.

"I don't know. He might just be taking extra precautions."

"Or someone else intercepted the delivery after Hans left. I'm not convinced. The bastard's bloody bonkers. I wouldn't put anything past him."

"That's why he does it," Bastian said.

Mercer didn't need to hear the words to know they were true. Unfortunately, that knowledge did little to calm his nerves, squelch his anger, or enable him to read this bastard's mind. The guy could do anything. Would do anything. He was a loose cannon. He'd act out whatever impulse came to mind. He fancied killing, at least that's what Mercer had deduced from their previous conversations and the man's cavalier attitude toward everything. "Dammit. Have you narrowed his location? You have his number. So where is he?"

"Working on it." Bastian glared at the screen. "The problem is he's still routing directly through his own uplink. He's not using the towers or networks here. He's going direct, even with the bloody internet number."

Mercer thought about the original drop, the people he saw, and the vehicles parked in the lot. No one would have taken the insulated bag. He didn't even think anyone saw him open the outdoor freezer. Who would want a container of leftovers, anyway? "I'll tell Zoe to prepare another meal."

"At least you can ring him to make sure he gets the delivery this time."

"If he answers." Something told Mercer that would be too simple, and nothing this bastard did was simple. Mercer left the room and knocked on Zoe's door. He told her a third party intercepted the package, so she had to prepare another meal for her daughter. Then he returned to the converted office with their files and research in hand.

"Jules, what are you doing?" Bastian asked as Mercer dissected each of the files, pinning the victims, locations, and details to the wall in neat rows. "I thought we wanted to keep this to ourselves, away from potentially prying eyes."

"We can't work like this. We need to see what we're missing. Just keep the Van der Bergs out. They won't notice any of this if they look in on us. But if they step inside, they'll get an eyeful, so keep them out." Mercer continued taping pages and maps to the wall. Then he reached for a pad of post-its and started making notes, adding them to the collection. "I should have done this from the start."

"Jules, keep in mind, we're less than twelve hours in. We're not behind. No need to play catch-up." Bas gestured at the preliminary work they'd put in. "If anything, we're ahead. And that frightens him."

"I don't believe he's frightened."

"I beg to differ." Bastian reached for a pen, tugging the cap off with his teeth. He scribbled down details from the screen while he chewed. Spitting out the cap, he held the notepad out to Mercer. "Those are coordinates for the outer perimeters. He's holed up somewhere inside with Annalise."

"Help me with the map." Mercer put the notepad down and unfolded the large map they'd been using. While he held the map in place, Bastian pinned the corners to the wall. Then the two men stepped back to admire their handiwork.

Grabbing a highlighter, Bastian read the coordinates off the notepad and marked the latitude and longitude. Then he took a black Sharpie and outlined the box. "This shouldn't be too bad." He reached for the laptop, supporting the base in his palm while he typed one-handed. "According to this, the population in this region is less than ten thousand."

"Before or after we add in the bloody tourists?"

"Before, but the locals congregate in certain areas. The residential neighborhoods are clustered together. It shouldn't take too long to search."

From the center of town, the search radius extended twenty kilometers in all directions. It would take months to search everywhere. The unsub wouldn't remain stationary long enough for them to find him. "This is rubbish."

"We've narrowed it considerably. And we'll

continue to do so. It's more than we had before."

Mercer noted the roads in and out. "You're sure he's in here?"

"Almost completely positive."

"Yes or no, Bas?"

"Yes, I'm sure. Mostly."

Mercer gave his best friend a cross look. He didn't like it when the analyst second-guessed himself, and that's all they'd been doing since Annalise had been taken. Reaching for a pencil, Mercer marked every road out of town that led to the highway or the diner. He paid careful attention to any back ways or side roads. While he did that, Bastian checked the internet for alternative routes.

"Any traffic cams on any of the routes?" Mercer asked.

"Negative."

Mercer counted the possibilities. Eight possible paths led to the diner. Six of which led to the highway. Two took back roads, or what Mercer assumed were roads. For all he knew, they might be hiking trails or ski paths. "Set up surveillance here." Mercer pointed to a spot on the map. "It's far enough from the diner that he wouldn't think to worry about us watching. And this way, we can see who comes and goes."

"On it," Bastian said. "I'll stick a wireless camera on the mile marker. He'll never notice."

"Make sure he doesn't. Make sure no one does. Will weather conditions pose a problem?"

"They shouldn't. Our equipment's handled far worse conditions than these."

"Scout ahead, Bas. And blend in. He could already be on his way. His actions are unpredictable. And I'm not certain he didn't spot Hans earlier."

"Do you think this is a trap? The first drop off might have been a test. This time, who knows?"

Mercer ignored the warning. It didn't matter what this was. Annalise had to survive. The delivery would help ensure that. And Mercer had to hope the kidnapper's willingness to accept a second delivery after the first one failed meant he wouldn't let the little girl perish.

"If it is, so be it." Mercer stared at the intel, absorbing as much of it as he could. The analyst quietly excused himself, radioed for Hans and Donovan to return to base, and grabbed a set of keys before setting out into the cold night.

When Mercer heard footsteps in the hallway, he stepped out of the office. "Is everything packed to the same specifications as before?"

"Yes," Zoe said, "with the exception of a piece of fruit, like you requested." She held the cooler bag out to Mercer. This one was white with blue stripes. They'd have to pick up more in the morning for future deliveries, assuming the funds weren't ready for the final exchange. "Did he say what happened to the first one?"

Mercer shook his head. "I'll make sure she gets this one." He pulled the office door closed behind him, wishing it had a lock. "I need to update your ex-husband. Would you care to join me?"

She snorted, practically rolling her eyes. "Might as well."

Again, Mercer gave her an odd look. While they spoke to Charles, Donovan and Hans returned. Bastian had already briefed them over comms, so Hans stayed in the main living area while Donovan went into the bedroom turned office to continue working on their limited leads.

"Good luck, Jules," Hans called as Mercer zipped his coat and set out to make a second delivery.

FIFTEEN

Mercer drove to the diner, passing Bastian along the way. The analyst was heading back to the chalet, which meant the camera was recording. Donovan and Hans were monitoring the traffic feed, but the kidnapper could be driving anything. So they'd have to conduct checks on every vehicle that passed. Luckily, no one was on the road.

Mercer pulled into the diner. Three cars were parked in front of the building. Another two were around back, probably belonging to the waitress and cook. Across the parking lot, the illuminated sign for the petrol station welcomed travelers, but not a single car idled in front of any of the pumps. A rusted truck was parked in a no parking zone, or what Mercer interpreted to be a no parking zone. The diagonal white stripes painted on the concrete usually signified such things.

Getting out of the car, Mercer stared at the truck, but no one was inside. It probably belonged to the clerk watching TV. Again, Mercer went around the side of the diner, turned the corner, and headed for the cooler. Stopping, he caught sight of a similar freezer at the side of the petrol station.

A gust of wind made him shiver, and he turned his collar up. The hairs at the back of his neck stood at attention. It wasn't from the cold. He stuck one hand into his pocket, gripping the Sig he had tucked inside for easy access. Staying within the shadows, he crossed the parking lot. Outside the petrol station, he opened the doors on the outdoor freezer. Unlike the one at the diner, bags of ice filled the interior.

Mercer released his grip on the gun and moved several of the bags, but this freezer was packed to capacity. He didn't make a mistake. It wouldn't be possible to leave anything inside. Closing the door, Mercer ducked down so he could get a better view of the bored clerk watching TV inside the convenience store. The man had a scruffy beard and unruly grey eyebrows. *That's not the kidnapper*, Mercer thought.

He exhaled, watching his breath turn into crystallized vapor. Again, he scouted for surveillance devices around the petrol station. This time, he noticed a camera near the door, covering the pumps. He tapped the radio in his ear but heard nothing but static.

Grumbling about the weather, mountains, and shitty reception, Mercer crept back across the lot. No one had come or gone in the last few minutes. Carefully, Mercer opened the diner's outdoor ice chest while he slipped the cooler bag off his shoulder. Leaning into the freezer, he searched the inside for the previous delivery. Perhaps the kidnapper didn't look hard enough.

"What the hell?" Mercer plucked three Polaroid photos from the freezer. They had been stuck to the inner wall with some type of tacky adhesive, which had frozen into a hard, cement-like ball.

Just as he reached for his flashlight, he heard a twig snap a few centimeters away. Mercer reached for his gun, feeling the muzzle of a weapon press into the back of his collar.

"Don't be a hero, Julian. No one wants to clean your blood and brains out of the cooler. They'd have to defrost the entire thing, and that's just a pain in the ass."

Mercer raised his hands slowly. "I thought you didn't want to meet in person."

"I changed my mind." The kidnapper tugged the cooler bag off Mercer's shoulder and lifted it over his raised hand. "I see you found the photos I left for you. That's your proof of life. Are you pleased? You should be. I followed through, just like you wanted." He shook the bag. "Isn't it nice to know we can get along? We're cut from the same cloth, you and me. We're birds of a feather. Two peas in a pod. A crumpet and tea, or whatever you British people say."

"What do you want?"

The kidnapper's chuckle turned into a cough. "I'm fine. Thanks for asking," he said pointedly.

But Mercer remained silent.

"Jeez, man, didn't your mother teach you any manners?"

"So you're not about to drop dead?" Mercer glanced at the kidnapper over his shoulder, the threat barely concealed beneath the surface. "Are you sure?"

"Nope, just too much cold air. I should have worn my insulated undies. I'm freezing my balls off out here. How 'bout you? Any shrinkage problems to report?"

"Are you sure you want those to be your last words?"

"Careful, pal. If something happens to me, the

package, as you like to call her, is as good as dead. Finito. Finished. No one knows where she is. She won't survive without me." He shook the cooler bag. "Without us. I hear she could go into a coma or ketoacidosis or whatever those commercials are always yammering on about. I don't exactly know what it means, but it's definitely not a pleasant way to go. And even if none of that happens, she'll starve to death. Or freeze. And you don't want that. Or do you?"

"What do you want?" Mercer was tired of dealing with this psychopath, especially when the guy had a gun pointed at the back of his neck. Didn't anyone ever teach him not to get that close with a gun? He was asking to have it taken away from him.

The sound of a zipper broke the deafening silence. "Hey, you brought fruit. I'm glad you listened. See, this works. You and me, we work."

"Do you mind if I turn around?" Mercer didn't make any sudden movements. This wanker was too unstable for that. Mercer knew the game. Ask permission, then knock the living daylights out of the git.

"Fine, fine." The kidnapper took a step back, possibly realizing the danger he'd face being in such close proximity to a former SAS commander. "But no funny business. And keep your hands where I can see 'em."

Slowly, Mercer turned. As suspected, the man didn't look much different from their previous encounters. He wore the same shabby coat from the promenade and the ski mask from their video chats. Beneath the coat were several layers. Mercer couldn't be sure if they were all wool, flannel, and fleece, or if the guy had some built-in insulation too. He was slightly shorter than Mercer. Like Bas had said, average height. Frankly, there was nothing remarkable about the kidnapper. That's how he blended in. That's how he got away with such atrocious acts. It might have even been what led his psychotic personality to abduct and kill. Perhaps no one knew who he was or even cared, so he'd make them care. Or so Mercer imagined.

He scanned the area behind the kidnapper. He didn't see any other vehicles near the diner or petrol station. One of the parked cars must belong to the kidnapper, unless he arrived some other way. But without mass transit or the conveniences of city life with taxis, limos, and ride-shares, that seemed unlikely. "Where's Annalise?"

"She's resting. She had a big day." The kidnapper nodded at the photos in Mercer's hand. "As you can see, she ate her dinner, we tested her blood sugar, and she figured out an adequate dose. And that snapshot, that's the updated numbers. Apparently, they can fluctuate. Who'da thunk it?"

"So she already ate?"

"Are you really this dense?" The kidnapper scratched his head with the butt of the gun, and Mercer inched forward. "No, no, no." The kidnapper stepped back, aiming. "I asked you here for a reason. The girl's fine. Everything's good. Don't go messing with the status quo. We're just finding our rhythm. The motion of the ocean and all that."

Mercer clenched his jaw, envisioning a dozen different ways to disarm this bastard. It'd be unlikely the guy would get a chance to fire off a shot, and even if he did, it was even less likely it'd prove fatal. The idea of breaking this guy's arm, his nose, his jaw, and other bones in his body held an undeniable appeal. Mercer could end this now. But something told him this guy would never give up Annalise's location. The sicko would let her perish to prove his bloody point.

"You're thinking of all the ways you can hurt me, aren't you?" the kidnapper asked. "I can see it in your eyes. That shimmer of joy. Lust. You want it so badly you can taste it. It's pulsing through you. Buzzing every pleasure synapse you have. It's addictive. The power. The control. The strength."

"Where's Annalise?"

"I'll never tell," he said in the same sing-song voice he used before.

Mercer had performed renditions and tortured men for information, but he always knew how it'd play out in the end. Men like the kidnapper would never talk or give up the location, at least not in time to save Annalise. This guy was too unstable. He didn't care enough about anything to allow someone to have leverage over him, and he obviously didn't give a shit about his well-being or safety because he wouldn't be standing a few meters away from Julian Mercer in the frigid cold after dark. Only someone insane would do something like that. And this wanker had proved time and time again he'd lost the plot.

"Why did you lure me here?" Mercer asked.

The kidnapper clucked his tongue a few times. "I didn't *lure* you here. That sounds so sinister. I just wanted to talk to you away from prying eyes and ears. I'd like to make you an offer."

Realizing the static in his ear was from a jammer, Mercer cursed his own incompetence. "I'm listening. So speak."

"You and I could have a good thing going. You convince the families to pay the ransom, and I ask for the ransom. We could have the perfect symbiotic relationship. We don't have to be on opposite sides of this. Sure, we could make it look like we are for the folks at home. Obviously, you need to convince everyone else you're a good guy, so you get to be cast as the hero. And I'm the evil villain. Mwahaha." He rolled his eyes. "But we save ourselves some time and effort. You don't have to track me. You just get me the money. Then we divide it up at the drop and go our separate ways."

"What about the package?"

"Again with the fucking package. Call her by her name or refer to her as the girl or something. I'm sure her parents would appreciate that. It'd help sell you as the good guy because right now you seem like a bigger asshole than me. And that just won't do. You have your role. And I have mine. This is what we convince people, and how we pull off the perfect kidnapping spree."

"I doubt that."

The kidnapper grinned, his teeth practically glowing in the dim light. "Is that a no?"

Mercer narrowed his eyes. He had heard some ludicrous demands but never anything this crazy. He couldn't even figure out if this wanker was on the level. And if he was, what would that mean for Annalise? "I will do whatever it takes to ensure the girl's safe return."

"That's more like it."

"I'm serious, sir." Mercer stared at him, watching the way the guy held himself. Confident and arrogant but not to the point of reckless. "Ensuring Annalise remains unharmed and returned to her family safely is my only priority."

The kidnapper dropped the salesman attitude. "You need to work on your priorities. You can't control what happens to her because you can't control me."

"But you proposed a partnership. If I were to agree, why should I believe you won't renege on the offer? What's to stop you from shooting me in the back, taking all the money for yourself, and killing the girl?"

"Absolutely nothing. But I could ask you the same thing. Since I came up on you, I've seen you clock my movements. You've been calculating your odds and determining the best angle for an attack. But you haven't tried anything yet. What's stopping you?"

"We need to build trust. You've already lied to me once about the first drop I made. I haven't lied to you. When I said I won't do anything to jeopardize Annalise's safety, I meant that. And taking you out would jeopardize her safety."

He tapped the side of the gun to his covered ear. "Glad to see you're listening, but you've probably thought about finding non-lethal ways to subdue me. Right?"

Mercer couldn't figure out what this guy wanted. "I have, but doing so would still jeopardize Annalise."

"So if I decide to shoot you dead, you'll let me?"

Mercer studied the man's face or what little of it he could see. "Perhaps."

"That just proves it. We're a match made in heaven. You're even more fucked up than me." He took several steps back until he had crossed the parking lot and was now under the petrol station's awning. He jerked the barrel of his gun in the opposite direction, toward the diner's parking lot. "Get going. But think about what I said. We could take this show on the road and make millions. Hell, billions. The sky's the limit, baby. I'm sure it's better money than whatever scraps they throw at you now. I'll call you in the morning. This second delivery should hold *the package*," he made air quotes with one hand, "over until lunchtime. By then, I'll want an update on my money and an answer to my question." He jerked the gun toward Mercer's parked car. "Now, get."

SIXTEEN

After a few hundred meters, the static in Mercer's ear abated. The comm link was no longer jammed, so he tapped the radio and updated the team. Keeping an eye on the rearview mirror, Mercer slowed his speed, whipped the car around, and doubled back. Trees lined both sides of the road, too dense for Mercer to conceal the vehicle in the forest. So he pulled the car onto the shoulder, half in the grass, cut the lights, and checked the time.

"Do you have any idea where he came from?"

"No, Jules. I didn't spot any other vehicles on the road when I was setting up the surveillance. The feed didn't pick up any headed that way. Are you sure he drove? You said you didn't see a car in the parking lot."

"How else could he appear in the middle of nowhere?"

"No need to be sarcastic."

"I wasn't," Mercer said. "I want to know how anyone could just materialize at the bloody diner. The prick practically snuck up on me." No one had ever done that before. Mercer was always on alert, his senses constantly scanning for oddities. "You have to figure this out, Bas."

"Do you want me to retrieve the footage from the petrol station's camera?"

"Not yet. I want to make sure he's gone. For all I know, he's waiting for us to return. Since we don't know how or when he arrived, I can't be positive he's left yet." This would explain why Hans never spotted him making the pick-up either.

"He might think you're a lone wolf. I could show up with a clipboard and some coveralls, so he won't realize we're together, especially if he thinks you're a solo act."

"That won't work. You heard him. He knows I have a team."

Bastian sighed. How much did the kidnapper know about them? The four of them had tried to maintain a low profile, but in a small town, that was impossible. Their first visit to speak to the local police force had resulted in gossip, but since they hadn't asked about the abductions directly, Mercer thought they were in the clear. Now he wasn't sure.

"If he calls back, handle it," Mercer said. "And reassure the Van der Bergs that I've received proof of life. I'll forward you the images for further analysis. But Bas, we need to figure out who he is and where he's keeping her. He has something planned. Something big. I don't think she'll survive without an intervention."

"I thought he just wanted the money. He even offered to cut you in on the deal. Why would he harm her?"

"He offered to cut me in if I align myself with him, if I stop worrying about her. About the outcome. That tells me one thing. This won't be a positive recovery. Once he gets the money, she's as good as dead."

"And if we delay?"

"We've seen what he's done when faced with previous delays. We can't risk that either."

"Bloody hell, we're damned either way."

Headlights approached, and Mercer sunk down in the seat. But the lights belonged to a lorry, a freight logo painted on the side. Annoyed by the false alarm, Mercer let out a frustrated growl. "Find him. I'll head back once I've exhausted all possibilities, but hopefully, he left some clues behind that will lead us to Annalise. If I encounter any issues, I'll let you know. I'm hoping his trail hasn't gone completely cold yet."

"Are you sure you don't want us to meet you?"

"Negative."

But Bastian didn't sign off. Instead, he hesitated. Mercer could hear his nervous chewing through the earpiece. From the loud crunch, it sounded like pretzel rods or possibly bagel chips. "For the record, you're not considering his offer, are you?"

"Don't you know me by now, Bas?" How could his friend think he'd work with a disgusting, depraved, murderous kidnapper? The idea turned his stomach. It took Mercer a moment to recognize the emotion for what it was. Only his disbelief dulled the hurt disappointment.

"I do. And I know you'll say or do whatever it takes to get the girl back alive. Do not make a deal with the devil, even if you plan to double cross him the first chance you get. We don't know enough about him or the situation. You can't do this alone, Jules."

Mercer chuckled, oddly relieved. "No worries. I'm not doing anything unless we're all on board."

"That'll be the day."

Rubbing his palms together, Mercer worked the stiffness out of his fingers. He regretted not shooting the bastard. He could have tossed the plonker's body into the empty freezer. No one would have found him until spring. But innately, he knew the op would go pear-shaped if he did that. He also knew if he waited too long, Annalise wouldn't make it.

"Bollocks." Frustrated, Mercer checked the time. Twenty minutes had passed. After grabbing his gear from the glove box, he climbed out of the car, carefully shut the door, and crept along the tree line. He followed the highway back to the diner.

This time, he stayed hidden in the shadows. The same three cars remained parked in front. He crouched down and peered through his binoculars. He didn't see the shabby coat anywhere inside the diner. Switching to thermals, he checked for heat signatures. He spotted seven inside the diner and another inside the convenience store. He didn't spot anyone in the nearby woods.

He scanned for RF signals but didn't find anything suspicious. No piggy-backed loop. No unidentified networks. As far as he could tell, the kidnapper had vanished. He tapped his radio. This time, he heard the same intermittent interference caused by the mountains and weather.

"Jules?" Bastian asked. "You all right?"

"He jammed us before. I'm guessing this means he's gone. I'll check inside the diner and then head back."

"Bring back some pie."

"I thought you're watching what you eat."

"You need a cover story, and that's a bloody good one. Get blueberry or cherry, if they have it."

Mercer would have chuckled if the situation weren't so dire. "Focus more on finding this prick and less on your stomach."

After entering and performing a sweep of the interior, including the bathrooms, Mercer took a seat at the counter. The waitress, a busty woman named Bev, pulled a chewed pencil from behind her ear and stood sideways, resting her hip against the counter. She eyed him, the fatigue evident in her eyes and the lines of her face.

"What'll it be?"

"A piece of pie, to go."

She arched an eyebrow. "Anything else?" She leaned down a little, making a show of looking out the front windows. "You need me to call you a tow truck or something?"

"No."

"You sure? I don't see your ride out there." She gazed at him, her eyes traveling up and down. "You don't look much like a hitchhiker. You don't sound like one either, unless you've been hitchhiking for a while."

Mercer forced his facial muscles to relax. His mates were much better at asking questions without appearing threatening. But he could be charming when he wanted to, or so Michelle had told him on numerous occasions. Plus, he'd seen Bastian do this a hundred times. How hard could it be?

He chuckled politely. "No, love. I popped a tire. My mate's working on it. He sent me to bring back pie." He winked at her. "Do you get many hitchhikers around here?"

She shook her head, scribbled down his order, and lifted the glass lid off an elevated cake plate. "Not many. We get a few. They usually look homeless. My momma always said they were ridin' the rails." She scooped a slice of blueberry pie into a foam container. "Do you want whipped cream?"

"Actually," he stopped her as she raised the metal canister, "if it's not too much trouble, maybe I'll just take a whole pie instead."

"Suit yourself, sugar." She slid the spatula underneath the slice, put it back on the glass stand, and covered the plate. She grabbed one of the uncut pies from a rear display case, put it in a cardboard box, and folded down the flaps. "That'll be twenty dollars."

Mercer didn't quibble over the price. Instead, he pulled out two twenties. "Sorry about my indecisiveness." She tried to hand back one of the bills, but he shook his head. "That's for you."

She gave him the first genuine smile since he arrived. "Thanks, mister."

"My pleasure." He firmly gripped the sides of the box and stood. "Any riffraff out there I should worry about? Hitchhikers and railway riders?"

She laughed. "You look like you know how to handle yourself. Where are you headed?"

"To the resort. Thought I'd arrive early for some skiing."

"Don't worry. The locals won't bother you. But you won't get much skiing in until they turn on the snow machines or until the weather cooperates. Maybe you'll have some luck by the end of the week. Weatherman predicts we might be getting a blizzard."

"I guess you don't get many walk-ins."

"Nowhere to walk from."

Mercer filed the thought away, unsure how the kidnapper could have made the pick-up without the use of a motor vehicle. "Did anyone give you any trouble tonight? I thought I saw a rough looking gentleman outside earlier. He had a long shabby wool coat and a ski mask. He looked like he was prepared to go hiking or knock over the petrol station."

"Was his coat moth eaten?" she asked.

"Perhaps."

Bev tucked the chewed pencil back behind her ear. "That's Earl. He doesn't mean any harm. He wanders around these parts, just kinda comes and goes."

"Earl? Does Earl have a last name?"

"Sure, he does. I just don't know it." Her brows knit together, the kindness leaving her eyes. "Why do you care?"

"You mentioned hitchhikers. I thought he might need a ride."

"Nah." She wiped the counter. "He always finds a way to take care of himself."

Earl, Mercer thought as he left the diner. That didn't give him much to go on. But it was a start.

SEVENTEEN

"You're sure she said Earl?" Bastian asked. "I've only found three living in the area."

"How far out did you expand the search?" Hans picked up one of the forks and snagged the corner of Bastian's piece of pie.

"Fifty kilometers. He can't be beyond that point. Honestly, that's probably too far." Bastian gestured to the map. "Those are the Earls within our grid."

"Run backgrounds." Mercer examined the three Polaroids and rubbed his fingers together, annoyed by the sticky residue. "Any idea what this is?"

"Chewing gum, maybe. I scraped it off and dropped it in the post. The lads in the lab will get around to it once they receive it." Donovan cleaned the barrel of his handgun and began reassembling it. "When do we move?"

"As soon as Bas gets us an address." Mercer held up one of the photos. "Any idea where he took this?"

Bastian glanced at the snapshot. "I'll let you know when I have the bloody address. Showing me the photo won't help. It's the same location as the video proof of life he initially supplied. The bedroom's the same."

"So he hasn't moved. That'll make this easier." Mercer picked up the pastry box and went into the kitchen. Zoe and Charles were sitting at opposite ends of the table. Mercer put the pie down, placed the photos on top of the box, and went to the cupboard to retrieve two sets of plates and forks.

"You bought pie?" Disdain dripped from Charles' words. "And now you're going to serve it? Is this what we're paying you for?"

"You're not paying me." Mercer put the plates and forks down in the center and pulled out the nearest chair. "I needed intel. Sometimes, one must blend in. Hence, the pie."

"Yeah, whatever. You said you spoke to him. That you saw him. Why didn't you do something?"

Mercer's volume dropped, along with the temperature in the room. "I would have preferred to end this outside that diner. Under different circumstances, the man who took your daughter would be dead or imprisoned by now, but killing him won't get Annalise back. He didn't bring her to the drop. Until we know where she is, we can't move on him."

"Still, you could have done something. You could have had him arrested. Interrogated. Hell, give me a few minutes with this guy and I'll make him talk."

"How many fights have you been in, Mr. Van der Berg?" Mercer asked.

"What does that have to do with anything?"

"How many interrogations have you conducted?"

"Honestly, I don't see the point. He took my baby. I'd find a way to get answers. To get her back. It's more than what you've done."

"I don't believe your assessment is correct. Had I thought such action would have resulted in a desired outcome, I would have done whatever was necessary. But I couldn't hurt or capture him, and he knew it."

"Why?" Charles asked, grabbing one of the photos off the top of the box.

"Until we have the location, this plonker is the only one keeping Annalise alive. We have to play along for now. Her condition requires it. Even if that weren't the case, the frigid temperatures would still give me pause. She could starve or freeze without him. We can't risk it. Not yet."

Zoe bit her lip to keep from crying. "But you gave the man food. He said he'd give it to her, so she's okay."

"For tonight."

"What about tomorrow?" Charles asked.

"It turns out he received the first delivery. That means she has enough medicine and food for the morning. It gives us some time."

"That's good," Zoe said.

"How is that good? It gives this shithead more time to do god knows what to our little girl," Charles said.

"We're making progress," Mercer said.

"What kind of progress? I want to see this progress with my own two eyes."

"When we have something solid, I'll let you know."

"This is bullshit." Charles shoved away from the table. "If he so much as touches a hair on her head, it's on you, buddy." He stormed up the stairs and slammed the door.

Zoe flinched at the sound, but she had yet to look up from the photograph of her daughter. "Did he say anything? How she is? What he wants?"

"He didn't say much, just that he wants his money. That's what he keeps insisting. Are you sure this isn't personal?"

"I don't know anyone who would do something like this." Finally, she tore her gaze from the photograph. "What's to stop him from hurting her once we pay?"

"Me. Bastian. Hans. Donovan. We'll stop him."

She snorted, but it didn't alter her expression. "I appreciate the sentiment." She narrowed her eyes at the pastry box. "Why did you bring us pie?"

"Bas wanted it." Mercer shrugged. "I don't know. My wife used to bake whenever she was upset. I thought it might help."

"Do you have children?"

"No."

"Does your wife want kids?"

Sorrow tugged at Mercer's insides. "She's dead."

"I'm sorry. How did it happen?"

"That's not your concern." Mercer didn't discuss his personal life with clients. He rarely discussed it with anyone. "You should get some sleep. Tomorrow will be another hard day. You need to prepare yourself as best you can. All the days will be hard until we make the recovery." Though the voice in the back of his head questioned if they'd recover the child intact or if they'd only bring back her body for her parents to bury.

"I doubt I'll sleep."

"Try."

"You'll wake me if he makes contact in the middle of the night?"

"Yes, or one of my teammates will."

"Okay." She took the photo of her daughter and wandered down the hallway toward the bedroom. From her unsteady gait, she looked like a sleepwalker. Unfortunately, this was worse than any nightmare.

Mercer let his head sink into his hands. They had to figure this out. The only way he could see to do that was by identifying the kidnapper. They identified the cat, but that didn't lead to anything. Bas checked the cat café, but they didn't employ anyone named Earl. Bev, the waitress at the diner, said Earl wanders. He might be transient or living on the fringes and observing while the rest of society turned a blind eye. He could have wandered into the café, took the kitten, and grabbed the girl.

At least they had a name, but based on the ransoms the kidnapper had collected in the past, he wasn't poor. Far from it. So that must be an act. After all, he would need top of the line computer equipment and a strong knowledge base to conduct his business. But with only three Earls in town, it shouldn't be hard to find him. Mercer would bang down each of their doors in a preemptive strike if it meant rescuing Annalise.

Tonight, the kidnapper wouldn't know what hit him.

EIGHTEEN

"Switch to thermals," Hans suggested over comms. "I can't see shit." After a brief argument, Mercer convinced the reconnaissance expert to remain at the chalet and function remotely as overwatch. Someone had to stay behind to guard the Van der Bergs and wait by the computer in case the kidnapper called again. Though the doctors had cleared Hans for active duty, so to speak, Mercer felt better knowing he was somewhere safe. "I'm getting a lot of static on my end."

"It's the bloody mountains." Bastian switched to infrared. "I don't see anything either."

"Are you sure this is the right address?" Donovan crept along the side of the house and peered around the corner. "It looks abandoned."

"I don't know if it's the right address." Bastian cycled back to night vision. "But Earl Hilty owns this place. I didn't find any record of sale."

"And the other two locations?" Mercer asked as he crept to the other side. The neighborhood, if one used the term loosely, contained a dozen houses, spread so far apart it was nearly impossible to make out the next nearest house through the dense woods. This house was only ten kilometers from the diner, if one were to take the back roads.

"Well, Earl Stanhope is eighty-three and lives in an assisted living facility. That probably rules him out as our kidnapper." Bastian let out a huff. The mask over his face limited the plume of crystallized vapor. "And Earl Taylor didn't check all the boxes."

"How many of them did he check?" Mercer asked. "Our profile is nothing more than a best guess. We shouldn't assume we know anything about this arsehole except his eye color and height."

"And his fashion sense," Hans added.

"Earl Taylor's flat isn't an ideal breach point," Bastian said. "He lives in the center of town. We would have spotted his vehicle if he had gone to the diner to meet you."

"You can't be certain of that. And since when do we concern ourselves with ideal breach points?" Mercer asked.

"We bloody well should. If our strike doesn't result in a recovery, then we've blown our load. At least out here, we're less likely to get caught."

"Let me be the judge of that. Where's the third location?"

"It's just a few kilometers from the resort. You remember those high-end condos and rowhouses we passed?"

"Bollocks." Mercer knew Bastian's logic was sound, but that didn't matter. If Annalise was being kept there, Mercer would find a way inside.

"With so many shops within walking distance, someone would have noticed if Earl Taylor arrived home with a little girl. Small towns have plenty of nosy neighbors," Bastian continued.

"So we're in the middle of nowhere because this is your best bleeding guess?" Mercer hadn't realized selecting this location had been nothing more than a toss of the dice. At the chalet, Bastian made this address sound promising. But now that they were two seconds away from knocking down the doors, the location felt wrong. The lack of heat signatures and network activity indicated no one was inside. The small bit of hope Mercer had that they could find this bastard and save the child evaporated as quickly as his puff of breath.

"Jules," Bastian grunted, "we've been over this. Earl Hilty, the owner of this house, fits our profile to a tee. He's within our estimated age range. He isn't married. He lives alone. He works at one of the upscale restaurants which every one of the victims visited."

"Fine, but that doesn't coincide with the drifter status Bev described."

"Maybe his name's not Earl," Donovan said. "She could have it wrong. Or she could have been talking about someone else. We could hold off and collect more intel."

But Mercer didn't want to wait. "Move into position. We breach on my count."

In full blackout gear, the three took up positions at various entry points. Bastian covered the front door. Mercer took the large side window, and Donovan crouched at the rear exit.

Mercer ran his gloved fingertips around the frame, but the double-paned windows were sealed. He'd have to break the glass, and that would make noise. "Hans, monitor police frequencies. Let us know if someone reports the break-in."

"Aye, commander."

"On my mark." Mercer turned away, silently counting in his head. Donovan and Bastian would need a few seconds to retract the fiber optic cables they'd used to check the interior of the house. None of the equipment showed movement inside. "Three." Mercer took a deep breath and pressed his back against the house. "Two." He lifted his gun, holding it in such a way to break the window. "One." He pulled his arm back and swung hard. The leather gloves and thick insulation in his winter weather gear kept the glass from cutting into his flesh. But it did nothing to muffle the noise.

Long, glass shards fell to the floor, nearly drowning out the sound of the front and rear doors popping open. Mercer hopped in through the side window, which placed him in the master suite. Flicking on the torch, he scanned the room for signs of life but found none.

"Clear," Bastian said in his ear.

"Clear," Donovan echoed. "I'm heading upstairs."

"Moving to the kitchen," Bastian replied.

The interior of the house didn't look much better than the exterior as Mercer scanned the room. The bed didn't look anything like the one from the video. Neither did the walls or the door. Nothing about this room was familiar. Mercer checked the closet, bathroom, and beneath the bed. Then he made his way to the wood-burning fireplace. From the looks of it, no one had used it in a long time.

"Bedroom's clear." Mercer reached for the light switch but thought better of it. If the neighbor to the left looked outside, he'd notice the light. And Mercer didn't want to risk it.

Leaving the bedroom, he checked the rest of the first floor. He found Bastian in the laundry room. The machines had been removed. The connections hung from the wall like a robot's exposed innards.

"The place is dusty," Mercer said. "And cold. No one's been here in a long time."

Donovan came down the steps. "Upstairs has been cleared out. Looks like maybe it was in the middle of a renovation when somebody pulled the plug."

"He could have left in a hurry," Bastian suggested. "But according to the bistro's employee database, Earl Hilty hasn't missed a single shift this week. Perhaps he found better accommodations and gave up on this place. Not that I blame him."

"Okay, so where is he?" Mercer asked.

"Maybe he's with a bird," Donovan suggested.

"I checked the usual places on social media but didn't find anything on Earl Hilty," Bastian said. "No profiles. No tags. It's like he doesn't exist. Like he intentionally wanted to stay off the grid, except he has a job and bank account."

"What about his recent transactions?" Mercer asked.

"Nothing but cash withdrawals. As far as I can tell, he uses cash to pay for everything. He just has his paycheck deposited there. And before you bother asking, the ransom money isn't hiding in his account either."

Static burst in their ears right before Hans spoke. "I'll see if I can find anything on the restaurant's page or other social networks. Are you returning to base camp?"

"Negative," Mercer said. "We'll finish our search here and move on to the next suspect's location. If you find anything, let us know."

"Roger."

Bastian reached for the light switch, but it didn't turn on. "Electricity's been turned off."

"This could be our guy." Mercer left the laundry

room and went into the kitchen. He found the cabinets and fridge empty. "He could have stopped living in this dilapidated hovel after he received his first ransom demand."

"Could be." Bastian went into the living room, tossing pillows and cushions aside as he checked the couch and chair for any indication Annalise Van der Berg or any of the kidnapper's previous victims had been here. "I didn't know the place was abandoned, Jules. Nothing in Hilty's records indicated he abandoned his home. He's holding down a job, acting normally, at least based on his work schedule and financial activity."

"Do you recall seeing any charges for the diner or petrol station?"

"No."

"Did he use any foreign ATMs?"

"No, he always accesses the same one in town."

"Why would he abandon his house? Where would he go?" Mercer tried to think. "He must have another property or rental. We have to find it."

"That shouldn't be too difficult. He has a shift tomorrow afternoon. When he leaves, we'll follow him," Bastian said.

"If he shows up. He might not bother going to work if he's responsible for kidnapping Annalise. After all, he has a captive to handle." Mercer cursed. "Is it possible he only abandoned this house after grabbing Annalise?"

"Doubtful." Donovan opened the linen closet, finding thick cobwebs. "With the amount of dust and spiders, I'd say it's been at least six months since anyone's been here. Maybe longer."

"Where has he been living all this time?" A sick thought twisted Mercer's insides. "You said you thought the kidnapper was keeping Annalise inside a commercial property."

"Well, a rental or hotel," Bastian said.

"But he's local, so he probably has contacts at the area lodgings. He could be staying elsewhere without registering or paying for the room. And even if he does pay, he probably uses cash." Mercer returned to the bedroom, searching for clues. After giving the bathroom a good tossing, he pulled apart the bed, leaving the coverings in a heap on the floor.

"Find any girly magazines?" Donovan asked from the doorway.

"Nothing."

"Damn."

The two men were sifting through the ashes in the fireplace for clues or burnt receipts when Bastian joined them. "I checked for radio frequencies and networks, but there's nothing here. I didn't even find a modem connection or router." He pulled out his own phone and held it up. "I'm not getting a signal. The calls didn't originate here."

"Nothing originated here. We need to find Earl Hilty." The last thing Mercer wanted to do was wait until tomorrow afternoon. But without solid intel, there was nothing else the team could do.

"Are we giving up on the alternative, then?" Bastian gestured around the room. "This could be construed as breaking and entering. Maybe we should limit our criminal activities until we know more."

"We've done far worse in less time," Donovan said.

"That's not the point." Bas waited for Mercer to look up. The commander was stubborn and rarely listened. His skull was too thick for anything to penetrate, so making eye contact often helped drive a point home. "Jules, the more attention we attract, the faster the kidnapper will go to ground. This is a small town. We already know word spreads like wildfire.

Are you sure you want to risk exploring a less obvious possibility?"

"We'll be careful." Mercer stood. He couldn't see the soot on his black gloves, but he wiped his hands on his trousers anyway. "I don't believe anyone will report this break-in. And we'll be careful at Earl Taylor's flat. We've found our way in and out of tighter spots before."

Donovan put the poker back on the stand and clicked off his torch. "I doubt Hilty or anyone else has stopped by this place in a long time. I don't see why that would suddenly change. Our presence here won't be noticed, Bas. This doesn't pose a risk to our operation."

"For the record, I don't like it. What if we're wrong?" Bastian asked.

"What if we're not?" Mercer didn't wait for an answer. He left the bedroom and headed for the front door. It was nearly two a.m. They only had a few more hours until the townsfolk headed back to work. And since the second location was considered prime real estate in the idyllic town, the chances of getting caught would grow exponentially the closer they got to morning.

NINETEEN

"Is this everything you have on the layout?" Mercer studied a digital copy of the blueprints on Bastian's tablet.

"That's it." Bastian tapped impatiently on the dash. "It's rather straightforward, which is what poses a problem."

The two-story rowhouse was wedged right in the middle of the busiest residential street. This was prime real estate, and much newer and nicer than the forested area they just left.

"I see two entry points. The front and back doors, and they're in a near straight line. If you and Donovan stay on the doors, no one can slip out."

"But we have to be quiet." Bastian pointed to the display. "The walls are thin. Neighbors on either side could report a disturbance."

Mercer tapped the radio. "Donovan, anything?"

"No silver sedans. I haven't found any vehicles matching the descriptions or license plate numbers you gave us from the diner. The neighbor two doors to the east has a doghouse in the backyard. No idea if any of these chaps have cats since they don't have houses."

"Cats have houses," Hans said. "They have the run of the main house. They get on the kitchen counter, put their arses in your food or face, and leave their bits everywhere."

"Didn't your mum used to have a cat?" Donovan asked.

"Enough," Mercer growled. "We have a mission. Stay focused."

"Aye," Donovan said.

"Fine, Jules." Hans sighed.

Mercer checked the time. They had to move. "Security system?"

"It's run-of-the-mill. I've pulled the manufacturer's master override code. It should deactivate it without an issue, unless it's been tampered with." Bastian shrunk the blueprint and brought up the security features.

"And this bloke's profile?" Mercer asked. "You said Earl Hilty checked all our boxes. What about this Earl?"

"Earl Taylor, twenty-seven, ski instructor." Bastian shrugged. "Only a third of the victims actually bothered with ski lessons. As you know, Zoe and Annalise never planned to ski or invest in lessons, so they never crossed paths with Earl Taylor."

"Not that Zoe remembers, but that doesn't mean he didn't take notice of them. He could have seen them walking around town. This is the main strip, after all."

"True, but Taylor's active on social media. He has bloody followers, thousands of them." Despite the dark mask concealing most of his features, Mercer knew Bastian's expressions and mannerisms well enough to know exactly what the analyst thought of that. "This guy is already a quasi-celebrity of sorts. People see him. Know him. He's recognizable. Think a small town version of a star footballer. He'd come under even more scrutiny than the oddball living in the woods," Bastian said.

"You don't think it's him."

"No." Bastian blew out a breath. "But we have to be absolutely certain."

"People said Ted Bundy was charming."

"Bad comparison, Jules. At least I hope it is. But I see your point."

"Some of these Yanks like to give their heroes the benefit of the doubt. They'd probably say he volunteers at an animal rescue or was the little girl's uncle or something. They'd find an excuse just because they idolize him." A thought crossed Mercer's mind, and he tapped the radio again. "Hans, check the cat café receipts and see if Taylor's a customer."

"All right. Give me a minute." Hans rifled through the receipts. "I don't know. I don't see his name."

"Can't imagine why," Bastian muttered.

"Donovan, what do you see on thermals?" Mercer asked.

"Two heat signatures on the upper floor. Looks like they're asleep."

"Same bed?" Mercer exchanged a look with Bastian.

"More than likely," Donovan said.

Bastian put a hand on Mercer's arm to stop him from rushing into the night, down the street, and bursting through the back door. "Hans, check Earl Taylor's recent online activity. Any hits on where he was tonight or if he had plans for company?"

Mercer waited. With each passing second, the tension grew.

"I don't see anything, mate. Sorry," Hans said.

Mercer took the binoculars and scanned the area. They had parked at the far end of the street, away from the traffic lights and a smattering of security cameras. Getting inside undetected shouldn't be too hard, if the override worked. But remaining undetected would be damn near impossible given the layout.

"I'll go in alone," Mercer said. "Bas, you keep watch on the front. If anyone comes out, stop them. Run them down with the bloody car if you have to. Donovan, you'll stand guard at the back. Get us eyes inside to make sure the coast is clear. I'm on my way."

"For the record, I think this is a mistake," Bastian said. "Think about what Bev said. Does some hotshot ski instructor sound like the type of guy who creeps around diners two exits from here in shabby woolies?"

Mercer didn't care. He had to do something. He couldn't go back empty-handed until he exhausted their only lead. "Should anything happen, focus your attention on Earl Hilty and that house in the woods. Unless we can definitively rule him out, we should focus on locating him and keeping him under surveillance."

"Okay, Jules." Bastian knew Mercer feared he might get caught or arrested for this venture, but that couldn't delay their mission. Nothing could. Annalise was running out of time.

Stepping out of the car, Mercer clung to the shadows, moving swiftly and silently to the back of the rowhouses. On this cloudy night, even the moon didn't provide any illumination. Julian Mercer was invisible. With the utmost stealth, he crept up to the fence of the proper unit and entered the unlatched gate.

Moving on instinct, Mercer crouched beside Donovan, who appeared to be nothing more than a shadow himself. Mercer examined the screen attached to the fiber optic cable. The kitchen was clear.

"Monitor thermals. Radio if you see any movement inside," Mercer instructed. "If things go tits up, evacuate and rendezvous at base camp."

"Right-o." Donovan retracted the cable and tinkered with the setting on his attached goggles. "Thermals are a go. They are in the front bedroom upstairs. Neither has moved since the last time I checked. I'd say they're sound asleep."

"Okay." Mercer worked the picks into the lock. Unlike the front, the rear door didn't have an extra bolt, just a screen door on the inside. After unlocking the outer door, Mercer was surprised to find the inner door didn't have any sort of lock. "Odd." Quickly, he opened the door. The alarm on the wall let out a single beep, warning it had been activated. Mercer typed in the code and waited. When no alarms sounded, he let out a breath. So far, so good.

Don't be hasty, Mercer's internal voice warned. As silently as possible, he started in the kitchen. If Earl Taylor kidnapped Annalise, her insulin should be in the refrigerator. So he opened the door and peered inside. The bottom shelf contained only fruit. The hairs at the back of Mercer's neck prickled. The kidnapper insisted Zoe pack fruit for her daughter.

Crouching down, Mercer examined the other shelves. He found lots of fresh vegetables, peeled, cut, and placed in individual glass jars, which took up the entire second shelf. The top had an assortment of milks, none of which came from a cow, a foam takeout container with half a steak, and an opened bottle of wine.

Instead of shutting the fridge door, Mercer opened the freezer. He found cuts of meat, fish, frozen vegetables, and one family-sized frozen dinner. He closed both doors simultaneously and remained still, listening.

Once he was convinced the people sleeping upstairs hadn't heard the disturbance, Mercer turned on the kitchen light. He didn't find either cooler bag from the day's earlier drop-offs. Opening the garbage can, he poked around inside. Nothing.

"Jules," Donovan whispered through the radio, "is that you in the kitchen?"

"Uh-huh." Mercer barely spoke.

Donovan had been monitoring the situation, but turning on the lights in the middle of a blackout mission wasn't exactly protocol. Then again, this was K&R. Most protocols got tossed out the window once negotiations broke down.

Finding nothing conclusive in the kitchen, Mercer ventured into the living room. He opened doors as he went, but he didn't find Annalise. Holding a torch in one hand, Mercer searched the coat closet. But everything hanging was top of the line outerwear. It's what one would expect to find in a ski instructor's flat. He closed the door, disappointed not to find the shabby wool coat. More than anything, he hoped the night's outing would lead to Annalise. But he didn't want to find the little girl in some sicko's bed either.

Bugger, Mercer thought when the first step creaked beneath his boot. He held his breath, but he didn't hear movement above. Carefully, he continued up the steps. When he made it to the top, he scouted the second bedroom first.

Only the torch in his hand provided illumination. He caught sight of a furry lump on top of the futon, which rested against the far wall. A desk stood against the other wall with fancy computer equipment. A treadmill took up the entire middle of the room. Maneuvering around the exercise machine, Mercer went to the futon and picked up the stuffed animal. It was a child's plush toy. He turned it in his hand, examining it better beneath the torch's beam. It was a friendly tiger with a big smile on its face and a bubblegum pink nose.

Again, an unsettling feeling came over him. He put the tiger back where he found it and went to the desk. He had just opened the top drawer when Donovan interrupted his thoughts.

"Jules, we have movement. One of the figures just got out of bed. He's coming your way. You're trapped."

Mercer killed the torch and pressed against the wall. He inched closer to the door, hoping to subdue the man before the situation escalated out of control.

"Five meters," Donovan said. A moment later. "Two."

Mercer held his breath and waited. A broad figure passed through the doorway. *Male*, Mercer surmised. The man felt around for the light switch on the opposite wall. Just as the overhead came on, Mercer spun around the doorframe and into the hallway. He kept moving. He didn't turn to see if his exit had been noticed. He had to find out who else was in the bedroom.

"You're clear for now," Donovan said, monitoring Mercer through the thermal imaging, "but hurry it up, mate."

Ducking into the master bedroom, Mercer peered through the darkness. A dim light filtered into the room from a streetlamp outside the window. From here, Mercer could tell the figure in bed was far too big to be Annalise Van der Berg. Pivoting on his heel, Mercer backtracked to the staircase.

"Shit," a voice said from behind.

Mercer kept moving, his pace quickening. He

stepped over the creaky bottom step and turned the corner, heading back to the kitchen and the rear exit.

"Jules, he's coming down the stairs. He's right behind you."

"Move," Mercer ordered. He burst into a run, racing to the back door and throwing it open without bothering to quietly pull it closed behind him. The screen door snapped into place as Mercer slammed the other door shut. In the pitch black yard behind the rowhouses, Mercer couldn't see Donovan, but he heard his teammate's muffled footfalls a few meters ahead.

By the time he made it to the end of the rowhouses, the patio light outside Earl Taylor's flat turned on. But by then, there was nothing for the unidentified man to see. Mercer and Donovan were gone.

"Should we split up?" Donovan asked.

"No," Mercer said as they remained in the shadows, heading for their getaway vehicle. "We stay put. Leaving now will only call attention to ourselves."

"But he knows someone was inside."

"That doesn't matter now." Mercer opened the car door and slid into the seat. Donovan got in behind Bastian. "We have to wait. We'll see if he calls the police and what kind of attention this attracts. Once we know the coast is clear, we can pull away."

Bastian and Hans had heard the situation unfold over comms. Hans would monitor police chatter. They'd find out soon enough if the break-in was reported.

"Did you find anything inside?" Bastian rolled his mask up high enough so he could chew on a licorice twist. "Any sign of Annalise or proof this is the proper Earl?"

"He had a child's toy in the spare bedroom. A tiger." Mercer squinted through the dark. By now,

Earl Taylor, or whoever else was sleeping inside the flat, had turned on the interior lights and the porch lights. "I didn't get to complete my search."

"Do you think he heard you?" Bastian asked. "Is that what woke him?"

"No," Mercer pointed to the time, "he got up to exercise. He also has an affinity for fruit, just like our kidnapper. We need to keep an eye on him." Mercer reached for the tablet. "Let me see his license photo again."

Bastian tapped on the screen a few times. "Here."

Earl Taylor had Nordic features and hazel eyes. No wonder he had a following. This blond-haired man with broad shoulders, defined biceps, and a chiseled jaw had movie star good looks. However, the trimmed beard and scruff on his face was enough to explain why the kidnapper on the video chat might have wanted to scratch at his upper lip.

"You think it's him," Donovan said, more as a statement than a question.

"I don't know," Mercer admitted.

"He doesn't have a tattoo," Bastian said. "At least not in any of his shirtless photos." He reached for another licorice twist. "Take a look."

While Mercer flipped through the hundreds of photos this man posted of himself, wondering how anyone that vain could have the time to orchestrate so many kidnappings, a police car drove past their parked car and continued down the street, double-parking outside Earl Taylor's flat. Without lights or sirens, no one else in the neighborhood would notice. After all, who was even awake at four a.m.?

A single patrol officer exited the vehicle, went up the front steps, and knocked on the door. Earl Taylor opened it with a ski pole in hand. The three former SAS watched the flat, transfixed. Twenty minutes passed before the cop exited.

"Hans?" Mercer asked.

"Cops will keep an eye out, but the responding officer thinks Mr. Taylor was dreaming. The alarm wasn't tripped. Taylor didn't think anything had been disturbed, and nothing was missing. His companion didn't hear anything either."

"Jules, if Taylor's the kidnapper, would he have reported the break-in?" Donovan asked.

"I don't know." None of it made sense. Mercer considered the possibilities. His suspicions weren't baseless, but he had to admit, there were too many discrepancies. "Everyone in this bloody town looks like a suspect."

"Let's wait him out," Bastian suggested. "We'll see when he leaves and maybe catch a glimpse of his mystery guest. We can follow him and take it from there. All right?"

"No." They didn't have the time or resources to waste, especially if Earl Taylor wasn't the kidnapper. After all, Earl Hilty checked all the boxes. He might actually be the better suspect, like Bas had insisted all along. "Bloody hell."

"You need to take a step back. You need to stop," Bastian said. "Donovan, stay here and keep an eye on prime suspect number two. Jules and I will head back to the chalet. We'll leave you this car. We have another rental parked in the lot a few blocks from here. Radio if anything pops off."

"You're sure?" Donovan asked, his focus on Mercer.

The commander nodded. "Bas is probably right about this bloke. He's always bloody right about everything, isn't he?"

Bastian chuckled, grabbing the package of licorice twists. "I'm glad you finally realized it."

TWENTY

Julian Mercer couldn't stand it. He had to figure out who the kidnapper was and, more importantly, where he took Annalise. At the moment, they had two viable candidates, but something about the situation irked Mercer. The more he learned about the two Earls, the more frustrated he became. As far as he was concerned, everyone in this bloody town was to blame. They allowed this bastard to function within their society, to prey on the weak, to exploit others for personal gain or as sport to hunt and kill. This killer or kidnapper, whichever term he preferred, thought of himself as clever, but he was nothing more than a rabid animal. And Mercer was determined to put him down.

After tacking Hilty's current work schedule to the wall, Mercer clicked through the restaurant's payroll files, courtesy of Bastian's hacking. Hilty worked as a busboy and dishwasher. He had no formal education or technical training. He could observe the affluent from a safe distance without any of them noticing him. Hilty's job fit perfectly with what little they had deduced about the kidnapper's mental state.

"What do you think?" Bastian asked, opening one eye.

"He looks good, but only two of the kidnappings took place during a prolonged absence from work. How did he pull off the others?"

"Not sure." Bastian rolled onto his side to face Mercer, glad their office was actually a bedroom. "He might have had someone cover for him. Until we visit the restaurant and see how things work, we can only speculate. We ought to speak to management while we're there."

"Need I remind you, if Hilty is the kidnapper, questioning his boss could trigger a violent reaction? We don't want this bastard to turn vindictive and take our investigation out on Annalise. Frankly, I'm certain our presence is the entire reason he abducted her yesterday afternoon."

"Again with that?"

But Mercer knew it was true, even if he had no solid proof. He marked the corresponding dates of Hilty's work absences with the names of the kidnapper's victims. Still, that only explained two of the abductions. What about the rest? "According to this, Hilty worked the lunch shift yesterday and helped prep for the dinner rush. If he took Annalise, he would have had to grab her while on break, contact us, and return to work."

"It's feasible." Bastian closed his eyes. "Is the sun up yet?"

"Almost."

"And Donovan?"

"No word yet. Taylor must not have left his house." Mercer thought for a moment. "Do you think they're working together?"

"Who?"

"Taylor and Hilty."

"Jules, come on." Bastian let out a dramatic sigh. "That's paranoid, even for you."

"No, hear me out. The kidnapper offered me a partnership, and I'm the fucking opposition. Why wouldn't he have offered someone else, a friend, a colleague, someone with access and skills, an opportunity to make a fortune by assisting him?"

Bastian reluctantly sat up. "You might be on to something. Though, I'm still not sure Taylor has anything to do with this. He's this town's golden boy. A star ski instructor or ski instructor to the stars. Either way, he wouldn't want to get mixed up with a kidnapper."

"Then why did he have a child's toy in his spare room and a fridge full of fruit?"

Bastian blinked. "Do you hear yourself?"

Mercer pushed away from the desk. "It hasn't even been twenty-four hours yet. The first day is crucial. And we have nothing. We've done nothing. We aren't even sure what this bastard's name is. All I have is the word of an overworked waitress. She could be in cahoots with the kidnapper."

"Cahoots." Bastian laughed. At this point, sleep deprivation made a lot of things funny, even when nothing about this situation was amusing. "All right." He went to the duffel and grabbed his gear. "I'm heading to the petrol station to get a copy of their footage. If I leave now, I should get there at the beginning of the breakfast rush. That'll make it easier to blend in. Plus, with everyone's cell phones, I can mask my presence with all the other network activity. I'll be back soon."

"Careful, Bas."

With Bastian gone, Mercer shifted his focus to

Taylor. Aside from the man's first name, the rest of the so-called evidence against him might have been circumstantial. This wasn't how Mercer and his team worked kidnappings. They were far too professional to conduct witch hunts, but that's exactly what the night's outings were, bloody witch hunts.

No matter how Mercer twisted the facts, his behavior came down to two things—the kidnapper's glib indifference and Mercer's own guilt. If they hadn't come here looking for this wanker, Annalise Van der Berg wouldn't have been kidnapped. She'd be asleep in the upstairs bedroom, dreaming of building snowmen and sipping hot cocoa by the fire. This was his fault. And he didn't know how to fix it.

Hans appeared in the doorway. "Jules?"

"Hmm?" Mercer looked up from the screen.

"Since I'm up, you should sleep now. I'll monitor radio communications and wake you if Bas or Donovan encounter any issues or if this bastard calls back."

The last thing Mercer wanted was to sleep, but he had to be sharp. He had to be on his game. He'd been in enough scrapes and warzones to know it was key to get sleep whenever possible. Right now, they were in a lull. No amount of online research would get them answers. They had to wait. Unfortunately, Mercer had never been particularly patient. "Thanks."

"Sure, mate. No worries."

Mercer had just settled onto the bed and closed his eyes when someone said his name.

"Julian?" It was Michelle's voice.

"What?"

"You have to get up, darling."

"Not yet." He reached for her. "Just a few more minutes."

She laughed, that familiar sound that made him

smile. "You always say that."

"I want to stay here. I don't want to leave you. Not again, my love. Not again."

"But you can't stay. You have a job to do."

Those words forced his eyes open. But his lids felt weighed down, and he couldn't quite see clearly. A small part of his mind understood why, but he ignored it. Dreams were far better than reality. "It's my fault. All of this is my fault."

"You know that isn't true."

"No, it is." He rolled over, wrapping his arms around her. She let out a delighted squeal, and he breathed in the smell of her shampoo before kissing her.

"Enough of that," she said, her tone teasing. "You know there isn't time for these shenanigans. You have a mission to complete."

"You never used to say such things."

"That was before." Her expression changed, and though she ran her fingers along his jaw, he could barely feel them. "Julian, this isn't your fault."

"It doesn't matter. That makes no difference. I have to stop him. I have to save her." Sadness pulled at his heartstrings. "I should have saved you. That was my fault. Just like this. Just like now." He held her tighter, unwilling to let go. "I'm sorry, Michelle."

"Julian, get up. Go. Save her." She pushed against his chest. "You have to save her."

"I know."

She tugged the covers off of him. "Jules, you have to get up." Michelle's voice faded, blending with Bastian's. "Jules," the bed shook, "he's on the phone."

Mercer gasped, his eyes popping open. The pain in his chest was almost more than he could bear. He took a few deep breaths, hoping to steady himself. The computer faced the other wall, so the bastard couldn't see him. And Bastian had muted the microphone, so the kidnapper couldn't hear their exchange either.

The dreams tortured him, but he'd take every single moment because it gave him that much more time with his wife. He rubbed the grit from his eyes, his hands shaking.

"I spoke to him," Bastian said, knowing Mercer would pull it together long enough to deal with the current situation. "He said the girl's fine, but he won't provide proof of life. He says he'll only speak to you."

"Fine." Mercer stood, his breathing measured. "Did Donovan come back yet?"

"Yes. Nothing conclusive. I'll brief you after."

"Very well." Mercer stepped into view and unmuted the microphone. "Sir, how is Annalise today?"

The kidnapper grinned and pointed at the screen. "See, you learned something. I'm glad you've been paying attention. We're good for each other. Admit it."

"Fine."

"Oh, come on, where's that spunk? This isn't any fun if you don't play along." The kidnapper cocked his head to the side. "Are you feeling okay, buddy? You look like the dog crap I scraped off my shoe this morning. Maybe you need a spot of tea?"

"How's the girl? Did she eat and check her blood sugar?"

The kidnapper sighed dramatically. "Yes, she ate. I'm not a monster." He held the blood sugar monitor up to the screen. "See, she's fine. Just scared. She wants to go home. She misses her momma. When are you going to let her go home?"

"That's not up to me. That's up to you."

Bastian caught Mercer's eye from the other side of the screen and nodded. At this point, it was best to make sure the kidnapper felt he had control. From what they knew, he enjoyed having power over others, and as long as Annalise remained alive, he had influence over Mercer. Once she was eliminated, that power would disappear. It might just buy her more time. And time is what they needed.

"True, but part of it is up to you. When are you getting my money?" the kidnapper asked.

Mercer glanced at Bastian who scribbled down a time and held up the notepad. The money transfer wouldn't happen until late tonight. The cash probably wouldn't be delivered until the next morning, but the Van der Bergs had spoken to several banking officials and Charles' accountant and hoped to get everything moved before end of business today. However, Mercer knew not to overpromise and under deliver. That was a surefire way to lose the hostage. "Tomorrow morning. First thing."

"That's acceptable, I suppose, but I've changed my mind on a few of the conditions. And honestly, I'm not sure I should trust you. You have too many cooks in your kitchen."

"You mean Bastian? He works for me. You can trust him. He won't deceive you."

The kidnapper rubbed the top of his ski mask, making the eyeholes shift from side to side. "I dunno."

"You have no reason not to trust me. I haven't lied to you. I've met your demands so far."

"An apple and banana don't mean shit, man, not when I'm dealing in dollars and cents."

"So let's talk dollars and cents."

"Ah, music to my ears." The kidnapper made a show of looking at the far corners of the screen. "Are you alone, Julian? Or is Benjamin still in the room?"

"Bastian," Mercer corrected automatically, though he wasn't sure why he wasted his breath. "He won't interfere."

"Did you tell him about my offer?" The kidnapper

didn't wait for a response. "You did, didn't you? I figured as much. I bet the two of you don't have any secrets. You share everything. What about bodily fluids? You share those too?"

Mercer's patience was waning. "What are your new demands?"

"You're no fun. I'll have to remember what a grumpy puss you are in the mornings. Are you better after a cup of joe? Or tea? Whatever the hell it is you drink. What do you drink?"

"Tea. Now your demands."

"Yeah, yeah. I was getting to that." The kidnapper waved his hand at the screen. His barely rolled up sleeve inching higher, but Mercer still couldn't make out the tattoo on the guy's forearm. If only he'd push up his sleeves, Bastian could ID him from the ink. "Negotiators talk a lot about good faith, or at least they do in movies. You brought it up yesterday when you asked for proof of life."

"Uh-huh."

"Well, I want you to do something for me as a show of good faith." The kidnapper smiled. "I want a portion of the money delivered by four p.m. today."

"How much?" Mercer asked. "A large portion of the family's funds are not liquid."

"I only want ten Gs."

"Ten thousand?"

"Yeah."

"American?"

The kidnapper snorted. "This is America, buddy. I'd like to be able to spend the money once I get it. None of that pounds sterling shit. I want good ol' American dollars and cents."

"Yeah, okay. That can be arranged. May I use the number you gave me to contact you once the funds have been collected?"

"Okay." This was the first time the kidnapper agreed so easily, and Mercer sensed this was a trick. "Get my coins together and we'll arrange a meet, so you can give me the money."

"Not a problem, but I'll have to verify Annalise is okay before I give you the payment."

"Sure." The kidnapper smiled. "There's just one other thing."

"What's that?"

"I want the ten thousand dollars in quarters."

TWENTY-ONE

"You can't be serious. Where am I going to get ten thousand dollars in quarters?" Mercer asked.

"The same place you get all your money," the kidnapper said. "I'd probably start with the bank. I have it on good authority the vault holds twenty boxes, and each box has fifty rolls. You do the math. It equals out. Easy peasy."

But Mercer knew that depended on the bank's delivery schedule and how willing the bank manager was to hand over their entire stock of quarters. More than likely, he wouldn't find a bank that had that many coins on hand or willing to fulfill his request. He opened another tab and entered a search. This town must have more than one bank. But he only found one within the town limits. To reach a larger town with more financial institutions would require a three hour drive. After all, they were in the middle of nowhere.

"Y'know, maybe twenty-five grand would be better. It's a quarter of a hundred thousand, and since I want quarters that would be rather apropos, don'tcha think?"

Mercer returned his focus to the kidnapper. He'd never get twenty-five grand in quarters. "Be practical. Ten thousand dollars in quarters is roughly 230 kilograms."

"227," Bastian whispered, having performed the calculation on a scrap of paper. "Well, 226.7 something."

"227," Mercer repeated.

"What the hell does that mean?" the kidnapper asked.

"It means it's bloody heavy. Think this through. Coins aren't practical. You won't be able to carry them. They'll slow you down."

"I didn't realize I was in a rush." The kidnapper snickered. "Are you trying to get rid of me? I thought we were chums. Aren't you having fun? I'm having fun. I'm not sure I want this to end."

"Coins are heavy. Too heavy for you to carry. You'll have to make arrangements to cart off the ransom."

"You can carry it. I mean you look like you could. I don't know what 227 kilograms translates too, but that doesn't sound like much. What is it? A hundred pounds? One-fifty?"

"Try five hundred."

The kidnapper attempted to whistle but failed because he was laughing so hard. "Guess you'll be getting a workout today, huh? Like I said, you have until four p.m. And Julian, if you can't act in good faith, neither can I." He slid his pointer finger in a line across his throat. "You know what that means for Annalise, don't you?"

"Don't do anything rash. You'll get your money in quarters."

"I better. Oh, and I want it delivered by four, so let's say you have it ready to go by three, just in case.

I'll expect your call precisely at three, not a minute later. After all, you said it might be difficult to transport, and I'd hate to have it slow me down to the point where I don't get home in time to feed poor Annalise or make sure her blood sugar stays within a safe level."

Before Mercer could voice a threat, the screen went blank. He rubbed a hand down his face and turned away from the computer. "He's absolutely psychotic." Spinning back around, Mercer continued his bank search. "I'm only finding one financial institution in this shitty town."

"There's the main branch of Mutual One and another branch, but it's not a full-service location." Bastian clicked the mouse several times. "I'm seeing a few ATMs. And the resort cashes checks. They have a vault on hand. They must receive deliveries. It could be promising."

"You think the resort bothers with quarters?"

"They must bring in some. Money drops are often dollars and cents. I'll speak to the Van der Bergs and call the agency. One of us should be able to convince Mutual One to hand over whatever they have. And we'll just scrape together the rest. I'll handle this while you get everything in order." Bastian eyed his friend. "It's okay. You can take a minute."

Mercer nodded. His team knew he hadn't recovered from the devastating personal loss, even though it had been years since his wife was killed. But it still felt fresh, particularly upon waking from a dream or nightmare. He needed a few minutes to collect himself and compartmentalize. If he didn't take the time now, he was liable to snap. And with the kidnapper's demented nature and irritating behavior, Mercer would lash out and botch the negotiation. They couldn't afford that, not when they were close to identifying the arsehole.

After a quick shower, Mercer dressed and went into the kitchen. Zoe sat at the table, relentlessly stirring the cream in her coffee. From the dark circles beneath her eyes and her dazed expression, Mercer doubted she slept which made him feel guilty for the four or five hours he managed. Charles leaned against the counter. While he looked rested, the sour expression on his face indicated a fight was brewing. Donovan sat at the head of the table, cleaning the equipment and keeping an eye on the estranged couple, like a corrections officer expecting violence to break out.

"Where's Bas and Hans?" Mercer asked.

"At the bank and performing recon," Donovan said.

"Did Bastian update you on your daughter's situation?" Mercer glanced from Zoe to Charles.

She nodded, but Charles' scowl deepened.

"I did some research last night. According to what I read, the first twenty-four hours are crucial in these types of cases. If a person isn't recovered within a day, then it's not likely she will be," Charles said.

"That's for missing persons, not kidnapping victims," Donovan stated. "Matters are different here. The timeline is different. Nothing is set in stone. It changes as the negotiation progresses."

"But you don't know where she is," Charles argued. "So my little girl is missing. The longer he has her, the farther away they can get."

"They aren't traveling," Mercer said, but that had been an aspect of the kidnapper's MO when it came to his other victims. "We've pinged their location. He's in the area. We haven't been able to narrow it down to an exact address yet, but we know he's within an hour's drive of here. And they haven't moved since."

"But he wants more money," Charles said. "What's to keep him for asking for even more once he gets his original asking price?"

"Charles," Zoe snapped, "she's our baby. Money is no object."

"That's not what I meant, dear." He put a bitter emphasis on the word.

Mercer held up his hand. "I know what you meant, Mr. Van der Berg. We'll take every precaution, establish numerous safeguards and contingencies that will guarantee he doesn't get a dime unless we get Annalise."

"Oh, really? Then what the hell are you hoping to safeguard by giving him ten thousand dollars? That's just a fraction of the ransom. What's he going to do? Give us a piece of Annalise in exchange for the money? I've read about shit like that happening."

Zoe went ashen. Her already sickly pallor went stark white. "You don't think he'd really do that, do you?"

Mercer swallowed. This bastard was capable of anything. "I won't let that happen."

"So what are you going to do?" Charles crossed his arms over his chest and stared over the rim of his glasses at Mercer.

Mercer filled the kettle with water and placed it on the stove. "For starters, I don't let arseholes with god complexes push me around." He took a mug from the cupboard and placed it on the counter. "Second, the kidnapper wants a portion of the money as a show of good faith on our part. It's payback for accepting the food last night and taking care of your daughter's medical needs. However," Mercer turned away from the kettle, finding Zoe's teary eyes staring at him, "I intend to use this to our advantage. Annalise only has enough food and medicine for breakfast. He wants a four p.m. delivery. I trust she'll be able to hold out until then."

Zoe nodded, dabbing at her eyes. Mercer hated when women cried. It was his kryptonite. "That should be okay."

"Will it? Annalise is normally on a better schedule. Her meals come more regularly. This isn't good," Charles said.

"It's not ideal, but it is manageable," Zoe said.

The kettle shrieked, and Mercer turned off the flame and poured the hot water into his cup. "This is the best way to ensure she gets another meal and enough medication to keep her stable until the full ransom arrives."

"So your plan is to let him fuck with us until payday? That's ridiculous," Charles fumed.

"Charles," Zoe snapped, but her warning didn't hold its usual zing. She might have objected to her ex-husband's annoyance and language, but even she thought he had a point.

He marched over to Mercer and stabbed his pointer finger repeatedly into Mercer's chest. "You better come up with something better. I want my daughter back. I'll pay if that's what it takes, but according to FBI statistics, paying a ransom doesn't guarantee anything. If you find a way to get her out before then, you better do it."

"You need to stay off the internet, mate." Donovan popped open a case and placed the freshly cleaned accessories inside. "Nothing good will come from reading that shit. You'll just drive yourself batty."

Charles turned to glare at Donovan. "What else am I supposed to do?"

"Stop poking me unless you want your fingers broken. Now sit your arse down and let us work." Mercer picked up his tea and blew on the rising steam. The silence spoke volumes. Eventually, the upset father backed down.

Charles took a seat closer to his wife. "We should cook something special for her. Something she likes. Something to let her know we're thinking about her and trying to get her home."

Zoe nodded. "Yeah, you're right."

While Annalise's parents focused on the one thing they could do for their daughter, Mercer and Donovan excused themselves and went into the makeshift office. "What happened with Taylor?" Mercer asked.

"He left his house at 6:45 this morning. He had a bird with him. I found her profile on his social media page. She's twenty-four and works at the resort's pro shop. They grabbed breakfast at the café on the promenade before splitting up. I followed him, but since there's no snow on the mountain yet, he went to the gym and taught skiing techniques to some kids. I checked his schedule, but he's booked for the day with group classes and private lessons."

"How can he teach someone how to ski without snow?"

"He's more of a personal trainer. Plus, the gym has machinery to simulate the skiing experience." Donovan pulled a brochure out of his back pocket. "In case you're interested."

Mercer flipped through the booklet. It looked like nothing more than an extensive advert to buy time with the local celebrity athlete. "Did you place a tracker on his car?"

"Of course, but he's at work."

"Just because his vehicle hasn't moved, that doesn't mean he hasn't."

"I don't know, commander. He's fully booked. If he skips out, someone's bound to notice. But I'll inquire further." Donovan gave Mercer an uncertain look. "Do you want me to head back to his flat and finish what you started last night?"

"No, it's too risky. In broad daylight, you will be noticed. Someone will tell him, and after last night, we know Annalise isn't being held there. We'll table that idea until nightfall."

"Right-o."

Mercer opened Bastian's laptop, entered the password, and searched for last night's surveillance footage from outside the diner. In the dark, the petrol station's security camera barely glimpsed the kidnapper, and just like on the promenade, the bastard never turned around. "Dammit."

"I know. It doesn't give us much. This plonker knows what he's doing. He has everything scouted. Memorized. He plans better than we do."

"Or just the same. He said something odd to me this morning." Mercer squinted, hoping to recall the exact words, but he couldn't. "He said something about how we conduct negotiations. He mentioned the tactics we use. Good faith and proof of life. He's familiar."

"Do you think he's one of us?"

"He's too unstable and far too irreverent. He wouldn't risk tipping his hand. But he studied up. He probably had to since he's done this so many times." He clicked a few keys, bringing up the profile on Earl Hilty. He checked the man's financials, found his phone bill, and got the number. "Why isn't Bas monitoring Hilty's calls? Or pinging his location?"

"Because I'm not an octopus and don't have a dozen techs at my disposal," Bastian said, entering the chalet. "Plus, his phone's turned off. But I have it set to automatically check. Once he turns it back on, we'll know where he is."

Mercer eyed the bag thrown over the analyst's shoulder. "How much did you get?"

"Thirty-five hundred."

"It's not enough."

"I know that, but it's all the bank had. They get deliveries twice a week. The next one is scheduled for tomorrow. This is all they had left in the vault, with the exception of maybe a hundred dollars." Bastian dropped the heavy bag onto the chair. "I checked with the resort staff. They don't get much in terms of coins. The manager offered to check the vending machines."

"That's brilliant," Donovan said.

"Well, it would be, except someone came to refill the machines last night and emptied out the tills." Bastian bit his lip. "It could be a coincidence."

"This bastard knows everything that goes on inside this town. He knew about the bank's delivery schedule and the vending machines. He did this on purpose. He knew we wouldn't get the money. He wants to screw with us." Mercer pondered the kidnapper's logic. Only terrible thoughts came to mind. "Did you get anything from the machines?"

"Six dollars and fifty cents." Bastian slid into the seat beside Mercer and yanked the computer away. "The concierge suggested we check with the arcade. Apparently, it's a popular hangout." Bastian minimized Mercer's research and conducted his own search. "They open at 10:30."

"That's in a few minutes," Donovan said. "I'll leave now."

"Call us and let us know how much you can get," Mercer said.

"Jules," Bastian said, "should we set out for the next nearest bank?"

Mercer checked the time. They didn't have six hours to wait. The kidnapper expected Mercer to call and prepare to drop the money off by three. "We don't have time."

"C'mon, with the way you drive, we could make it

there and back with plenty to spare."

"No, Bas. He says I have to call for further instructions at three. I don't know how quickly he'll expect delivery. But I can't miss the call. The only reason he changed the time was to make sure we couldn't get the funds from an outside source. He wants us to fail, or he's planning something else. I just don't know what."

"I could set up something remote," Bastian said. "You could call from another location, and I can make it look like it's coming from here. With six hours, I have the time to make it happen."

"And then we're lying to him, and it's still game over." Mercer strode to the window and pushed the drape aside. He stared at the snow-capped mountains and the thick, grey clouds. A storm was brewing. He could feel it. "What have you found on Earl Hilty?"

"Jules, maybe now's not the time to worry with that."

"It bloody well is." He gestured vehemently around the room. "This isn't about ten thousand dollars. The kidnapper wants to keep me busy and distracted so I can't go looking for him."

"You think he knows we're on to him? That we might be getting closer?"

Mercer thought about the two B&Es they pulled last night. Neither resulted in much of anything, but maybe the kidnapper heard about their crimes or picked up the police chatter. Or Taylor was the kidnapper and had glimpsed Mercer escaping the flat, and today's call was about getting payback. Or Mercer was paranoid, like Bastian insisted. However, there was another option. "Either that, or he wants us to fail. He needs an excuse to kill her."

"Do you really believe he needs that kind of justification?"

"No, but he'll blame me for it. He wants to do that. He wants me to know this is my fault."

"How can you be sure? Granted, he likes to push your buttons, but that sounds personal, mate. Like he has an agenda focused on taking you down."

"Doesn't he?" Mercer kicked the door closed. He didn't want the Van der Bergs to overhear him. "We know why he took her. We triggered it. And he offered me a partnership. I can't be sure what that was about, but paying us off proves he's won. That his way of doing business is the best way. The only way. That he can't be stopped, or that no one is willing to stop him."

"And what better way to prove that than by turning the enemy into an ally." Bastian pursed his lips and exhaled. "It's also possible he wants you to take the fall. He could be setting a trap to make you look responsible for the kidnapping, like this is some elaborate ruse to extort money from the Van der Bergs."

"How? We can't be in two places at once."

"No, but he's done his research. He knows this town. He knows everyone in town and their business. He could plant seeds of distrust with the police, the government, the establishments. They'll start eyeing us."

"Did you tell anyone what we're actually doing here?"

"No. When I was at the bank, I told them this is an exercise. A practice run."

"They'll see through it eventually. I assume you used the same excuse with resort management."

Bastian nodded. "It's best to limit our lies."

"Do you think he intends to frame us for all the kidnappings and killings? Or just Annalise's?"

"It doesn't matter. Either way, he'll get away with

it, and by doing this, he'll make sure we're not in a position to stop him." Bastian chewed on his fingernail. "If we're not careful, we're fucked."

They couldn't worry about that now. They had to take this one step at a time. They needed to collect ten thousand dollars in quarters. Hopefully, Donovan would convince the arcade manager to help them. If not, they'd have to get creative.

TWENTY-TWO

"He'll give us what he has but at a price," Donovan said.

"Fine. Get every last one." Mercer handed the phone to Bastian and updated Annalise's parents on the situation.

"What are you going to do?" Zoe asked.

"We'll find another way." Mercer returned to their office. The only way they'd get ten thousand in quarters was if they split up. This wasn't the only ski resort in town. He'd have to check the others. And the hotels too. Tucking the radio into his ear, Mercer updated Hans on the current situation and asked the reconnaissance expert to divert his efforts from hunting this bastard to hunting for quarters.

"Shall I panhandle?" Hans asked.

Though the question was cheeky, Mercer didn't dismiss the possibility. "If we become desperate enough. Right now, Donovan's at the arcade. I'll move east from here and check the other resorts and hotels along the promenade and see if they have a stockpile of coins. I'm hoping they have different vending machine delivery schedules."

Bastian stepped into the office and closed the door. The analyst caught the tail-end of Mercer's side of the conversation. "Who are you talking to?"

Mercer pointed to his ear. "Hans."

Bastian picked up his own earpiece, adjusted the dial, and clipped it on. "I'll reach out to the insurance firm who originally hired us and see if we can get an emergency delivery."

"All right, Jules. I'll start on the east end and move west. We'll meet in the middle. What happens if we can't get the vendors to open the machines for us? Are we allowed to borrow what we need?" Hans asked.

"Just don't get caught. The last thing we need is to get arrested over a few quid. Something tells me the bobbies won't care about our motives." Unzipping one of the bags, Mercer selected a few tools he thought might be necessary. He never realized last night's B&Es were the beginning of their crime spree.

"I'll do what I can from here and radio in whatever updates I receive," Bastian said into the mic, making sure everyone could hear him through comms. "Whatever coins you get, let me know. I'll keep up with the total so we don't lose track." He turned to Mercer. "If we can't get a delivery here in time, I'll research other promising locations to collect the coins and start scouting."

Nodding, Mercer left the chalet. It was barely 11 a.m. The wind had picked up. Thick clouds blanketed the sky. It remained light out but hazy and grey. Mercer tugged on the insulated leather gloves he had stowed in his pockets as he headed away from the resort and stepped onto the wooden boards of the promenade.

The main strip had about as much life to it today as

yesterday. Though he intended to visit the next nearest hotel, which loomed less than a block away, he stopped at the clothing store first. It hadn't even been twenty-four hours since the last time he visited. But the clerk at the counter seemed to have already forgotten him.

The man barely even glanced toward the front door when the bell chimed. A young woman in her early twenties folded sweaters on a display rack in the corner. She smiled at Mercer. "May I help you?"

"Were you here yesterday?"

She shook her head. "Jared, didn't you work yesterday?" The man behind the counter let out an affirmative grunt, his eyes glued to his cell phone screen. "He was here, but can I help you with something?" She lowered her voice. "He's not what you'd call employee of the month material."

"No, I just need to speak to him in private for a moment." Mercer marched to the counter. "Outside. Now."

Jared, the unhelpful clerk, looked up from the counter. For the first time since Mercer entered, Jared noticed who was in front of him. "Hey, man. Did you ever find what you were looking for?"

Mercer snatched the phone from Jared's hand. "If you want this back, follow me." He went outside, remembering how pitiful the store's security system was. Mercer moved to the far end of the main thoroughfare, entirely out of sight of the cameras. Jared followed. "Show me your arms."

"What?" Jared held out his hands, confused, and Mercer yanked the other man's sleeves up. But he didn't find any tattoos. "Hey, stop that."

"Are you working with him? Did you help him?"

"Whoa. What are you talking about?"

"The little girl and her mum from yesterday."

Jared stared, not a single word registered on his face. "What girl?"

"The one I asked you about."

Jared wrapped his arms around his middle. "I don't know." He shivered and held out a hand for his phone. "It's freezing out here. Give me back my phone. Or I'll call the cops."

"How? I have your phone."

Jared stared at Mercer, not comprehending the question. "Dude, come on."

The apathetic attitude reminded Mercer of the kidnapper, and again, he wondered how many people in this town were involved in the kidnappings or aiding the psycho. But this sod was too stupid to be involved, or he did an excellent job of playing dumb. "Fine." Mercer shoved the device into the man's hand. "But I need your quarters and whatever's in the register."

"Whatever, man."

The two went back inside. The young lady gave them an odd look but didn't inquire further, much to Mercer's relief. After exchanging twenty-two dollars for quarters, Mercer left the shop. He didn't get answers, and at this rate, they'd never obtain the ransom in time.

Mercer entered each shop along the way. By the time he reached the first hotel on the strip, he'd only managed to collect a little over a hundred dollars in quarters and was almost out of cash. He stopped at the ATM in the lobby, withdrew the maximum on one of the cards, and spoke to the manager. When that failed to produce worthwhile results, Mercer inquired about the vending machines. But unless the operator was on the premises, the hotel had no way of opening the machines or emptying the tills. So Mercer would have to get creative. However, knocking over the machines after asking about them wasn't smart, so he exited and marched to the next hotel on the strip. But this time, he didn't ask about the vending machines. Instead, he took the elevator to the top floor, made sure to conceal his identity as best he could beneath the hood of his jacket and a pair of wraparound sunglasses, and stepped into the snacking alcove at the end of the hallway.

While he waited for housekeeping to pass, he pulled the lock picks and a few other tools from his jacket. Once the coast was clear, he unlocked the soda machine, opened the door, and removed the metal box. After jimmying it open, he poured the coins into an abandoned ice bucket he found beside the ice machine, repeated the process with the second vending machine, and shoved the lid on top of the ice bucket. He tossed a handful of bills into the metal boxes, closed the vending machine doors, snapped the locks back in place and headed down the hall.

When he happened upon the housekeeping cart on the next floor, he grabbed a towel and a plastic trash bag. Then he repeated the process on this floor and every level of the hotel until he reached the bottom.

He spread the towel out inside the bag, poured the coins on top, and twisted the bag closed. Then he tucked the lump inside his jacket. As he walked, he could hear the clinking of the coins, but the towel muffled most of the sound. As long as he didn't get too close to anyone, no one would notice.

He set out for the next hotel. He'd have to find a better place to stow the coins as the bag grew heavier, but for now, this would have to do.

Conducting business in this manner was slow going, but Mercer didn't know what other choice they had. The kidnapper had left them with few viable options. He did this on purpose. Mercer just didn't know if the kidnapper's goal was to complicate matters, ensure the team failed, or humiliate them in the process. Probably all three. But Mercer was sure of one thing. Everything this bastard did, he did for a reason.

TWENTY-THREE

"How much have we collected so far?" Mercer asked.

Once he caught up to Hans, Mercer took their collected coins back to the chalet while Hans continued to seek out other viable locations where coins would be stockpiled.

"$8745.25." Bastian kept a tally. "There must be other places we haven't checked. More shops, more vending machines."

"What about newspaper stands?" Donovan asked. After returning with the arcade's entire stock of quarters, he tried the bank branch inside the grocery store but had brought back little to show for it. Afterward, he returned to the chalet and had been counting and rolling the quarters in preparation for transport.

"How are you going to break into those without anyone noticing?" Hans asked. "They're practically in the middle of the street. The soda machines were easy enough, but they're always in those little alcoves. With a proper cap and a work shirt, no one pays any attention." And they hadn't while the team conceivably robbed every vending machine in the neighboring hotels and resorts. They'd hit sixteen places and come up with nearly two thousand dollars. Luckily, this resort and the others didn't use the same vending machine supplier. And they hit the jackpot at a few locations.

"Let's try the area shops and markets." Bastian pointed to the map. "I've sectioned off the town into grids. It'll optimize our efforts."

"We only have an hour and a half to collect the remaining funds." Mercer glanced at the computer.

Their plans for today had been shot the moment the kidnapper phoned this morning. Mercer's research on the two Earls had fallen to the wayside, as did Donovan's attempts to follow up at the cat café and search for the tattooed man with easy access to kittens, and Hans' attempts to scour employee records for anyone with absences that corresponded to the previous kidnappings.

"Have you hit the vending machines at the gym where Taylor works?" Mercer asked into the radio.

"No," Hans said.

"I didn't think you wanted us getting that close," Donovan replied.

Mercer looked at the tactician. "Check it out, and make sure the bastard's where he's supposed to be."

"Aye," Donovan said.

Mercer contemplated what other locations besides the arcade might have change machines. The arcade had provided the largest single sum. If they could find another promising location like that, they'd get the rest of the money in time, even if it required a bit extra. Those two thousand dollars in quarters had cost nearly double since the owner had to be reimbursed for the coins at a premium since wiping out his supply would result in lost business. And by now, Mercer was sure the town was growing wary of the K&R team and their odd requests. "What about laundromats?"

"I found two in the area. One on the east side of town, and the other off the main strip," Bastian said. "But with a town this size, I'm guessing they don't get much business. We probably won't get more than a few hundred. Everyone has a bloody washing machine in their flat nowadays."

"But they should have change machines," Mercer said. "That's what we need."

"In that case, we should scout the automated carwashes too," Hans suggested. "I passed three on my way here. With the constant snowfall and salted roads, they must do a good business. And since it hasn't snowed yet, they shouldn't have had to dispense that many quarters yet. The machines should be full."

"Again, assuming everyone isn't paying with plastic," Bastian said.

"I thought you were supposed to be the optimistic one, mate," Hans quipped.

Mercer gave the analyst a look. They'd been sleeping in shifts, but aside from Hans getting a few hours on the couch, no one else had slept except Mercer. And he could tell lack of sleep and stress weighed on Bastian. "You okay, Bas?"

"I'm bloody brilliant." Bastian pulled up the addresses, cursing himself for not thinking of the possibility sooner. "The carwashes have heavy surveillance, so I'll go there and jam the signals before trying anything. The last thing we need is to get caught, especially when we're so close."

"All right. I'll hit the laundromats," Mercer said. "Hans, see what you can get at the few remaining shops and then get back to business. I want Hilty under surveillance, and Donovan, get eyes on Taylor. The kidnapper should be expecting a call soon. I want to know if either of the men disappears to answer it. If either leaves, follow him. We need Annalise's location."

"Aye, commander," the two men said simultaneously.

"Everyone stay in contact. Radio in whatever you get. We need an accurate tally. Worst case, we'll hit the newsstands if all else fails." Mercer hated to leave the Van der Bergs alone in the chalet. But he didn't think the kidnapper would make a move on them, but he might try to make contact while the team was out.

Bastian promised the calls would be rerouted to Mercer's cell, but Mercer worried something might go wrong.

"Bas and I will rendezvous back here in forty minutes, whether we have the ransom money or not. I don't want to cut it any closer than that. If you've picked up significant funds, let us know and we'll meet you to collect. I don't want to risk missing an opportunity to ID the kidnapper and discover his location."

"But if we don't have the ten grand by then, what will you do?" Hans asked.

That was a good question. Hopefully, Mercer wouldn't be forced to lie about the ransom because he feared the consequences, but telling the truth could result in Annalise's termination. "Let's make sure that doesn't happen. Now move out."

TWENTY-FOUR

"That's the last of it," Bastian said, emptying his pockets on the table.

"What does that make?" Mercer reached for another coin wrapper and started sliding stacks of ten quarters into the sleeve. "Do we have ten thousand?"

"We're nine quarters shy."

"Have the Van der Bergs check their pockets. If that doesn't work, stop people on the street and ask for change. We've gotten this close. We can't miss it by nine fucking coins." Mercer wrapped another ten dollars in quarters and stared at the pile of silver discs in front of him. What could anyone want with this many quarters? Thoughts of homemade bombs came to mind, but he didn't think the kidnapper had any desire to blow up the town. His preferred method of killing was far more personal.

"Knock, knock," Zoe said from the doorway. "How's it coming along?"

Mercer looked up, but she didn't enter the room. She understood this was where he worked. "We're almost there. We'll figure it out. We're too close not to."

"I know." She tried to paint a smile on her face, but it didn't look quite convincing. "Charles is checking the car. He has this terrible habit of tossing change into the cupholder and leaving it there indefinitely. Anytime he picks up the dry cleaning or goes through a drive-thru, he dumps his change. Annalise loves it." This time, the smile was real at the fond memory of her daughter. "Charles lets her keep whatever she finds. She always makes out like a bandit." She focused on the stack of coins, the rows of rolled quarters, and the bag Mercer hadn't counted out yet. "Why would anyone want this many quarters?"

"I don't know. But now we have what he wants." Before Mercer could say anything else, the computer alerted him to an incoming call. He checked the time. It was 2:43. The kidnapper was calling ahead of schedule.

"Is that him?" Zoe asked.

Mercer nodded, reaching for the headset. "Go get Bastian."

Zoe ran out of the room, and Mercer executed a few commands to record the conversation and trace the origin of the call. Then he clicked the green accept button and steadied himself in front of the screen. The kidnapper wore the same ski mask and non-descript winter weather gear. The puffer vest was basic black over a thick, knit black sweater.

"You're early," Mercer said. "Is everything okay?"

"Wonderful," the kidnapper replied in a smarmy voice, "thanks for asking. I see you've learned some manners. Do you think I'm on track to turning you into a real boy?"

"Piss off."

"Ah, there's that Julian." He squeezed his eyes shut

and crinkled his nose, or at least Mercer assumed that's what he was doing since the ski mask bunched in the middle, but it didn't expose any other characteristics about the guy. "You know I love you. The only question is how much."

Mercer contained his growl. "Is ten thousand in quarters enough?"

"You got it?" The kidnapper's tone was flat, and Mercer sensed the news came as a disappointment.

"Almost."

"What does that mean? Either you have it, or you don't. This isn't horseshoes, Julian."

Footsteps sounded outside the door, and Bastian came in with a charcoal grey plastic container in his palm. He took a seat on the bed, out of sight of the camera, and dumped the contents onto the spread. "We're over by six."

"I have your money. All forty thousand quarters." Mercer tightened his jaw, making sure he didn't appear smug. Any flinch or mannerism could be off-putting to the kidnapper and botch the negotiation.

"Let me see it," the kidnapper said. "Just pop the camera around and show me."

"Jules," Bastian warned.

"It's fine." Mercer turned the webcam around, focusing it on the piles of coins and not on the walls where they had placed their intel. But Mercer knew that's actually what the kidnapper hoped to see. He wanted a look at their operation, fearing they were getting closer to figuring out his identity or where he stashed Annalise. That's why he distracted them with this wild goose chase. "Happy?" Mercer swiveled the camera back around.

Like a cartoon villain, the kidnapper rubbed his palms together. "They're so sparkly. And you're sure that's forty thousand quarters? Did you count each and every single one of them? I don't want you slipping in any of those Canadian quarters or shit like that. Every single coin in those bags and wrappers better be official U.S. currency. I accept no substitutions."

"They are."

"Okay, because I'm gonna check. And if they aren't, well, you know what that means." The kidnapper ran his finger across his throat again. The threat getting old the second time around. "So you're sure, right? You checked each one personally?"

"Of course."

"Great, now I just need you to deliver them by four p.m. No tracking devices or dye packs or anything sneaky or underhanded. If you pull something like that, we're done. Got it?"

"I understand, but I can't agree to deliver until I see Annalise and verify that she's okay."

"Jeez, man," the kidnapper let out an exasperated huff, "can't any of these calls just be about us? Those are my quarters. And you're going to bring them to me. Why can't it be that simple? If you want to make it complicated, maybe we should call the whole thing off right now." He reached for the screen as if to disconnect.

"Stop." Mercer kept his eyes on the kidnapper. He could sense the tension growing. Bastian returned to his previous perch behind the other computer and gnawed on a drinking straw. "You know the conditions. The money's here. It's ready to go. I just need to know the girl's okay first." Mercer waited a moment, letting the reality of the situation sink in, but the kidnapper didn't seem to care. "It's the only way you get the money."

"All right. I'll tell you what. You bring her dinner and insulin with you and make the drop by four p.m., and maybe, just maybe, I'll let you see her."

"I need a guarantee."

"Here's a guarantee. If you don't do what I say, none of your efforts up until now will make a damn bit of difference. You feel me, Julian?"

"Yes, sir."

"Good." The kidnapper's serious tone faded. "I want you to bring my coins to the outdoor ice skating rink. Make sure you put them in something inconspicuous. I don't want to draw unnecessary attention to ourselves. Just think of the children. We don't want to ruin anyone else's day, now do we?"

Mercer bristled. "No, sir."

"Excellent. Oh, and make sure you come alone. I don't want to see your partner or mate or whatever cutesy labels the two of you have for one another anywhere around there. This is about you and me." He made a heart shape using his thumbs and pointer fingers and held it up to the screen. "If we decide on a ménage, I pick the third. It'd be best if you keep that in mind. I better not see anyone other than you, or the deal's off. And the girl's dead. I figure that goes without saying, but I wanted to say it anyway. It's kinda fun. You want to practice?" The kidnapper grinned. "Say it, Julian. Say *the girl's dead.*"

Mercer saw red, but he forced the anger down. His grip on the edge of the desk tightened to the point his knuckles turned white. But he couldn't react. He could tell that's precisely what the kidnapper wanted, and the threats would eventually escalate to violence if he knew it riled Mercer. So instead, he remained focused on the exchange. "How do you expect me to carry five hundred pounds alone without drawing attention to myself?"

"Again, that sounds more like a you problem than a me problem. But you're smart. I'm sure you'll figure it out. You've probably had all day to think about it. I mean you just had to make a quick trip to the bank. After that, what did you have to do except wait for another opportunity to talk to me? This must be the highlight of your day. I bet you've been catching up on your soaps and napping because you look a hell of a lot better now than you did when we spoke earlier. Did you go to the spa? They have a sugar scrub to die for. Well, I'm sure someone could die from it. Y'know, people with sugar issues." He slapped his palm to his forehead. "I just realized Annalise has sugar issues. Do you think she'd survive a spa treatment?"

"Enough with the theatrics."

The kidnapper glared. "I decide when enough is enough. I'll see you in an hour. Don't keep me waiting." The call disconnected.

"He's got a bee in his bonnet. I don't like it." Bastian pushed away from the screen.

"Neither do I." Mercer released his grip and slammed his fist on the desk. "We need to know who we're dealing with and where he has the girl."

"I can't get a lock on his location. It could be due to the mountains or lack of cell towers. All I can say for certain is he's somewhere in our search grid." Bastian went to the map. The new ping landed within the previous search box he'd marked, but this time, they were able to narrow the search parameters. "He's somewhere in here." Bastian drew a second circle with a fourteen kilometer radius. "We're getting closer." He squinted at the map. "Most of this is woods."

"That doesn't help much."

"I'm sorry, Jules."

Mercer shook it off. "He didn't expect us to get the money. Now he doesn't know what to do." The aerial view of the town showed the outdoor skating rink. It was positioned off the promenade, almost at the center, across from the shops and restaurants. It shared a parking lot with the other nearby businesses, making it impossible for Mercer to drive up to the location and toss out the bags.

"He's unstable." Bastian mused. "You shouldn't go alone."

But Mercer wasn't listening. He tucked the radio back into his ear. "Any updates?"

"Taylor finished teaching his last class. He's in the locker room changing," Donovan said.

"Are you certain?" Mercer asked. "Do you have him in your sights?"

"Negative, commander. The locker room is members only. I can't get near it without the perky redhead at the desk chasing after me with her clipboard."

"It sounds like you need backup," Hans teased.

"Report, Hans." Mercer didn't have time for the usual back and forth.

"Not much to report. According to Gloria, Hilty hasn't shown up yet for his shift today. He called in sick."

"Did you get his address?" Mercer asked.

"Or a phone number?" Bastian chimed in since the one they had was turned off.

"Working on it," Hans said. "Give me a few more minutes."

"Donovan," Mercer said, "get inside that locker room through any means necessary and find out if Taylor made a call. You know what the background looks like on the video calls. See if it could be him. Just make sure he doesn't see you."

"That's not possible. If I go inside, he'll notice me. He'd have to be blind not to."

"How long has he been in there?"

"Twenty minutes," Donovan said.

Mercer glanced at the clock. "Fine. Do whatever it takes. Let me know what you find."

"Aye."

"Bas," Hans interrupted, "I might have a fix on Hilty. Gloria gave me a landline. Think you can work some magic." He repeated the number while Bastian entered the information into the computer. "Anything?"

"The address links to the house we visited last night." Bastian skimmed the rest of the details. "It's been turned off."

"Shit," Hans swore. "I'll see if his mates know where he might be staying."

"All right," Mercer said, "stay on him. I have to deliver the ransom to the ice skating rink. I'm supposed to go alone."

"Jules," Donovan cut in, "Taylor's not our guy. He's in the shower, and I'm pretty sure he's not alone. The locker room doesn't look anything like the background in the video calls, and I've gone through his things. He's not involved."

"It's best we learned that now," Mercer said, though he regretted the time they wasted. "Head over to the restaurant and help Hans. If Hilty's the kidnapper, I'd like to know before we make the exchange."

"I'll see what I can do," Donovan said.

"Jules, once we finish up here, I'll head over to the ice rink. You could use a set of eyes to scout ahead. But I'll maintain a safe distance and monitor the area from the end of a scope, so he won't spot me." Hans paused a moment. "What are you supposed to do with the money?"

"He expects me to have it on me."

"How?"

"I guess we're going to find out."

TWENTY-FIVE

Mercer tugged the last of the rolling suitcases up the small hill and checked the time. 3:47. He parked the suitcase next to the duffel bags and two other rolling suitcases he'd already lugged to the drop off location. He hadn't had time to roll all the quarters, but since the kidnapper didn't ask for the coins to be rolled, Mercer hoped that wouldn't be an issue. Wiping his brow with the back of his hand, he took a seat on the bench.

Two teenagers hung out inside the hut beside the skating rink. Based on their matching outfits and name tags, Mercer figured they worked at the rink. However, they'd been snogging since he dragged the first two duffel bags to this location. So he couldn't be sure how much work they were doing, but given that only a toddler and her dad were out on the rink, he doubted it mattered.

Mercer watched the little girl stumble, her feet scrambling against the ice before she landed on her bum. The dad reached down, scooping her up by the arms and helping her get back on her skates. Mercer watched the two slowly circle the rink, contemplating ways to encourage them to leave. He didn't like having civilians in the area. They made great targets, and the kidnapper had already proven repeatedly he had no problem preying on children and families.

Looking around, Mercer didn't spot Hans, but he knew the recon expert was close. Mercer had insisted they maintain radio silence since the kidnapper had a working knowledge of computers and negotiations. It's also why Mercer wore a Kevlar vest beneath his parka. The kidnapper was unpredictable and unhinged. Mercer couldn't take any chances.

His gaze drifted from the father and daughter to the two teenagers. He had to get them to evacuate the area. But when static filled his ear, he knew it was too late. The kidnapper was close. The same happened last night outside the diner. This bastard didn't take any unnecessary risks.

Gripping the Sig concealed at his side, he searched the area. At first, he didn't see anyone, but then he glimpsed a dark, tattered coat coming down the steps from the promenade. "He's coming from the north," Mercer whispered, even though he doubted Hans could hear him or that he'd even need the warning.

As predicted, the kidnapper wore the same mask he had on during their video chats. The only difference was the tattered coat. He must have worn the same thing the previous day when he abducted Annalise. Even if the abduction had been caught on camera, they wouldn't have been able to recognize him. This bastard was careful.

Spotting Mercer, he gave a friendly wave, sauntered over, and slid onto the bench. "I should have told you to come unarmed. Take your hand out of your coat, or those lovely people might think you're fondling yourself while watching the kids make out. You don't want that. The last town pervert got locked up, and once he was released, he was chased out of town by an angry mob carrying torches and pitchforks."

"Is that what happened to you?" Mercer holstered the weapon and eased his hand away.

"Ooh, burn." The kidnapper laughed, throwing an arm around Mercer's shoulders. But then he hissed in his ear, "I'm not a pervert. You and the Van der Bergs should be pretty fucking happy about that. Let me tell you. I bet when she grows up, little Annalise is gonna be one hell of a knockout. Well, if she grows up. That possibility is still up for debate."

"You're a sicko."

"Now, now, stop with the name calling. I told you that's not my cup of tea. Eighteen and over only."

"Your photograph makes me question that."

"Oh, is that the image keeping you warm right now?" The kidnapper kept his arm where it was. Despite the mask, Mercer could smell onions and garlic on the man's breath and something else spicy.

"Remove your arm before I break it."

"Again, I wouldn't advise it. Someone will call the cops, and things won't turn out so well for you or little Annalise. Have you forgotten that's why we're here?" But the kidnapper let go of Mercer and leaned forward, examining the suitcases. "Are these for me? Is it Christmas already? I'm surprised you don't have a giant red bow stuck to the top." The kidnapper glanced over his shoulder at Mercer. "I said you should put the money in something inconspicuous. This makes it look like your wife just threw you out or you're working baggage claim at the airport."

"No one's paid any heed to the bags. I've followed your instructions. Now I want to see proof of life. And if I find out you laid a finger on the girl, you'll die slowly and painfully."

The kidnapper nearly giggled. "I like it when you're feisty. Do you want to pull my hair a little and spank me?"

For a moment, Mercer couldn't see or think. Infuriated, he fought his baser desire to strangle the man or break his bones. Surely, he could find creative ways to get the answers he needed. And the only thing he needed from this bastard was Annalise's location. Once he had that, it'd be game over. Taking a deep breath, Mercer let out a puff of air. "Proof of life, or I walk away." Or kill you.

"You can't. Everything's at stake. The girl's life. Your reputation. Everything. If you botch this, you fail."

"It's a job. There will be others."

The kidnapper snorted, rubbing a gloved finger over his exposed lips. "A job, huh? What exactly is your job, Julian?"

"To safely recover the package."

"Again with the package. I knew you were a pervert."

Mercer stood, but the kidnapper grabbed his shoulders and shoved him down onto the bench.

"Don't walk away from me," the kidnapper warned, but by now Mercer had the Sig pointed at the kidnapper's ribcage. He kept it concealed from the few civilians nearby by keeping it underneath his coat. "And stop pointing that thing at me unless you plan on using it."

"I'm tired of this game. Either cooperate, or it ends here. You won't see another cent. If you want the two million, you'll do as I ask."

"You first." The kidnapper turned sideways on the bench, pulling one knee up in the space between them. "I asked you a question about your job. Last night, I offered to join forces. But you scoffed at the notion. Is that beneath you?"

"I already have a job."

The kidnapper's eyes narrowed. "You were snooping around before there even was a job. Why? What brought you here?"

"You fucked up. We traced your other crimes to this town."

"So you came here for me." The kidnapper clutched his chest. "I'm touched." He glanced down at the gun. "Well, only by you, if you play your cards right, handsome." He winked.

"Is that why you took her?"

"Don't flatter yourself. You really think I had nothing better to do than kidnap some kid just to get your attention?"

Mercer didn't answer. The wind picked up, and thick, heavy snowflakes started dropping from the sky. The child on the ice skating rink let out a delighted squeal, and her father scooped her onto his shoulders. They circled the rink a few times while she waved her hands in the air and turned her face skyward, catching a flake on her tongue.

"Y'know, you haven't exactly been doing a great job of maintaining a low profile." The kidnapper had lost interest in keeping an eye on Mercer and watched with amused fascination as the father skated around the rink with no other purpose than to please his child. "The entire town's been whispering about the real reason you and your partner came here. The townsfolk are suspicious. Again, you need to be careful. I'm not joking about the torches and pitchforks."

"Are you trying to bore me to death? Let me see proof of life."

The kidnapper held up a hand for Mercer to be

patient, while still watching the figures circle on the ice. "Look, man, you have a job. A ridiculous one. But who am I to judge? But see, I also have a job. And last night, I made you an offer. You didn't exactly give me a response. Definitely not the one I wanted. So why don't you reconsider? Your antics at the diner caused a ruckus that people in town are talking about. And the diner is two freaking exits away. They don't trust you. That's bound to make your life more difficult. Y'see, I hear things. I know what you've been doing all day." He made a tsk sound. "Naughty, naughty, Julian. How hard do you think it'd be to link the vending machine burglaries to you and your mate?"

Mercer ignored the threat. But he wondered how the kidnapper knew so much about their exploits. What else did he know? Did he realize Mercer worked with three other men? Were Hans and Donovan compromised?

"You need to stop drawing so much attention to yourself. Bev couldn't stop talking about the Brit who sampled her pie." He licked his lips. "Yum, yum."

"You picked that drop location. Not me."

"No, no, no." The kidnapper shook his head, the collected flakes falling off the top of his ski mask and onto his coat. "I'm not talking about the drop. I'm talking about later on. After I left. You went back, didn't you?"

Mercer hesitated. He hadn't lied yet, and starting now seemed pointless, especially since he wasn't convinced he wouldn't shoot this bastard in the gut as soon as the civilians left the skating rink. "I needed pie."

The kidnapper laughed. "Blueberry. Good choice. Personally, I'm more of a cherry man. There's just something about popping a sweet cherry into my mouth."

Ignoring the innuendo, which was meant to gain a rise out of Mercer, he filed the pertinent information away. Since the kidnapper knew what kind of pie Mercer ordered, he might have been inside the diner. He tried to think back to the men eating, but he couldn't reconcile those images with the masked man before him. Something didn't fit.

"What's a matter? Cat got your tongue?" the kidnapper asked. "Or are you just worn out? I'm guessing after the sugar rush hit you decided to go looking for trouble. The report of a break-in at the ski instructor's townhouse, I'm guessing that was you." The kidnapper tapped his temple. "See, I'm not stupid. Bev must have given you what she thought was my name."

"Earl?"

"Yes?" The kidnapper animatedly gasped. "Crap. You've found me out."

Mercer stared blankly at him.

"Jeez. I'm just shitting with you. You seriously thought it'd be that easy to ID me? Fuck. You know how long I've been at this. Did you really think I'd make an amateur mistake like that?" Reaching down, the kidnapper unzipped one of the suitcases. "Did you also try to hide a tracker in the bags?"

"No. I followed your instructions to the letter."

"Amazing, at least you did something right." The kidnapper took a fistful of coins out of the bag and examined them. "Good job." He tossed them into his pocket.

"I've done everything you asked. Provide proof of life so we can continue the negotiation."

"Change of plans, Julian. You haven't been playing by the rules. You play by your rules and pay close attention to what you say to avoid lying, but that's what this is. It's all a bunch of lies. It's time you start being honest."

Mercer waited. The staticky snaps in his ear only infuriated him further. He could feel the shift. The negotiation had derailed. Every attempt to appease this bastard had been for naught. Things were about to pop off, and no amount of backpedaling or compromise could get this derailing train back on track.

"What do you want to know?" Mercer asked.

"Do you care if the girl lives?"

"Yes."

The kidnapper nodded, zipping the suitcase closed. "That means you'll do whatever I say to make sure I don't harm her."

"That's not how negotiations work."

"I hate to break it to you, buddy, but you screwed this one up. This negotiation is over. I'm calling the shots now." He stood, tapping the nearest suitcase with his foot. "Grab those and follow me. The snow's not going to let up. I gotta get on the road before it gets too bad, or Annalise could starve or freeze while she waits for me to get home." He picked up the cooler bag from the bench. "I hope you remembered her insulin. She looked kind of pasty when I left. Oh, and I hope you packed fruit this time. I'm not coming back for a second pick-up when it's coming down like this."

TWENTY-SIX

"Stop." Mercer rose from the bench, the Sig Sauer in his hand. He didn't care who saw them. Hans could provide cover fire if necessary. "Prove you haven't harmed her."

The kidnapper turned around. "Again, I'll remind you, if you kill me, you're pulling the trigger on the child too. She'll die if I don't get back to her." He stared into Mercer's eyes. "Do you think I'm lying?"

Mercer remained poised to fire. Again, the same thoughts he entertained during their previous encounter played through his mind.

"Let me make this easier for you." The kidnapper took a step closer, but Mercer didn't back away or flinch. He was too well-trained. "Pull the fucking trigger and see what happens. I dare you."

Mercer held his ground. "Show me proof of life."

The kidnapper reached into his pocket. Suddenly, the staticky buzz in Mercer's ear vanished. Slowly, he removed his hand, opened his jacket, and reached for a phone. "Fine, but I don't like being strong-armed.

You get one of these, Julian. One." He clicked a few buttons and turned the screen around for Mercer to see. "I took that before I came here. As you can see, she's alive but not so well. The longer you delay, the worse it'll be. So how sadistic of a killer are you? Do you want the girl to die a slow, torturous death because that's what will happen if you don't stop pointing that gun at me?"

"Commander, what's going on?" Hans asked in his ear, but Mercer didn't reply. He couldn't.

"How do I know she's not already dead? Send me the photo, so I can see the timestamp and metadata. You could have taken it hours ago."

The kidnapper glanced up. "Toss your gun away first." He nodded to the rubbish bin beside the bench.

Mercer took a step back, noticing the area had gone silent. The fat snowflakes continued falling, limiting visibility. By now, the green grass was quickly vanishing beneath the blanket of white. The father and daughter were on the other side of the rink, taking off their skates. No one had seen Mercer pull a gun, except Hans.

"Okay." Mercer dropped the gun into the waste receptacle with a clang. Even the metallic echo was muted by the snowfall.

"What the bloody hell are you doing?" Hans asked.

Mercer ignored the voice in his ear.

"Take out your phone and ask the Van der Bergs if they got the photo. I assume your boyfriend's monitoring communications from afar," the kidnapper said.

"Bastian's with the family." Mercer dialed the analyst's number. "Did you receive a photo?"

"Yes, Jules, but she doesn't look so good. Do you know her numbers?"

"When was it taken?" Mercer asked.

"The timestamp says just after three."

"I need you to verify it."

Bastian sighed. "This isn't what I would call an exact science."

"Do your best." Mercer held the phone away from his mouth. "How was her blood sugar?"

The kidnapper sighed. "Not great. It'll be worse by the time I get back. If I get back. So how long do you want to continue with this pathetic show of dominance?" He jerked his chin at the phone. "Ask the Van der Bergs how they'd like you to proceed. Since you work for them, it's time you let the family call the shots. I offered you a better alternative, but I can see you're not the man I thought you were."

"Jules?" Bastian asked.

"Her sugar's not great," Mercer repeated. "How do her parents want to proceed?"

"You have insulin and food for her. Let's hope that will stabilize her condition for now."

Hans' voice piped in, and Mercer figured the entire team could hear the phone call exchange on comms. "Do you want me to take him out?"

"Not yet," Mercer said, hoping Hans would catch on. "He just texted that photo from his phone."

"According to the data, the image is less than an hour old," Bastian said. "I have no reason to doubt it. It hasn't been altered or tampered with."

"What else?" Mercer kept his eyes on the kidnapper.

"I have the number. Obviously, you already know his location. I'm pulling up the phone records now. You're not going to like this. It's registered to Joe Doe. It's your typical burner. Bogus address. Even the credit card on file was a prepaid. But if he keeps it on him, I'll be able to track him."

"Very well," Mercer said. "We'll carry on with the

exchange."

"Got it, Jules. I'll follow him," Hans promised. "As soon as we get a location, we'll move in and rescue the girl and end this wanker."

"Understood." Mercer pressed the disconnect, but he'd remain connected to his team via their comms as long as the kidnapper didn't reactivate the jammer.

"Well? Are we one big happy family again?" The kidnapper jerked his chin at the bags. "Now let's get going."

Mercer stared at the kidnapper's retreating back. "I can't carry them all. You have to help me, or this will take even longer."

The kidnapper shrugged. "It's no skin off my nose. You weren't in a rush before, so neither am I." He continued down the path, sliding a little on a slushy patch.

Mercer strapped the two duffel bags in a cross pattern over his chest, grabbed the handle on a rolling suitcase, and followed the path from the outdoor skating rink across the street to the parking lot.

The kidnapper opened the rear doors of a white van and crossed his arms over his chest, waiting. "Are you coming or just breathing heavy?"

Mercer dragged the bag across the pavement, huffing beneath the weight strapped to his body. Based on the ski shop logo, the van was used to deliver equipment and gear. He noted the name and the license plate as he hefted one duffel off his chest and tossed it into the van. While he repeated the process with the other, the kidnapper opened the first bag.

"Should I be concerned about trackers?"

"No." Mercer bent down, hefting the suitcase into the back. "I already told you there are no trackers."

"Would you tell me if there were?"

"Probably not." Mercer stepped away from the van, moving at a faster clip now, desperate for a moment of privacy. He jogged across the parking lot, his boots keeping traction with the slick pavement. "Do you see the van?" Mercer asked, hurrying up the hill to grab the other two bags. He noticed the two teenagers had left the hut. One pulled down the gate while the other poked around the remaining luggage.

"Yes, Jules. I'll keep an eye on it. Donovan's ready to pursue once it pulls away. I'll get into a second car and follow," Hans said.

"Whatever happened with Hilty?"

"Still working on it."

"Very well. Bas, do what you can remotely." Mercer rattled off the plate number and store logo before static burst from the comm. He glanced back, finding the kidnapper heading his way with a gun at his side. Mercer approached the closest teenager. "Those are mine. Leave them be." More than anything, he wanted the kid to disappear. He didn't trust the kidnapper not to open fire. "Get away. Now."

"Cool it, man," the teenage boy said. "I was just looking. I didn't hurt nothing." His girlfriend finished locking up and jogged over. One lethal look from Mercer, and she tugged on her boyfriend's hand.

"C'mon, Petey. Let's go." She gave Mercer another uncertain look. Unlike Petey, she knew to be afraid. Women were usually smarter when it came to dangerous situations. And Mercer capitalized on that knowledge, glowering at her. She tugged more vehemently on her boyfriend's hand, and they headed in the opposite direction.

Mercer extended the handle on the first rolling suitcase, relieved to find the father and child had disappeared. Based on their footprints, they'd wandered back onto the promenade. They'd be safe there.

"Hold it," the kidnapper said as Mercer reached for the second suitcase. He aimed at Julian's chest. "Let's see how you like being held at gunpoint."

Mercer stared at the gun. "Fine. Shoot me. Take the money. And help Annalise."

"You're serious?"

"If that's what it takes."

The kidnapper swore. "Then who the hell's going to carry all these coins back to the car?" He moved around Mercer and the luggage. "Don't stare at me. If I shoot you in the back, I shoot you in the back. That's my call. Now get moving."

Tugging on the handles, Mercer dragged the two rolling suitcases through the deepening snow. The left wheel on the second bag locked in place. An ice chunk kept it from rotating, but Mercer continued to tug on the bag. His back muscles, shoulders, and triceps strained under the effort. Finally, he made it to the parking lot. With the locked wheel, the bag flopped onto its side. The coins jangled loudly, but the parking lot was empty. Everyone had gone inside due to the unexpected storm.

"Load them in the back." The kidnapper remained a few steps behind Mercer.

"There." Mercer didn't turn. He just hoped Hans wouldn't take the shot or return fire.

"That's everything?"

"All ten grand."

"Good. Now get in the back." The kidnapper jerked his gun.

"What?"

"You tried to fucking shoot me. Do you honestly think I'm just going to let bygones be bygones? Get in the fucking van."

"If I don't return, my team will come looking for

me."

"Good. That's what I'm counting on." The kidnapper shot Mercer in the back, catching the former SAS operative before he could slump to the ground. After shoving him into the van, the kidnapper went around to the front, got behind the wheel, and pulled away.

TWENTY-SEVEN

Mercer rolled onto his side. The pain made it hard to concentrate, but he forced himself to focus. He heard the driver's door slam and felt the rumble of the engine. He pulled one of his gloves off with his teeth and reached behind his back. He checked his hand. No blood. The bullet didn't penetrate, but it hurt like hell.

"Hans?" Mercer asked, but he didn't hear anything but static and the rushing of blood in his ears. "Bas? Donovan? Does anyone copy?" Wincing, Mercer moved his right foot, then his left. No paralysis. He tried to sit up, but the van veered hard to the left. He rolled, bumping his back against the wall and cursing.

"Dammit," the kidnapper turned around, looking through the mesh wire that separated the rear compartment from the cab, "you mean that didn't kill you?" He slammed his palm repeatedly against the steering wheel. "Fuckity, fuck, fuck."

Mercer glared at him. "Not yet. Give it a few minutes."

The kidnapper stopped cursing. The melodrama forgotten. "Try not to disappoint. You better not be placating me with what you know I want to hear."

"Sod off."

The kidnapper turned the wheel hard again. The heavy duffel slid across the floor, slamming into Mercer and pinning him against the side of the van. For a moment, his vision swam, and he struggled to get his lungs working again.

The back wheels locked up, shrieking as the rear of the van skidded back and forth. Finally, the kidnapper got the van straightened out. "Told you the roads would get treacherous. The weatherman didn't call for snowfall until later. The salt trucks and plows figured they'd wait until five to get started. They like to get overtime whenever they can. And since the tourists aren't here yet, no one's going to bitch or moan about it."

Mercer remained pinned against the wall behind the driver's seat. The kidnapper couldn't see him unless he fully turned around, and with the current road conditions, such action was ill-advised. Aside from the pain, Mercer didn't worry about the extent of his injuries. The Kevlar had taken the brunt of the impact. A few bruises didn't matter. A fracture would heal. Worst case, he could live without a kidney, just as long as the other one functioned. But none of that mattered. *I have to save the child,* Mercer thought. He just wasn't sure how. Normally, he'd be planning a retaliatory strike, but he couldn't. Not until the girl was safe. How did he end up in this no-win situation?

The van swerved on the icy roads. Mercer focused on the turns, but with the constant bumps and the erratic way the kidnapper drove, it was difficult to keep track. Each bump felt like a knife in his back. For a moment, he thought he blacked out, but he wasn't sure. The van continued to totter along. He tried his phone, but the kidnapper's jammer blocked that too. *It doesn't matter,* he told himself. *Hans and Donovan are in pursuit. Bastian has his cell number. They'll find him. They'll recover the package.*

Suddenly, the van lurched to a stop. Mercer slid forward a few inches, along with the heavy bag of quarters. No longer pinned, he unzipped the bag and removed several of the rolls. His training kicked in. He wanted to fight. The coins would make that easier. He could fill his glove and use it like a blackjack to strike. He'd knock the killer out cold with little effort, but he knew the consequences of such action. Instead, he stuffed the rolls into his pocket, just in case. Shorting the kidnapper wasn't wise, but his gut said today's delivery wasn't about the money. He just hoped he was right.

The driver's door slammed, rattling the frame, but the engine continued to rumble, letting out an unexpected shudder. The rear doors popped open, but Mercer resisted the urge to fight back. Instead, he shut his eyes, making his body go limp.

"Oh, Julian," the kidnapper sang, grabbing Mercer's ankle and tugging him toward the doors. That yank sent a shockwave of pain through Mercer's body, emanating from the base of his spine and running down both legs like white-hot razorblades. "Are you still alive and kicking?" The kidnapper took a step back, as if Mercer might actually kick him. But Mercer remained still. He wouldn't act until he knew where they were. Hopefully, it was the same location Annalise was being held. Then he'd give this bastard what he truly deserved. "Guess you're not kicking, huh?"

He pulled Mercer out of the van. An unexpected *oomph* escaped Mercer's lips when he hit the ground.

The kidnapper leaned down, poking at the K&R specialist.

"Are you playing dead?" He pressed the barrel of his gun to Mercer's forehead. "Keep it up, and you won't be playing."

Mercer opened his eyes. Thick plumes of exhaust billowed up from the tailpipe. He couldn't see beyond it, so he turned the other way, finding nothing but snow and trees. They were no longer within city limits. Trees lined the road on both sides. The roadway was covered in white. The tire tracks they just made were already fading beneath the heavy snowfall.

"Get up." The kidnapper took a step back, his head whipping back and forth to make sure no one was around. As far as he could tell, they hadn't been followed.

On the two-lane road, it'd be impossible for anyone to sneak up on them. Where were Hans and Donovan? Weren't they supposed to be in follow cars?

Slowly, Mercer rolled onto his side, getting his hands and knees beneath him before pushing up to his feet. The twinge in his back nearly knocked him to the ground, and he used the open van door to steady himself. He shifted his weight from one leg to the other until he became accustomed to the pain. That made it easier to ignore.

"Where are we? Where's Annalise?" Mercer didn't see anything, but as he spoke, his ears popped. They must have been driving for a while. Those few moments Mercer thought he blacked out must have been longer than he realized. Where was his team? Something must have gone wrong.

"Those are two things you no longer need to worry about." The kidnapper jerked the gun to the side. "Get moving."

"Where?"

"Up the hill, just a little ways."

Playing up his injuries, Mercer limped slowly up the road. With the constant, blowing snow, he couldn't see more than a few meters in front of him. The road turned sharply, and he turned with it.

"Not that way," the kidnapper poked Mercer in the back.

Mercer howled and dropped to his knees. For a moment, he wondered if he'd been too dramatic. Did the kidnapper actually believe he was in that much pain? But the giddy snicker answered Mercer's question.

"Damn, I've forgotten how much fun this is. Y'know, if I didn't have to rush back home, we could perform our own reenactment of the 'The Most Dangerous Game'."

"Kipling?" Mercer asked.

"Actually, no. Well, I don't know. I should look that up. Now it's going to drive me crazy." He poked Mercer hard in the back. "Stop doing things to irritate me."

"Too late." Mercer climbed to his feet, catching a dizzying glimpse of nothing but swirling white below him. He couldn't tell if there was anything beneath it on account of the visibility. "You're already bloody daft."

"Like a fox." The kidnapper circled, stopping in front of Mercer. "And what exactly does that say about you? I'm holding all the cards, so to speak, and you're standing there with a bullet in your back. I guess that means I win. You should have taken my offer. It didn't have to go this way. We both could have walked away, rich and happy."

Sensing this might be it, Mercer made one final plea. "Don't hurt the girl. She's an innocent. You have me. Let her go."

"Mmm...no." The kidnapper rubbed at his upper lip, the knit fabric chafing his skin. "Dammit." He tugged on the bottom of the mask, pulling it just above his nose, so he could scratch his face.

"You were in the kitchen at the cat café."

"No, I wasn't." He tugged the mask back into place. "But thanks for playing." He pulled the trigger. The booming report echoed off the mountains.

The impact sent Mercer sprawling backward. Everything slipped away, but ice on his neck brought reality crashing back to him. He felt the rush of earth beneath him, and then he was falling. He reached out, searching for a hold as he slid backward down the mountainside.

His hand latched onto a branch or root, but it wasn't strong enough to stop his descent. It broke away in his hand. His left heel caught on something, and his body jerked. The constant throbbing in his back momentarily replaced the fresh new sting in his chest, and then he was sliding downhill on his stomach.

He twisted, wet snow blowing up into his face as he tried to see what was ahead. He couldn't tell much, but he spotted a tree with a thick trunk coming up on the right. Shoving all his weight to one side, he did his best to maneuver toward the tree. His shoulder collided with a rock on the way, knocking him high into the air. He landed sideways, the momentum forcing him into a somersault, and he continued to roll. End over end, the world moved faster and faster. Then he hit the tree. And everything went dark.

TWENTY-EIGHT

Mercer blinked. He couldn't see anything except blinding white. And he was cold. So cold.

"Bloody hell." He thought death would be more peaceful than this. Where was Michelle? Shouldn't she be here? And why wasn't it warmer? Mercer snorted. Perhaps he should be relieved it wasn't.

Shaking off the pile of snow that had been dumped on top of him when he collided with the tree, Mercer filled his lungs, gasping and choking at the cold air's assault. It hurt to breathe. It even hurt to think. Images flooded him. He recalled the bottom portion of the kidnapper's face. It had to be the same bastard he'd seen in the kitchen at the cat café. He had to get word to his team. At least getting shot twice had been worth something.

He unzipped his parka and plucked the newest slug out of the Kevlar. The kidnapper fired dead center. If he was a better shot, he would have aimed a few centimeters to the left. Gasping again, Mercer coughed a few times, his vision growing dim. His lungs weren't meant for this kind of assault. It hadn't been that long since he had one resected. He didn't want to have to go through a surgery like that again.

Pulling the vest away from his body, Mercer looked down to make sure the bullet hadn't penetrated. His chest was purplish-blue and swollen. "Just a bruise." He imagined the one on his back must look about the same. Convinced he'd live, he tried to make heads or tails out of his surroundings. But the snow hadn't let up. Even the trees didn't offer much protection from it.

He tapped the radio in his ear, finding it missing. "Bollocks." Carefully, he got onto his hands and knees. He could have lost it anywhere during his tumble down the mountain. But he still had his phone.

One bar.

Tugging off his glove, he dialed Donovan.

"Commander?" Donovan asked. "Are you all right? We saw you get shot and taken, but we lost sight of the van."

"I'm fine." Tucking the damaged copper-colored bullet into his pocket, Mercer took in his surroundings. "I saw his face. He's the bastard from the cat café. He was in the kitchen. The bloke that kept staring at us."

"The kidnapper?" Donovan asked.

"Yes. Where is he? Are you still tracking his phone?"

"Let me dial in the rest of the team. Hang on."

"Jules?" Bastian asked.

"Here," Mercer replied.

"I saw the arsehole shoot you," Hans said, "and stuff you in that bloody van. Are you okay? I was going to put a hole through his head, but you said we had to save the girl."

"Good call," Mercer said. "Where is he?"

"He gave us the slip on the back roads, so we doubled back," Donovan said.

"I'm tracking his coordinates," Bastian said. "But the signal's weak. I keep losing it. From what I can tell, he's still moving. Once he stops, it'll be easier to pinpoint his location. Are you still with him, Jules?"

"Negative, but I've identified him." Mercer repeated the same thing he told Donovan.

"Jolly good." Bastian entered several commands. "Two men work there. What does he look like?"

"Curly, brown hair. Hazel eyes. Average height. Medium build."

"Okay, I'm checking DMV photos." The entire team waited for Bastian to come up with a name. "That sounds like Joe Robbins. I've got his address and phone number." Bastian rattled off the intel.

"That's in town," Donovan said.

"Hans, get over there," Mercer said. "Figure out where he's going and where he's keeping Annalise."

"What about you?" Hans asked, while the team listened to Bastian's typing. "Where are you, Jules?

"Somewhere on the mountain."

"Where?"

"I don't bloody know." At least letting this bastard use him for target practice had paid off. "Don't lose him. Bas, run everything you can. We have to stop this guy. Donovan, remain at the bottom. If he makes another run into town or tries to go back home, stay on him. The bastard's slippery. In this storm, he won't encounter many other cars. He might try to make a run for it."

No one replied. And Mercer pulled his phone away. The signal strength blinked. "Bas, are you reading me? Anyone?"

A garbled response came back.

"Say again."

"Jules," Hans said, "just hang on. I'm coming to get you."

"Negative." Mercer stared up the mountainside. It was too steep. He wouldn't make it back up without climbing gear. Just the thought made his back ache. "Follow orders." Using the tree for support, he got to his feet. A sudden gust of wind pushed against him, but he managed to stay upright.

"I'll follow the road and pick you up," Donovan offered.

"I'm not on the road."

"Where are you?" Bastian asked.

"I went over the side. I'm not sure exactly how far down I fell." Mercer stared into the swirling white, unable to see how far he had traveled. "I'm by the tree."

Hans wouldn't give this up. "Which tree? There's a whole bloody forest covering the side of the mountain."

"It doesn't matter. Get your arse to this bastard's house and find out where he's keeping her."

"Jules," Bas's voice came through the earpiece, calming Mercer's nerves, "what's your condition?"

"Bruised. And bloody angry. Hans, go. If we don't locate Annalise and stop this bastard, he'll kill her and dozens of others after her. We can stop him. We know who he is. Now all we have to do is find him. Follow the plan."

"Bloody orders," Hans mumbled, the phone only picking up a few words here and there, "...daft...if you think...probably bloody well dying."

"Bas, you're in charge until I climb down," Mercer said.

"Aye." Bas waited. "Hans, let me know what you find at Robbins' home address. Stay on comms. Donovan, maintain position. I'll do my best to monitor his cell signal from here, but it's spotty at best. If it goes out completely, you're our eyes and ears."

"What about you, Jules?" Donovan asked.

"I'll get Jules," Bastian said.

"Bas," Mercer growled, "stay where you are. You have to coordinate and provide overwatch."

A burst of static came through the earpiece. And Mercer's phone dropped the call. "Bollocks." He tried to ring them again, but the call wouldn't connect.

Mercer knew his team. If he didn't get back to them, they'd find a way to get to him. And they didn't have time for that.

There was only one reason the team would sacrifice a mission, especially one involving a child, and that was to save him. They were brothers, not by blood, but by something far more important. Breaking off one of the weaker branches, Mercer fashioned it into a walking stick of sorts. And then he set out to find a path that would lead him safely down the side of the mountain without tumbling over the edge.

He'd only gone a few meters when his phone rang. It was Hans. He always had trouble following orders he didn't agree with.

"Hans, she's only seven. She needs you more than I do." Mercer knew that would get the recon expert moving since ordering him around didn't work, but emotional manipulation did.

"Fine. Just stay away from the bloody edge," Hans said. "It's a long way down."

More static crackled in Mercer's ear. And the rest of the message came out garbled. Mercer pulled off his glove again to tinker with the device. But he couldn't make it work. He should have brought a SAT phone with him. No wonder the kidnapper used a direct uplink to make contact. It's the only thing that worked out here.

Giving up, Mercer fought against the blowing snow and moved into a more densely wooded area. He figured the trees might keep him from tumbling down the mountain. But the incline remained steep, and the footing uneven, especially with the centimeters of freshly fallen snow.

Unsure of his bearings, Mercer turned one way and then the other. They'd worked a lot of missions under different conditions. This wouldn't be the first time he hiked down a mountain in a snowstorm. He just hoped he could avoid the avalanche this time.

Setting out to the south, Mercer picked his way along the path. He tried to stay within the trees to make sure he didn't get blown off his feet by another strong gust. Plus, they aided his balance and provided a bit of shelter from the storm.

As the sky grew dark, the temperature dropped, but Mercer kept walking. At one point, he started leaving quarters near the base of the trees to make sure he didn't end up moving in a circle. But the coins quickly vanished in the snow.

Stopping, he looked around. The swirling snow and winding path made it impossible to continue in a straight line. He wasn't even sure he was heading down the mountain. His hands were numb, like most of his body. Stopping for a rest, he took off his gloves and pulled his arms into his jacket, tucking his hands beneath his armpits for a few minutes.

Looking behind him, he couldn't see much of anything, but he felt the mountain's looming presence at his back. He had to be close to the bottom. Thirsty and tired, he reached for his phone. Two bars.

"Bas." His throat was sore and scratchy from breathing in the frigid air.

"I'm here, Jules."

"I need an update."

"We found Robbins' flat."

"And?"

Bastian hesitated. "The kidnapper phoned again. He told me you were dead and gave me one last chance to save the girl. He wants the cash left at the chairlift just before dawn. Once he gets his money, he'll give me her coordinates."

"I don't understand." Mercer blinked a few times. "We've identified him. Don't you have a location? What about tracking his phone?"

"His cell signal cut out and hasn't come back up yet. I requested satellite images. They should be in my inbox momentarily. We've searched property records, but according to the locals, there are a lot of old hunting cabins in the woods that no one ever uses. We think that's where he's taken Annalise and where he's holed up."

"Why aren't you moving in?" Mercer asked, confused. "I just saw him. The bastard shot me. I don't understand."

"In this storm, we don't have visuals. We don't have a signal. And until we know exactly where he's hiding, we can't risk stumbling around in the dark searching for him. It's not smart. If he spots us, she's dead. You know this. Right now, we have to focus our efforts on gathering intel."

Mercer knew what that meant. "When did it go tits up? Did Hans—"

"It's not his fault. The cell signal dropped hours ago."

"Why didn't you tell me before?"

"I mentioned it was spotty. I thought it'd come back. But it never did."

Mercer hauled himself to his feet. The anger overpowering his body's desire to rest. "Where are

Hans and Donovan now?"

"They're closing in on your position. They're bringing you home."

TWENTY-NINE

"Hold still. I'm almost finished." Donovan tugged the thread through the deep laceration on Mercer's shoulder, tied a knot, and cut the string. "How did you not feel that?"

Mercer shrugged, knocking back another shot of whiskey.

"Take it easy on the alcohol." Bastian circled the stool where Mercer perched, examining the contusions and other injuries.

"Why?" Mercer took another swallow before putting the bottle on the counter. "It's my kidneys you're worried about, not my liver."

"It's all connected with the filtering and the blood, and I don't know. Do I look like a doctor to you?" Bastian shook his head. "You're lucky to be alive."

Mercer turned the Kevlar vest around. "I've been shot before."

"We all have. More times than any of us want to count," Donovan said.

Bastian picked up one of the slugs Mercer had

pulled from the vest and examined it more closely underneath the light. "I did some checking on his previous victims. Our friends from the lab called an hour before you got back. He always uses the same type of bullet."

Donovan rolled up the unused medical supplies and placed them back inside the first aid kit. Then he took the tools he used to the sink to clean and disinfect. "I read the ballistics files in the police reports. They weren't even from the same caliber weapon."

"No," Bastian agreed, "but they were all non-lead bullets."

"He's a sportsman." Donovan abandoned the tools and returned to the table. He picked up the fragment. "It looks like copper." He picked up Mercer's vest and held it up to the light. "I'm surprised it didn't penetrate." He glanced over his shoulder at Hans. "How close was he when he shot Jules in the back?"

Hans cocked his head to the side, analyzing the room. "About the same distance I am from you."

"Bas is right. You are lucky, mate." Donovan put the bullet down. "Non-lead bullets tend to be harder. They don't fragment. They typically blow a hole right through their target."

Hans put down his empty beer bottle. "It's the extreme temperature change. It wasn't the bullet. It was the bloody gun that malfunctioned or, rather, the gun powder. Since it's freezing out there, when it ignited, it didn't have the same oomph. Less velocity. Less intensity. Less penetrating power. The cold saved your life, Jules."

"He should have known better than to keep his gun in the car." Mercer blinked a few times. He wasn't exactly drunk, but he felt pretty damn good. A lot better than he deserved, and that worried him. They had a mission to complete. Water. He needed water.

"My point is we know something else about him." Bastian eyed the other members of the team. "He's a hunter. With at least," Bastian rubbed his eyes, hoping to recall the details, "six guns?"

"Seven." Mercer passed Bastian the bottle. "Did you add it to the profile?"

"I updated everything as it came in and went over it again when he made contact."

"Did you get proof of life?"

"Yes."

"How is she?" Mercer was afraid to ask.

"Her blood sugar leveled out. Her mum thinks she needed protein. Again, not a physician."

"Speaking of," Hans said, "should I call Maggie? Donovan's no surgeon, and Jules doesn't trust anyone in town to take a look at him. But those are nasty bruises. It might be important to get a second opinion or even a first opinion."

"I'm fine." Mercer reached for his shirt.

"You're sure? No frostbite? No internal bleeding? No spinal cord injuries?" Hans asked.

"I'm fine."

"Okay." Hans waited for Mercer to pop his head through the shirt, and then he sucker punched him. The unexpected hit made Mercer stumble backward. "That's for letting us think you were dead and telling us to leave you behind." Before Mercer could say or do anything, Hans lunged again. But this time, he pulled Julian into a hug. "Stop giving orders you know I won't follow."

Mercer shoved him off. "Have you lost your damn mind?" Bastian and Donovan edged closer, expecting fisticuffs to break out. But instead, Mercer rubbed his jaw and glared at Hans. "Try that again and I'll toss you off the side of a cliff. Bloody nutter."

"Don't be such an arse." Hans went to the fridge and pulled out another beer. "You could at least thank us for picking you up. Had it not been for us, you'd be a popsicle by now."

Mercer licked his split lip. "You lost the kidnapper. That might not have happened if you'd done what I had asked."

"Enough," Bastian snapped. "You're going to wake the Van der Bergs. They don't need to hear this shit. What they need to hear is that their little girl will be returned safe and sound. Agreed?"

Mercer nodded.

"Yeah." Hans sipped his beer, a grin emerging on his face when he put the bottle down. "Let's hug it out, like they do on those family sitcoms." He spread his arms wide and stepped forward. The challenge in his eyes obvious. He knew Mercer was in pain, and hugging him proved it.

"Come near me again, and I'll shove that bottle up your arse." Mercer sidestepped around him and went to the freezer. Now that he was warm, he could tolerate an ice pack. He needed to get the swelling down before they headed out.

"I always said you were a pain in my arse," Hans teased. "Didn't realize you'd take it literally."

"No, he's a pain in my arse. But one I would greatly miss." Bas winked and went to the cupboard in search of a snack. "I'm knackered."

"You?" Mercer snorted. "I didn't realize you had to climb down a mountain."

"Piss off." Bastian tugged on the bag until it popped open. "I haven't slept in two days."

Mercer checked the time. "Take a nap. Until we figure out where they are, we're not going anywhere." Famished, Mercer took a handful of crisps from the bag. They had ordered room service, but it hadn't arrived yet.

"Are you sure?"

"In this blizzard, I don't think we'd get very far," Mercer said. "We should prepare to move once it slows down."

Bas stuffed a handful of crisps into his mouth and put the bag on the counter. "Guess you can take it from here. I'll just pop into the spare room and close my eyes for a few minutes. Wake me when the food arrives, and don't eat my burger."

"Aye, aye, captain." Hans saluted.

Bastian excused himself and went down the hallway to one of the empty bedrooms. Mercer tucked the liquor bottle away, filled a glass with water, and went into the office.

Fragments of intel covered the walls, and Mercer pulled down the bits he found irrelevant. "Hans, what did you find on Earl Hilty?"

"He never showed up for work, but his roommate said he caught a nasty stomach bug."

"Roommate?"

"Another busboy. The hostess said he's been couch-surfing these last few months. He's saving up to get his house renovated. He plans to list it on the web as a vacation rental during tourist season to up his income." Hans held out the man's driver's license photo. "Guess if he had the ransom money, he wouldn't have to go to all that trouble."

Mercer took the offered photograph and shook his head. "Nothing more than a wild goose chase."

"No harm done," Donovan said.

"That's debatable." Mercer stared at the wall, hoping to piece together the fragments of intel they'd gathered. "Have you contacted the previous victims? Did any of them go to the cat café?"

"Bas made some calls," Hans said. "No one stopped

by, but every person remembers passing it on their way to wherever. Robbins probably figured the crimes would never connect to him since he only targeted non-customers."

"It's right next door to that high-end boutique," Donovan said. "He watched the rich buy pricey baubles while he cleaned litter boxes and baked cat cookies. It must have driven him mad."

Mercer sat on the edge of the desk. "We need to search his flat."

"Already done." Hans reached for the camera and handed it to Mercer. "As you can see, he wiped everything down. He emptied the rubbish bins. He didn't leave anything behind. It looks like a professional cleaned it."

"Bugger. He's not planning to come back. We burned him. He has to leave now." Mercer reached for the open laptop. "He knows we have his name."

"But he thinks he killed you. Shouldn't you have taken his identity to your grave?" Hans asked.

"Robbins won't risk it," Donovan said. "Think about everything else he's done. He wouldn't take a chance like that."

"Bev's working with him. She has to be. She told me his name was Earl. She intentionally misled us. And he knew I went back to the diner and spoke to her. He even knew about the pie."

"It's a good thing it wasn't poisoned," Hans quipped.

"Robbins has been leading us around by the nose since the abduction. That's why he had us make the drop there. And when I didn't go inside the diner the first time, he called me back. He wanted me to speak to her. He wanted me to ask about him. Fuck." Mercer slammed his palm on the desk. "She must know where he is. We need to speak to her. Privately."

Mercer reached for his parka, wincing when a sharp pain traveled across his clavicle, down his chest, and around his ribs. But he shook it off. They had work to do. He palmed a set of keys and then thought better of it. "Donovan, maybe you should drive."

"You sure you don't want to sit this one out, Jules?" Donovan asked. "We're more than capable of picking up the bird and taking her back to our cabin for a chat."

"No, this is my mistake. I'll fix it."

THIRTY

Mercer stared at the abandoned white van. The familiar logo and license plate number taunted him. With gloved hands, he opened the rear doors, expecting to find Annalise's body. The suitcases and duffels remained spread throughout the back. But she wasn't inside, unless she was in one of the bags.

Taking a step back, Mercer peered around the side of the building. The storm hadn't let up. In fact, it had gotten worse. Ten cars were lined up in a row, most of them buried beneath several centimeters of snow. Understandably, motorists had stopped at the diner for a hot meal and refuge from the storm.

Donovan climbed into the van and unzipped each of the bags. "You were right. He left everything behind. All the quarters. He didn't care about any of it. He did all of this to fuck with us. Do you think he planned to eliminate you all along?"

"I don't know." Mercer checked the front of the vehicle, which smelled faintly of bleach. "It's been wiped. I don't think he left a single print or fiber in here. He doesn't want any of this to connect to him. But it connects to us. He knew we knocked over the vending machines. He must have been watching us. I just don't know how."

"We didn't know who he was or where he was. He could have followed us, blending in at the hotels and resorts. He's not exactly an amateur."

"No, he's not." Mercer thought about the way Robbins avoided the security cameras. "He knows security. He knows everything about this bloody town. How do you think he got the van?"

"It was reported stolen."

"Isn't that odd?" Mercer closed the door and stepped back, circling around. Based on the amount of accumulated snow on top, the van had to have been parked here for at least an hour. "He's been careful not to commit any other crimes. Why this one?"

"I don't know."

The only evidence inside linked to Mercer and his team. The teenagers at the ice rink could identify the bags, and the entire town knew the security specialists had gone to a lot of trouble to get lots and lots of quarters. "He did all of this to implicate us."

"Jules?"

A sick feeling wormed its way through Mercer's gut. Robbins didn't take risks. He didn't leave loose ends. And he enjoyed killing. "You never saw him drive back into town."

"No, he never came off the mountain."

"There has to be another path we don't know about. He has some back way of going. It's why we didn't spot any vehicles on the highway last night. He didn't take the highway. He bypassed all of that, came straight here, and then went back."

"He must have taken a side road."

"But where's the connection?" Mercer clicked on the torch and pointed it at the woods, but he couldn't see much aside from the falling flakes. "Scout around out here. I'll see what's taking Hans so long."

Mercer had been hesitant to enter the diner. He didn't want Bev to spot him and call Robbins. The last thing he needed was to freak out the kidnapper. At the moment, they had every reason to believe Annalise was still alive, but Mercer knew that could change at any moment. And if Robbins found out Mercer was still alive, he might move up his timetable, end the girl, and escape. But Hans should have returned with the woman. Something wasn't right.

Pulling the hood up on his parka, Mercer kept his head bowed as he entered the diner. He didn't spot Bev behind the counter. Another waitress bustled about, filling orders, while the cook brought out more food and delivered it to the tables. Mercer spotted Hans at the counter, attempting to speak to the waitress, this one a wispy, rail-thin blonde.

Ducking down the hallway, Mercer checked the bathrooms and office. Then he entered the kitchen. The cook didn't even notice. Mercer went past him and checked the walk-in fridge, but he didn't find Bev. He returned to the main dining area and took a seat beside Hans.

"Where is she?"

"According to Elaine, she went to take her lunch break an hour ago and never came back."

"So she left?"

"I don't know. Elaine says her car's still out back. She thinks she might have run across to the petrol station to get some smokes and decided to hang out over there until this mess dies down."

"Let's go." Mercer marched out of the diner and headed along the side of the building toward the petrol station. He moved through the shadows, as he had done the previous night. By now, he knew where the camera was and avoided it. He wasn't sure why, but something told him not to get spotted. When he got close enough, he crouched down, stabbing pain shooting through his back. He grit his teeth and ignored it, focusing his efforts on the figure inside. "He's alone. She's not in there."

"Want me to ask if he's seen her?" Hans asked.

"Might as well." Mercer sighed. "Just ask with an American accent."

"I'll do my best," Hans said in a manner that sounded vaguely Texan.

While Mercer waited, he crossed back to the diner, cursing himself for allowing Robbins to manipulate them. They hadn't had time, and with Annalise's life hanging in the balance, Mercer had been too focused on making progress and turning over every stone in their path that he hadn't seen what was going on. Even now, he still wasn't sure. Then he noticed red snow near the diner's outdoor cooler. He took out his torch. The top layer of snow only showed a few drops. But when Mercer brushed the fresh layer away with his foot, he found solid red ice beneath it.

He gripped his Sig, relieved that his team had recovered it from the rubbish bin, and glanced around. But he didn't sense danger. Slowly, he opened the cooler. "Bollocks." He didn't bother to check for a pulse. The busty waitress was already cold. A trickle of blood had frozen along her forehead and down her cheek where it had dripped from the bullet wound between her eyes.

Forcing himself to focus, he checked the inside of the cooler. But he didn't find anything.

"Jules," Hans jogged up beside him, "Jesus. I guess we can stop looking for her."

"He doesn't take any risks. He left the van here. He left the quarters, and he killed Bev." Only one thought came to mind. "He wants to implicate us in her murder. In the kidnapping. In all of it. That's why he made the offer. Why he tried to sow seeds of distrust with that very first conversation. He's been planning this since we stepped foot in this fucking town. He knows he's been caught, so he's blaming all his crimes on us."

"It's bloody brilliant." Hans stared at the corpse. "So what the hell do we do?"

"Get Donovan, we have to go. Now."

THIRTY-ONE

"Take a nap. That's what you said." Bastian ran a hand over his face. "Tell me this is a dream."

"It's a bloody nightmare," Hans muttered.

"Annalise?" Bastian asked.

Mercer shrugged. "I don't know. But if she's still alive, she doesn't have long. We have to move in before the drop."

"Do you even think he cares about the two million?" Donovan asked. "You said from the beginning this is about us. He may have no intention of picking up the ransom."

"No," Bastian said, "he wants the money. It might be his last big score for a while. He'll have to wait for the heat to die down and for the authorities to be satisfied that they've found the murderous bastard who's behind all these kidnappings before he can strike again."

"He should have plenty of money saved up from his previous kidnappings," Mercer said. "But he's spoken a lot about cutting me in on the deal. He probably wants the ransom to make it look like we stole it."

"How?" Hans asked.

"I don't know." Mercer couldn't see Robbins' moves. He didn't know enough about the man, and he didn't have the time to find out. "But he has a plan. While we've been trying to figure out who he is and why he chose this as his hunting grounds, he's been researching us. He waited to have everything in place before he made his move. I just didn't see it."

"No one could have," Donovan said. But that did nothing to comfort Mercer.

"He made it clear I'm to deliver the money to the ski lift at dawn. He'll pick it up on the other side, and once he has it, he'll text me coordinates to find Annalise," Bastian said.

"What about her insulin?" Hans asked. "Does she have enough to make it through the night? She's missing dinner. That can't be good."

"I argued that point, but he wouldn't budge. He showed me proof her blood sugar had stabilized. And her mum packed extra, so it should last. I hope." Bastian clicked a few keys, trying to stay on top of things.

"That won't make her bulletproof." Mercer flexed his fingers. He couldn't let the bastard kill again. "Did you get the satellite images yet?"

"Military intelligence sent us current ones, but they don't help on account of the storm. So they sent whatever they had from the last time everything was recorded." Bastian expanded the image. "As you can see, there are several structures in the area, any of which could be where Robbins is hiding."

Mercer tried to think. "His coworkers from the café might know something."

"Tried. I contacted all of them. They said Joe always kept to himself. Never invited anyone over.

Never spoke about hobbies or the things he did in private," Bastian said.

"Didn't anyone find that odd?" Hans asked.

"They just thought that was Joe." Bastian picked up a pen and chewed on the end. "They all said what a wonderful chap he is, how he volunteers around town, and helps out with charity drives and festivals. He does everything he can to build up this place and attract more tourists to the region. They think he's the cat's pajamas." Bastian winced. "That's a direct quote, by the way."

"That's bloody terrible." Hans scowled at the play on words.

"You haven't been inside that place," Donovan said. "Everything's about cats. As long as Robbins got along with them, the owner probably wouldn't notice his bad behavior."

"What did you find on Bev?" Mercer asked.

"Nothing conclusive. Robbins had called in several orders to that diner over the last few months, but so have plenty of other people. Aside from that, I can't connect the two. I'm guessing he ate there most nights. I don't know how much he shared with her or what she knew." Bastian gnawed on the end of a pen.

"She must have known something worth dying for." Donovan rocked back and forth on his heels. He didn't like the way they'd left her in the freezer, but there was nothing else to do. And hanging around and waiting for the police wouldn't have helped anyone.

"Or he told her to expect me and what to say, and she turned out to be nothing more than a means to an end." Mercer sighed. "It doesn't matter. We can't change that. We move forward. No one can help us find him. So we do it ourselves. We find the path he took. It has to be somewhere near the diner and connects to the mountain. Once we find it, we go up.

We'll use infrared to find the cabin. And we go in quietly and get Annalise out." He studied the map. "What do we need to make this happen?"

"A bloody miracle," Bastian muttered.

"Good thing you specialize in those." Mercer grabbed a pen.

"The first thing we have to do is combine everything we know, but it's still a guessing game," Bastian warned, opening several tabs on the screen.

"Then we make an educated guess." Donovan spread out the files, pulling out the relevant bits and pieces.

"Well, we know where he isn't, so that narrows things." Hans joined Mercer at the map and crossed off large sections of their search grid. "His phone signal cut out here. Jules, you were here. So he has to be beyond this point."

They had one shot at this. Their skills and training would only get them so far. When they were in Her Majesty's service, military intelligence made the call, painted their targets, or verified the data they sent back before they mounted a strike. But Mercer had done this enough to have a sixth sense about things. He stepped back and examined the big picture.

"It's not a road. At least not one on any map. It's something only he knows about." Mercer took a seat behind the other computer and searched for hiking trails and paths used by cross-country skiers and other outdoorsman. "He won't risk getting spotted. He's somewhere secluded. Someplace only he knows about and only he can access."

Getting up, Mercer leaned over Bastian's shoulder, examining the dated satellite images. Then he returned to his seat and searched for reports of wildfires or areas where there had been extensive logging, something that would explain the barren spots on the mountainside.

"They had a rock slide a few years back. Most of the trails were considered unsafe. The forestry bureau shut them down and redirected everyone to the more popular mountain paths for skiing and hiking." Mercer studied the updates Hans made to the map. Taking a pen, he marked a circle. "He's somewhere in here."

"You're sure, Jules?" Donovan asked.

Mercer looked back at Bastian, but the analyst didn't disagree. "We have to find a path up to be sure."

"Let me see what I can find." As usual, Bastian's fingers flew over the keys at lightspeed. "Bugger." He closed one window after another, entering new parameters and searching other sites for maps and locations. "I found a clearing half a klick from the diner on the same side. It disappears, but there might be a path up to those cabins." Bastian pointed to four different ones spread out over ten klicks. I just don't know if it's wide enough or stable enough to support a vehicle."

"We know he drove the van down the mountain somehow," Donovan said. "There has to be a path somewhere."

"But you've seen those woods," Hans said. "It could be anywhere."

"Bas?" Mercer asked.

"That's my best guess."

Mercer nodded. "Grab your gear. We move out in five."

THIRTY-TWO

"I'm only seeing residual heat signatures." Hans adjusted the thermal goggles. "Could be the insulation." The team spread out to check each of the cabins. "The house is warm, but I can't make out individual figures."

"What about the other possible locations?" Mercer watched the swirling snow through the night vision. The storm had tapered off but hadn't completely let up. The team wore solid white, making them nearly invisible. Even the trees were covered. Unfortunately, they wouldn't be able to hide their tracks. This was their only shot. They wouldn't get another chance.

Bastian muffled a cough. "Nothing at Charlie site. No lights. No heat."

"Donovan?" Mercer asked. The long-range tactician had spotted a hidden path a few kilometers up the clearing that led to a snow-covered dirt road. That road had taken them up a steep path which wound around. Hans remained at the first cabin they passed. The rest of the team had spread out to see if that might be a decoy. But none of the other cabins in the area had shown much promise.

"The roof's caved in. I don't see any other possibilities." Donovan sighed. "Should I keep going?"

"No," Bastian said, "you'll end up out of range. It has to be one of the four."

"We'll breach alpha site." Mercer remained flat on the ground, invisible to anyone who might peek outside. "I see one main entry point."

"The rear window's open," Hans said. "We need to cover it."

"Make that two." Mercer studied the building. "Any other points of interest."

"I'm coming up on the south," Bastian said. "Nothing but solid walls. Coming around now."

"Donovan how far out are you?" Mercer asked.

"Two minutes."

"Copy." Mercer wished they had the layout memorized. "Our primary objective is getting Annalise out safely. Our secondary objective is to neutralize Joe Robbins. Use your own discretion." Mercer waited for Bastian's protest. Normally, the analyst argued they weren't mercenaries who performed wet work, but after the number of lives this bastard had taken, the world wouldn't miss him if he happened to put up a fight. "Just make sure Annalise is clear. No civilian casualties."

"In position," Donovan said.

"Hans, remain outside. Cover the windows. Make sure he doesn't escape that way. Bastian, cover the front." Mercer took a breath. "I'll take the main door. Donovan, you take the rear." Mercer climbed through one window last night. He wasn't doing it again tonight. "We move on my count." Taking a breath, Mercer got off his belly and headed for the house in a low crouch. The mission focused him, dulling the physical discomfort. Nothing mattered but the mission. "One." He burst through the front door, clearing the front rooms and kitchen with expert speed and precision. He opened doors as he went. Closet. Bathroom. No sign of Robbins or Annalise. The end of the hallway forked, so he went left, knowing Donovan had entered on the right.

Mercer hit the light switch. He recognized the door, the bed, and the walls. "Where is she?"

Donovan finished clearing the house. "Not here."

"Robbins?" Mercer asked.

Donovan shook his head, and Mercer cursed again. They were too late.

"Bas, get in here." Mercer fought to keep his hands from shaking. He wanted to kill the bastard. "We need to figure out where he went and where he took the package." He checked the room. "You scanned for RF signals."

"He can't see us," Bastian assured, coming up behind them with his gun at the ready. He looked around the bedroom where Annalise had been held prisoner. Bits of the rug had been pulled up and torn. There weren't any windows. The team checked the floorboards and walls for possible hidden areas or trap doors, but they didn't find anything. "The door locks from the outside."

"But it was open." Mercer looked at it. The lock was engaged, but the door had been opened. "Maybe he twisted the lock automatically before he pulled her out."

"Maybe."

"Jules," Hans warned, "I see something. I'm picking up a heat signature. It's small. I'm not sure what I'm seeing."

"Stay here," Mercer told Donovan and Bastian. "Find something that'll tell us where he's taken her."

Remaining in a crouch, Mercer ran to Hans' position.

"Take a look." Hans offered Mercer the infrared scanner. "What is that?"

"Could be an animal. Or some kind of trap this bastard set. Let's find out."

Mercer and Hans moved silently through the snowy forest, giving the object a wide berth. When they were closer, Mercer switched to night vision. The blowing snow made it hard to see, but Mercer continued on the same path. The fallen snow concealed the object from view, and Mercer nearly tripped over it.

"Watch it," Hans warned.

Mercer brushed the snow off the slightly warm lump. "Annalise?"

Hans hit the radio. "We found her. Hurry." Hans gave them their coordinates while Mercer rolled the child over. The grey kitten had been tucked beneath her, and it shook itself at the sudden disturbance.

"Annalise, love, can you hear me?" Mercer tugged off his gloves and felt for a pulse. Her skin felt ridiculously cold. He took off his parka and wrapped it around her, cradling her in his arms. "Annalise? Shit."

"Jules," Hans said softly, "is she?"

Mercer ran a hand over her face, brushing her snowy hair out of the way. "No, please, wake up." He cursed again and rocked her against him. Wrapping his parka tighter around her. "Come on. Don't do this. You have to wake up. Your mummy and daddy want to see you."

She coughed. Her voice was tired and weak. "Mommy?"

"I'll take you to her. Just hang on," Mercer promised. He lifted her off the ground, just as Donovan and Bastian ran toward them.

"Wait," she said, her voice weak and distant. "I

need mittens."

"We'll get you all the mittens you want, love," Bastian promised, adding his own parka on top of Mercer's to try to warm her.

"No, the kitty."

"I got him," Hans said, picking the grey kitten up by the scruff of the neck. He was nearly as cold as the girl. He unzipped his jacket and tucked the animal inside. "He's safe and sound. Now let's get you home."

THIRTY-THREE

Mercer paced the hospital hallways. Zoe and Charles hadn't come out of the room yet, and Mercer wasn't sure what that could mean. He just hoped they got to Annalise in time. If it hadn't been for Hans, they never would have found her.

"Ouch." Hans adjusted in the seat, pulling the kitten's tiny claws out of his skin. "You little bastard, is this what I get for saving your life?"

Donovan gave him an amused look. "Having fun?"

"No. Why don't you take him? You know how I feel about cats." Hans tried to pass the animal off to Donovan, but a nurse came down the hallway, so Hans had to tuck the animal back inside his jacket. Again, the kitten tried to climb up his chest, its tiny claws digging into him. "Stop that."

The nurse gave Hans a strange look but continued on her way.

After what felt like an eternity, Charles came down the hallway. He took off his glasses to rub his eyes.

"What did they say?" Bastian asked.

"She's cold and her blood sugar is low, but she should be okay. They want to monitor her to make sure her temperature and blood sugar remain stable." Charles adjusted his glasses and held out his hand. "Thank you for rescuing my little girl." He shook hands with Bastian and then Mercer. "What happened to the monster who took her? Where is he?"

"He wasn't there," Mercer said, "but we will find him."

Charles nodded, biting his lip. "I should get back."

"Go," Bastian encouraged. "Hans and Donovan will remain here to keep watch in case of anything. But you should be safe now. Annalise should be safe now."

Mercer and Bastian watched the man walk down the hall. It was just after six. The sun would be rising soon.

"Are you sure about this?" Bastian asked. "We could let the authorities handle it."

"Do you think they can?"

Bastian sighed. "Right. Let's go."

The two men left the hospital. It had finally stopped snowing, and though the sun wasn't up yet, everything appeared brighter and cleaner. They stopped by the chalet and picked up a briefcase. After filling it with copy paper, they set out for the chairlift.

"I'll make the call and tell him the money's ready." Bastian gripped the briefcase in one hand, his cell phone in the other. "Where are you going to be?"

"Somewhere he'll never see me coming."

"Jules," Bastian warned, "he might surrender."

"Do you think he deserves it?"

"You know what they'll do to a child killer in prison. That would probably be adequate punishment."

Mercer didn't reply. Instead, he slipped out of the car and scouted the area. He knew Robbins already had every inch of the place memorized. The kidnapper spent his entire life here. He knew everything about this place, but Mercer was a quick study. He stuck to the plowed roads and shoveled paths, noting the large snowdrifts, several meters high, and the walls of snow piled up, forming a maze. That would provide plenty of cover and opportunities to hide. Mercer just had to find the perfect spot.

Ten minutes later, Bastian stepped out of the car and made his way to the chairlift. He trudged through the half a meter of snow, which made it difficult to move quickly. On the bright side, it'd make it harder for Robbins to escape. Bastian had just placed the briefcase on the seat of the first chair when he heard someone cough.

"You came," Robbins said from behind, and Bastian turned around. "I wasn't sure you'd show. Guess you're really gung-ho about saving the girl. Is that because you couldn't save your partner?"

"He was a pain in the arse, anyway."

Robbins laughed. "In other words, I did you a favor."

"Sure."

The masked kidnapper jerked his chin at the briefcase. "Toss that to me and then take a seat. You're going for a ride."

"I'm not fond of heights," Bastian said.

Robbins waited for Bastian to grab the briefcase, and then he flipped a switch, activating the chairlift. After a few moments of grinding, the chairs started to move. "My money. Now."

"And the coordinates?" Bastian asked, playing along.

"I'll text you once you're on the other side."

"Why should I trust you?"

"Jeez." The kidnapper pulled a gun. "This isn't twenty questions. Do what I say or I'll shoot you."

"Like you shot Jules?"

The kidnapper laughed. "I knew you were bitter about that. Don't play me. I'm not a fool. You miss him." He pouted, mocking sadness. But the dramatics didn't elicit any type of response from Bastian. That struck the kidnapper oddly, and he eyed the briefcase where it sat on top of the snow. He trudged through the knee-high accumulation and popped open the case. "Is this a joke? What am I supposed to do? Print my own money."

"You're a smart fellow. I'm sure you'll figure something out."

"Where's the two million?"

"It's not coming."

"Then the girl's dead." Robbins came closer, shoving his gun into Bastian's ribs. "I hope you can live with yourself knowing you're the reason a little kid is dead."

"How do you live with yourself?"

Robbins shook his head. "No. This is your fault." He raised his arm to strike Bastian with the gun, but Bastian grabbed his arm and the two tussled. Robbins dropped the gun, and it sunk into the snow. He swung at Bastian, who ducked and hit the kidnapper hard in the solar plexus. Robbins wheezed and stumbled back, one arm wrapped around his middle, the other raised. "Fine. Whatever. I guess our business is done then."

"Not yet."

"Oh, you still want to know where the girl is." Robbins snickered. "I'll never tell, but I'll let you in on a little secret. It's already too late."

"Why?" Mercer asked, emerging from his cover position and coming up behind the kidnapper.

"Julian, you're alive. It's a miracle." Robbins faked enthusiasm. He glanced down at the gun in Mercer's hands. "Come on, now. You don't want to do that.

Remember, you never said you enjoyed killing."

"No, but you do. Is that why you killed Bev?"

"You found her?"

Mercer nodded.

"And we recovered the package," Bastian said. "She's safe and sound. We found her outside your hunting cabin. She nearly froze to death, you twisted shit."

"Outside?" Robbins' eyes narrowed, sensing this was a trick. "You're crazy. Why would I let her go outside?"

"We're not crazy, Joe," Mercer said. "But you are."

Robbins spun back around, surprised to hear his name roll off Mercer's tongue. "That's right. I'm just your average Joe."

"No, you're Joe Robbins. We know everything about you. It's over," Bastian said. "It's time you come clean."

The kidnapper chuckled. "Are you guys cops now? If you are, you have to tell me. If you don't, that's entrapment. Except, wait a minute, from what I remember, you actually committed several crimes. Vandalism, breaking and entering, burglary, assault, extortion, kidnapping, and murder, or at least that's how it appears. You see, gentlemen, I'm not an idiot. I left a trail of breadcrumbs," he walked his fingers across the air, "that points directly to you." He poked a finger in Mercer's direction.

"Bollocks. You killed the waitress at the diner and left her in the freezer after you told her to pass us some misinformation. You kidnapped Annalise Van der Berg. And let's not forget all your previous crimes," Mercer said. "Your other victims, the ones you kidnapped and the ones you killed."

"Except there's no evidence. If there were, you and

your boyband wouldn't have been tasked to investigate. That job would have been left up to the actual authorities. And this stuff, well, who's to say you didn't orchestrate it. You knew the girl had been kidnapped even before her mom did. And let's think about our little video chats. The times we met, just the two of us. And every crime you committed since. There might even be an account opened in your name with two million dollars sitting somewhere." Robbins grinned. "And let's not forget, this is a small town. People here know me. They trust me. I'm the guy who takes strays in off the streets. And boy, do I love taking them. Even if they arrest me, they'll never convict me. You, on the other hand, well, I wouldn't be so sure. Annalise can't recognize me. No one can." He tapped his temple. "Just like a fox."

"Roll up your sleeves," Mercer said.

"Why?" Joe looked confused, but the barrel of Mercer's gun insisted, so he tugged on the shabby wool coat and the sweater beneath, revealing the tattoo on his forearm. It was a skull with a dagger through it. "You like my ink?"

"No, but I saw the marking on your arm. I'm sure some of your victims have too. This is over." Mercer watched him carefully.

Joe Robbins was a cornered animal. He wouldn't give up without a fight. He tried to move toward the shoveled walkway. "Listen, fellows, I called the police before I came here. They think you killed Bev. Your prints were on the quarters, and the murder weapon was taped underneath the tailpipe. I even left some of the coins in her apron. It won't take long for the staties to link that to you. Oh, and did I mention, you also stole the van. An eyewitness saw you do it."

"What eyewitness?" Bastian asked.

"Me. Duh."

Mercer couldn't tell if these were lies or pathetic attempts to convince him and Bastian to let Robbins walk away scot-free. But Mercer didn't budge. "Stop moving. Since you called the police, we'll let them sort this when they arrive."

"I'm serious, man," Robbins said. "They're coming to get you. And they're going to lock you away. How's it going to look to them when they pull up and find you holding me at gunpoint? I'll tell you how it's going to look. Not great."

"They'll think I'm a hero," Mercer said. "You wanted me to play the part. So here it is."

"Fine." Robbins raised his hands over his head. "Then we'll just stand around and wait. I hope you enjoy your last few minutes of freedom. Maybe you should build a snowman or something." He stared up at the sky and spun in a circle. "I'd say maybe we should make snow angels, but we might suffocate. Ah, what the hell? It might be worth it." He flopped onto his back and rolled to the side, coming up with the gun in his hand. He fired at Bastian, who darted away, and spun around, firing at Mercer.

Mercer shot him twice in the chest, and Bastian shot him once in the back. Robbins fell to the ground and sunk into the snow.

Bastian looked around, but no one was close. He didn't know if anyone heard the shots. "That didn't go exactly as planned."

"I already let this bastard shoot me twice. I wasn't going to let him do it again." Mercer checked the body, but Robbins was dead. "You okay, Bas?"

Bastian rubbed a hand down his torso. "Just delightful."

THIRTY-FOUR

"He's been taken care of," Mercer said. "No one will hurt you. If the authorities have questions, tell them whatever you like."

Zoe nodded. Charles had left to take a few calls and have the money returned to his account. "I don't know what would have happened if you hadn't been here," she said.

But Mercer knew. More than likely, Annalise would have been safer. But Robbins' next victim probably wouldn't have been nearly as lucky.

"We're just doing our job," Bastian said.

"Please, let me pay you. I owe you everything."

"That's not necessary, madam." Mercer watched the kitten curiously climb through the covers toward the little girl, who let out a delighted squeal when she opened her eyes to find his whiskers tickling her cheek.

"He saved me, Mommy," Annalise exclaimed.

"I know, sweetheart. That's why we should thank Julian and his friends." Zoe smiled at her daughter and brushed her hair behind her ear.

"No, Mittens. When the bad man left the bedroom door open, Mittens ran out of the room. And then the bad man left. So I got up to look for Mittens, but he jumped out the window. I thought he'd get lost in the snow, so I went out after him. But I couldn't find him. It was too dark and cold, and there was so much snow. It was up to here." She gestured on her body to indicate the level of snow. "But Mittens found me. And he kept me warm." She cradled the cat in her arms. "Can we keep him? Please."

Zoe looked at the tiny stray curled up on the bed beside her daughter. "Of course, honey."

Mercer jerked his chin toward the door, and the team excused themselves.

"Sure, we come to the rescue and the bloody cat gets all the credit," Hans muttered.

"I saw the way you tucked him in your coat," Donovan said. "You like him. You were hoping we could keep him instead."

Hans glared but didn't respond.

"Should we be concerned about the threats Robbins made?" Mercer asked as they left the hospital.

"I didn't find anything, Jules. No accounts. I think it was rubbish," Bastian said, "but the authorities will have questions for us. Some we might not be able to answer so easily."

"In that case, we should leave town before we cause any more trouble. The mission's over. I see no reason to hang around. Agreed?" Mercer asked, and his teammates nodded. As usual, it was best to keep moving.

WANT MORE JULIAN MERCER? CHECK OUT THE CROSS-OVER THRILLER ZERO SUM
(ALEXIS PARKER #22)

DISCOVER OTHER SERIES AND MORE.
VISIT US ONLINE AT
GKPARKS.COM

ABOUT THE AUTHOR

G.K. Parks is the author of the Alexis Parker series. The first novel, *Likely Suspects,* tells the story of Alexis' first foray into the private sector.

G.K. Parks received a Bachelor of Arts in Political Science and History. After spending some time in law school, G.K. changed paths and earned a Master of Arts in Criminology/Criminal Justice. Now all that education is being put to use creating a fictional world based upon years of study and research.

You can find additional information on G.K. Parks and the Alexis Parker series by visiting our website at
www.alexisparkerseries.com